Spurred On
A Windy Peaks Novel
Elle Jordan

Contents

Dedication

To my bestie for convincing me that ditching my other manuscript to write this one was the right move. This was the most fun I've ever had writing a book. As a writer, I needed this book to remind me why I love to write in the first place, and it wouldn't have happened if it wasn't for Cait.

Preface

While keeping things 100% accurate has its place, this book will not be one of them. I have twisted some laws, some rules and some logic to make the story work. There will be some things that couldn't happen in real life, but that's why it's fiction! I hope you enjoy the ride, and come to love Mav & Ava as much as I have. Thank you so much for reading!

Content Warning

This novel contains strong language, (Friday is my second favorite f word), sexually explicit scenes, brief violence, scenes and discussion of anxiety, discussion of parental death (not on page) and on page injury. Some humor can be deemed as offensive, read at your own discretion.

Content Warning

Chapter 1
Ava

"I look ridiculous." I almost choke on the cloud of hairspray coating the air as Erin sprays my golden locks down. My hair is one millimeter away from entering heaven and speaking to Jesus. Eyeing myself top to bottom, I feel a ball of dread form. Why did I agree to do this?

"You look hot," my best friend, Erin, says, smiling at me through the mirror as if she can already sense I want to back out. But I flew all the way out here from Wyoming so I need to make this time away from job hunting worth it.

After passing my boards, the girls insisted on a weekend-long celebration in good ol' Las Vegas.

I'm a long stretch out from being done with the stress. Nursing school was the hardest ten years of my life. It wasn't actually ten years, but it feels like it aged me that much. I'm still on the hunt for a job. I've been itching to spread my wings and leave, and this might be the kick in the ass I need to do it.

A knock at the door makes Erin put the can of hairspray down. She flips her long, bouncy brown hair off her shoulder and skips to the door. If only we all felt as joyous about life as she does.

The sound of high-pitched screeching enters the room as Josie and Cami make their way in, and I can't help but smile at the excitement in the air. I deserve to have a little fun tonight. I haven't been out with the girls in over a year, and if we're only here for two nights, I need to make them count.

Walking out of the bathroom, I head into the main room to meet the rest of the girls.

"Holy crap, Ava. You look amazing," Cami says. I don't know if I should be offended or flattered by the way her jaw is hitting the floor right now.

After months of living in the scrubs they assign to us during clinicals, it feels nice having clothes on that are actually made for a woman. My black long-sleeve bodysuit hugs my body like a second skin. Rhinestone-covered mesh climbs up from the flare of the bell-bottoms all the way to the top of my hips. A little saucier than I'd usually wear but Erin insisted, and I didn't have the energy to argue with her.

"Thank you. You don't think it's too much?" I nervously look down and run my fingers over the fabric.

"No such thing. And even if it was, you pull it off so it wouldn't matter. Now get the boots and the hat on," Erin instructs.

The rest of the group is decked out in their own western wear. Are any of them actually western? No. Cami and Josie are about as city as they come. Erin and I grew up together in Wyoming. She went to college in Denver and added the two girls to our girl gang. We all fit together somehow, no matter how different our personalities are. And all of the crazy in this room is about to take Vegas by storm.

Cami's denim bell bottoms hug her hips, showing off her shape perfectly. Her shirt's belled sleeves flare out at the elbow. Her personality comes through with the delicate floral design. She's our soft-spoken one. Until you get tequila in her, then Cami 2.0 comes out.

Josie is decked out in all black. Distressed black denim, with a lacy long-sleeve shirt peeking out behind her Bud Light T-shirt. Perfectly edgy and perfectly her. Now Erin? Her light-wash jeans are so tight, she might end up having to cut them off. Her button-down hot pink shirt is tucked in, and she's got the pink cowboy hat and boots to match. Confidence radiates off her in waves.

I plop down on my bed that is now covered with discarded clothing that didn't quite make the cut for a night of rodeoing. Should I clean this off now? Yes. Because there is a good chance drunk me will not care enough to clean it off later but I hear Erin call out, "Alright girls, hats on, tits up. We need to get a picture before we ruin all our hard work."

Skipping the cleaning, even though it's killing me, I slide my cowboy boots on and pull my bell bottoms over them. We all gather in front of the large, illuminated mirror in the bathroom. Erin snaps the picture and then looks at it. "Ava, I swear to sweet baby Jesus, if you don't learn how to keep your eyes open, I will fight you." I roll my eyes, which is a dangerous move because she might choose now to throw hands. She takes picture documenting very seriously, while I do not. I can't remember the last time I even took a picture of myself. Probably on my first day of clinicals two years ago, if I had to guess. We all smile and go through the poses until Erin is satisfied, taking no less than one hundred pictures. My cheeks hurt from smiling for so long, but I'm sure in a year's time I will be happy to have this snippet of a memory documented, because I really am happy to be here, even if it's out of my comfort bubble.

"Uber is on the way. Everyone have their IDs?" Cami asks. Mine is tucked into my small purse, so I nod. Locking up, we leave our completely wrecked room behind. We can clean that up tomorrow.

Stepping out of the Uber, we feel the cool Vegas air as we walk up to the Thomas & Mack Center at the University of Las Vegas. National Finals Rodeo signage is everywhere if that didn't give away what we were walking into, the smell of livestock would. All questions I had about being overdressed are quickly squashed. Girls are decked out with big belt buckles and even bigger bell bottoms. There's hardly a head here without a hat atop it.

"Look at all these cowboys," Josie says. I'm pretty sure she's got little cartoon hearts in her eyes right now. Taking a glance around the arena, I see she isn't the only one affected. If you look close enough, you can see the drool hanging off everyone's chins. The effect isn't lost on me. These cowboys fitted in wranglers and boots are a sight to be seen.

Making it through security, we get inside and are met with vendors and beer stands galore.

"Let's grab a beer and then find our seats. I want to see how these boys ride," Erin says with a wag of her eyebrows.

"Oh, I'm sure you do." I laugh as she links her arm through mine, and our group navigates through the crowd.

After stopping at a nearby stand for an overpriced beer, the cold cans chill our hands as we find our seats.

"Holy cow, Cami. How did you get seats for this?" I can't help but gawk at the scene before me. We're so close to the action. She had all our tickets on her phone, so I didn't get a chance to peek at where we would be sitting.

"My dad's company buys a ton of tickets every year. I told him about our Vegas trip and he had the hookup."

"Remind me to thank him extensively next time we see him," Erin says, smiling widely as she looks at the horses trotting through the dirt floor below us.

The announcer's voice begins booming through the stadium. "Welcome to the National Finals Rodeo." He drags out the words "welcome" and "rodeo," inciting cheers and hoots from the crowd. "We have the pleasure of watching these boys battle it out on this country's meanest, bucking bulls."

The overhead screen displays the riders we will be watching tonight. My eyes scan the screen, noticing one in particular: grey eyes, dark brown hair, and a smile that could break a million hearts without even trying. His name, Maverick Ryder, comes over the intercom as the announcer names off the participants, and the stadium goes wild. The distinct sound of women fangirling rises above the rest of the stadium and I can't help but laugh. I see what most of them are here for. Not that I can blame them. I know next to nothing about bull riding, but I can see trouble a mile away. And *that* man is probably trouble.

Chapter 2
Maverick

"Alright, Mav, you know the drill," my manager, Doug, chastises. His voice barely audible over the cheers of the crowd. My glove-covered hand brushes the sticky rosin over my rope, making sure it's primed for the ride and making sure my glove gets nice and coated while I'm at it.

I stand behind the corral bars next to my designated chute, getting my head in the game. I'm getting old and the promise of another title is so damn close. My coach's eyes stay locked on the current rider, taking in the competition. Sully's been in this game a long time; no one knows bull riding quite like him.

"Yeah, yeah. Hold on for dear life. Squeeze my thighs, spur him a little to make him extra pissed off." My manager and coach are both unimpressed with my lax approach but I've been doing this since I was six. I didn't get three titles under my belt by not knowing what the fuck I was doing. "Calm down, boys. This isn't my first rodeo." The look Doug shoots my way could kill me. His perfectly styled hair doesn't fit in here. Neither does the sport coat, but he always wears it anyway, sticking out like a sore thumb against our cowboy hats, boots and chaps.

"You need to score an eighty-seven. The bull you pulled is mean, but you'll need more than that to take the leaderboard and the title tonight. Make sure you rile him up to get as many extra points as we can," Coach says. It's my last ride of the National Finals Rodeo, and it needs to be my best.

The announcer's voice booms over the PA system, "Up next, we've got Maverick Ryder riding Diesel." The arena erupts in cheers as adrenaline fills my system. Getting up on the bull, the team gets me ready. We wrap the bull and my hand in, making sure I'm not going anywhere. My vision begins to tunnel as I get myself mentally prepared. This is how I do it, this is how I win time and time again. Complete and total focus. Voices in the background fade to silence. And the only thing I can see, hear, and feel is me and Diesel. The sound of the bull's hooves stomping the ground hits my ears as dust kicks up around us. He's one of the most ruthless bulls in the system. His snarling grunts add to the adrenaline pumping through me. My grip tightens on the rope as they open the chute, and we're off.

I just need eight seconds. It doesn't sound long until you're on the back of a bull, hanging on for dear life. My body instinctively moves with his, anticipating his next move and which way he's going to buck every time. I rattle my spur and give him a little kick. He bucks, causing me to lean all the way back, my hand in the air to counterbalance. One more kick and he swings his body left, I brace my body and hold on, squeezing my legs because I refuse to let the title slip when I'm this close. The horn goes off, and I slide off the bull, making sure to run my way to the pit before I get a horn up the ass. The bullfighters, dressed as flamboyant clowns with cheeks painted a bright shade of red and their big cowboy hats looking almost as ridiculous as their denim overalls, do a good job of distracting the angry beast.

Once I'm safe, I rip off my helmet, hop on the gate, and wait for my score. My chest is heaving with heavy pants as I try to catch my breath and settle my heart rate back down. A large board backlit with bright lights goes through the previous riders' scores and recaps all the events until the judges submit my score. It hangs from the ceiling in four sections, making up a box so everyone from every angle can get a peek. Seconds pass before the number eighty-nine flashes across the screen. I throw my hands up in celebration. My crew circles around me with slaps on the back. That'll be next to impossible to beat. With two riders left, I can almost taste the victory, and boy, is it sweet. This buckle is mine.

"Good job, kid," Doug says with a wide smile. It's rare that I get any praise from him, so I take it with a smile and nod.

Being this close to payout makes my hackles rise with every second of the other contender's rides. It's been my life mission to prove I'm the best, to shut up all the people who say I'm only here because of who my old man was. Every title I win, their voices get a little quieter. If I win enough, maybe I won't have to hear them at all. The rider after me does well, but with his scores, he's coming in fourth overall. Only one more. One more rider and the title is mine.

My luck feels just a bit shy; he drew the best bull out there. If he rides him well, he's guaranteed a high score. My hands grip the corral gates as he spins out of the chute, the bull putting on a show for everyone in attendance. The crowd roars as he holds on. Fuck. I'm going to lose. With three seconds left, the bull rears, back legs in full extension, and the rider slips. Not off the bull's back but enough to lose some points in multiple categories. I let out a small breath of relief, at least now I still have a chance. His ride ends and he's back on the safe side of the corral, ready to see how badly his slip costs him.

We all wait with bated breath for the score to flash up. My eyes squeeze shut, almost terrified of what I'll see when I open them. My hands shake at my sides from the nerves I can't seem to calm. Somehow, riding the bull was the most relaxing part of my night. The crowd roars, and I steel my nerves and peel my eyes open. My eyes scan the jumbotron, reading the scores. He came in one point under me. That's way too damn close. I like competition and all, but I like a bit of cushion so I don't have to sweat bullets like I did tonight. I've got to step up my game next ride.

Coach Sully pulls me down and into a bear hug. On the outside, I look pretty careless. But inside. I'm constantly trying to beat who I was yesterday—constantly trying to live up to the expectations others have set for me. Having a Dad who was a legend in rodeo is sometimes more of a curse than a blessing. Knowing I made Coach proud eases a little bit of the nagging voice in my head telling me I'll never be as good as my old man.

The grin that stretches across my face almost hurts. Winning feels so damn good. Hopping over the bars, I hit the dirt and make my way to the center of the arena. I pull my cowboy hat off my head, waving it to the arena of fans. The seats are full; my gaze catches on random fans, the joy on their faces make me feel mine tenfold. The screams rattle my eardrums; it's so loud in here from the cheering, the windows are probably shaking. I love this shit. This moment right here makes it all worth it.

My team rushes behind me as the media coverage team starts to fill the arena. Holy shit, I can't believe I won. I mean, I can, I've worked my ass off this year. It's been my best run yet and I don't plan on stopping anytime soon.

Hands, who knows whose, start clapping as cameras start being pointed at my face. The announcer, Sandy, comes to my side, a mi-crophone in her hand. Her boots are way too shiny to be on this dirt, but she doesn't seem to care. She's interviewed me multiple times, so I know she never asks shit questions.

"Maverick, tell us how you are feeling right now." She moves the cordless microphone in front of my face, smiling at me, waiting for a response.

"Really good. This is a huge win for me and my team. A big thank you goes out to my coach for making sure I put in the work. And to the founding members of the NFR for putting on such a great event. The bulls were excellent this year."

The crowd's cheers are so loud that I have to lean in and angle my head down to be able to hear her questions. "That's great to hear. Any big plans or goals for the next year that we need to know about?"

Easiest question of the night. "I'll be on the back of the bull, that's my plans. This has been a great year, but next year will be even better."

She smiles as she looks at the camera. "We love to hear it." Turning back to me, she says, "Well, congratulations on your big win. We were all rooting for you."

Nodding my head, I smile at her words, "Thanks, Sandy."

The interviews and media go on forever, and I have to say that this part of the lifestyle is the worst. I don't enjoy the cameras in my face, and I sure as shit don't like having to act a certain way just to keep my sponsorships happy. Say the wrong thing at the wrong time, and that hundred-thousand-dollar deal is going down the shitter.

It finally calms down enough that I can sneak off the dirt, my best friends are waiting for me. This part is fun, the celebration.

"So, what's the plan? We going to the NFR after-party or are we hitting the town?" Weston says. Rhett, always the quiet and reasonable one of us, leans against the corral bar.

"You know it'll piss Doug off if I skip that party," I say, gathering my bag from the side.

"So, what I am hearing is we have even more reason to skip the party?" Weston slaps my arm and I shake my head.

"Yup." Doug is such a pain in the ass, you'd think he pays me with the way he walks around. The only thing he's good for is keeping my sponsors happy and making sure my image stays squeaky clean.

Even Rhett gets excited. He claps and rubs his hands together. Both my boys showed up for me tonight. "Fuck yeah! Let's get out of here before Doug finds another camera to shove you in front of."

Like a group of teenagers, we sneak out. I throw on a hoodie and keep my face hidden. This place is fucking huge, and basically a maze. But if anyone can do it, it's the three of us. I know every adult in our life hated seeing us coming when we were kids. But now we're all on the brink of thirty or already thirty, and are the adults, even when we don't act like it. And we are about to unleash ourselves on Las Vegas.

Chapter 3
Ava

The margarita around my neck adds to the chill as we walk to the next bar. And by walk, I mean stumble. Laughter sounds behind me as Erin trips over her own two feet yet again. I need to get some water in her before she throws up. Then again, maybe I should take my own advice. But it feels so good to cut loose. I've been bound too tight, too long. The string has snapped courtesy of the strawberry margarita.

Walking into the Honky Tonk bar, George Strait blares through the speakers. The bar is packed full, and judging by the cowboy hats, they all came from the NFR too. A large mechanical bull sits in the middle, a rider already getting thrown off.

"*Okay,* girls, we need some tunes to set the night off right. I'm heading over to the jukebox," Josie says, strutting through the bar. At least ten men are watching her long legs pace through without a problem. Something tells me we won't be paying for a single drink.

Within seconds, Shania Twain's *Let's Go Girls* fills the bar. Our hoots and hollers are met with every other girl's as we run to the dance floor and throw our hands in the air.

"We need to do a round of saluting our girl. She did the damn thing, and now maybe, just maybe, we can teach her how to have a good time again," Erin says, and I roll my eyes at her.

They always tease me about this, but I didn't have the same liberties as them. I had to figure out the whole college and adult thing completely on my own, which meant I had to grow up a hell of a lot faster. I can see why they thought I was boring, but I was pouring everything I had into just getting by. But those days are about to be over. All my hard work has paid off, finally.

"Yeah, yeah. I'm so sorry I became such a bore while I was working nights and going to school during the day."

She puts a hand over her heart and fakes sincerity, "Thank you for your apology. And I'm proud of you, Grandma." I can't help but laugh at her because I do feel like a grandma most days. I was the second oldest in my nursing school graduating class at the ripe age of twenty-eight. Barb was forty-seven and trying something new after her divorce. She was my best friend and probably the only reason I didn't pull my hair out. While the girls lived on campus and were partying, I was pulling overnights stocking shelves to pay my rent. But maybe now that I have more than seven minutes of free time, I can figure out what fun is again.

"I'll head to the bar and get us a round," Cami says, practically skipping back to the bar. Her usual shyness has long drifted away, and her alter ego, social butterfly Cami, has arrived.

They were right, this is fun. I watch Josie get on top of the mechanical bull, and the crowd around her goes wild. The controller just smirks at her and she mean-mugs him back. Our little spitfire. "Turn her on, bull boy."

The bull starts spinning and rocking, and she makes a show of it with her hand in the air, somehow staying on. "Go, Jos!" Erin hollers.

Apparently, the controller was taking it easy on her because two seconds later, he picks up the pace, and she flies through the air. The bar erupts in cheers, but we ignore it, rushing to make sure Jos isn't hurt. She hops to her feet, but the crowd once watching her is gone, all gathering and cheering near the front of the bar.

"Are you okay?" I ask, the nurse in me taking over as I scan her head to toe. But she looks almost giddy, we can probably thank the liquor for making her a bit more rubber-like.

"That was amazing! You have to try Ava!" Jos says with far too much enthusiasm. I'm shaking my head no before she can even get the sentence out. Erin saves the day by jumping in, replaying the whole event, causing us all to be bent over in fits of laughter. I'm not sure what it is, but when Erin tells a story, it sometimes becomes twenty times funnier than the actual event.

"Bet you a cold drink that I could out ride you?" a male voice comes from behind me, causing me to jump a little. I was far too lost in our conversation to even hear someone sneak up.

Turning my head, I eye him. He's way too attractive for me to make a fool of myself in front of so I shake my head. "I bet you could but I'll pass, I am happy to watch."

He cocks his head at me, his grey eyes glinting with a little wildness. "Come on, don't tell me you're a fun sucker." A playful smirk causes one side of his lips to tilt up.

That little comment right there spurs something in me. I'm tired of being told I'm not fun. Responsible does not mean *not* fun. I had other shit to worry about. So you know what? Fuck it. Maybe it's the tequila talking, but I'm going to prove to everyone just how fun I am.

"Fine. Hold this," I say to Erin. My drink sloshes over the sides and onto her hands, but she pays it no mind as she laughs.

"We've got a taker!" he hollers, and the crowd goes wild.

Erin looks at me with eyes bigger than dinner plates. I'm surprised too, girlfriend. But if one more person tells me I'm boring, I'm going to lose it. My eyes catch on him again. Why does he look familiar? I know I've seen those eyes before, they're piercing and impossible to forget. Probably saw him at the rodeo.

I hop into the bounce-house-looking pen and thank the Lord the floor is padded. I don't think tequila and bull riding go hand in hand, but what do I know? Every ounce of my body is screaming that this is a terrible idea. There's about a million and four ways I can get hurt. I probably won't last two seconds. For sure, I am going to embarrass myself, but thanks to the tequila sunrise in Erin's hands, I probably won't care about that until tomorrow morning.

Hopping up onto the bull, I swing my leg over, happy I wore pants and a bodysuit where there is no risk of anything popping out.

"Can I give you some pointers?" he asks, leaning his arms against the side of the pen. My eyes catch on the way his muscles bulge through the sleeves of his button-up shirt.

Quirking a brow up at him, I deliver a little more sass than necessary. "What? Does the cowboy hat make you a professional?"

He shrugs. "No, but I did just win the NFR. So I'd say I have some experience."

Well shit. Didn't know I was betting with a freaking god of bull riding.

"You didn't think to lead with that?" That's why the guy looked so familiar. Damn my liquor-hazed brain.

"Nah." He shakes his head with a cocky grin and I can't help but stare. It's no wonder why all the girls went crazy over him. He was pretty on the screen, but up close? No comparison.

"Well then. Come show me how it's done," I challenge, a little surprised at my own boldness. But I will never ever see this guy again, so who cares?

He gracefully hops over the side, which is impressive considering it deflates a little with touch, and somehow, my brain decides that it was really attractive.

"Alright, the trick is to stay loose." Funny. That's the first time I've ever heard a man say that to a woman. "May I?" His eyebrows raise with his question.

My gaze locks on his, and good lord, he may just be the most handsome man I have ever seen. I nod as his hands graze over the top of my thighs, and I feel flames up my body. His rough hands stick against the fabric of my body suit, and my skin erupts in goosebumps. "Except for these, your thighs need to squeeze this bull like your life depends on it." Little does he know I'm squeezing my thighs for other reasons. He's probably used to women fawning over him. So, I cool my features in a weak attempt to play it cool.

I make a show of squeezing my legs, and his hand drops away. "Good, now put a hand up to counterbalance." Regret already fills my body, even buzzed this is embarrassing. Maybe I should just wear my boring badge with honor from here on out. It's gotten me pretty far if I do say so myself.

Reluctantly, I put my hand up. He nods his cowboy hat to me, and I can't fight the blush that fills my cheeks. He looks over to the operator and waves before stepping back until his body is flush with the side of the pen, signaling it's go time.

Oh God. Now I'm nervous. My heart starts to race, and my palms suddenly feel clammy. I think he sees the flare of panic in my eyes. "Squeeze and stay loose." He gives me a thumbs up, and I nod my head.

The bull roars to life under me, jerking side to side and then front to back. Staying loose while you are scared shitless is not as easy as it would seem. I force my body to relax and figure out which way the bull will move next. When the back of the bull rears up, I lean back, hand in the air, somehow still firmly planted on the bull thanks to my thigh's death grip. I let out a laugh. This is actually fun.

I last one whole second after that before I go flying off the side. I land flat on my back, laughing. Mystery man is in front of me, a wide smile on his face. He grips my hand, the connection of skin making little zaps shoot through me. Maybe I'm more buzzed than I thought. He helps me to my feet and I realize I'm still smiling like an idiot.

"I was wrong, you do know how to have fun." He keeps his hands on mine, and I feel a flush rush over my body.

"Be sure to tell my friends that. I'm tired of them calling me grandma." He shakes his head. He lifts the hand still holding mine in the air, as if I'm the heavyweight champ who just won a boxing match. The crowd goes wild and I nervously look at his profile, admiring the sharp line of his jaw and the way his nose is slightly crooked. Probably broke his face flying off a bull.

He turns his head to look at me. "Think they're louder for you than they were for me." I shyly shake my head. "Now, I think you owe me a drink." He drops my hand, and we start our exit from the pen.

"Sure, but only if you tell me your name."

"What, you don't know?" He looks genuinely shocked.

"Not a clue. I remember seeing your face on the screen but I have no idea who you are."

He looks a little surprised but holds out his hand for me to shake. "Maverick Ryder."

A little chuckle bubbles up. "You ride bulls and your last name is Ryder? How original." We exit out the back of the ride, nodding to the operator.

He scoffs. "Hey, it's not like I came up with my last name." I roll my eyes, and he leads us to the bar. It isn't lost on me that he still hasn't let my hand go. And it isn't lost on me that I'm not sad about it. Maybe I could have one night of fun with him. Just one. Then I can go back to real life and start fresh on Monday.

We sit at the bar and start talking. Sharing embarrassing stories I wouldn't dare tell someone I planned on seeing again.

"Oh, you think that's bad? In high school, I walked around half the day with a pair of my underwear stuck to my leg." The mortification from that has haunted me every day since.

He laughs into the beer and takes a sip before spilling another of his stories. "If it makes you feel better, one time I had to dart out of the locker room, covering my junk with my hat, because my best friend thought it would be funny to steal my clothes." The people around us gawk as uncontrollable laughter seeps out of me.

Erin not so secretly walks by about every three minutes to make sure I'm not freaking out. I eventually give her the leave me alone look and she stays back. I'm not freaking out or wanting to get away. Just the opposite. It feels good to flirt. It feels good to let loose and laugh.

With every drink, I feel more relaxed, a little lighter. He goes round for round with me until his eyes start to look a little hazy.

"I like your hat." I flick the tip of it, a girlish giggle bubbling up.

"Want to try it on?" he asks. It then dawns on me that I lost my hat at some point tonight. It probably flew off when I got bucked off the bull.

"Are you sure? You might not want to wear it anymore when you realize it looks better on me." I wink at him and his face lights up.

"Oh, I'm sure." His hand rests on my thigh and sparks erupt in my core. How can a light little touch do that?

Taking his hat, I place it on my head, and the smile that stretches across his lips is absolutely sinister. His hand no longer rests on my thigh, it grips it, and good lord, I think I might combust.

"You know what they say about a man's cowboy hat?" he asks and I shake my head. He leans in close to my ear, his hot breath on my neck makes me suck in a breath. "Wear the hat, ride the cowboy."

Chapter 4
Ava

My eyes blink open from the light streaming in through the white curtains. The pounding in my head leaves me a little disoriented. Trying to clear the fog, I blink my eyes a few times, struggling to keep them open. My whole body feels like it was hit by a Mack Truck. I'm never doing a girl's weekend again in my life. This right here is why I stay home. Nausea rolls through me and I fight it, breathing through my nose. It's then that I realize there is a soft snore next to me.

Why is there a snore next to me?

My heart starts hammering away when I realize I am not alone. Sitting up in bed, I look around to see men's clothes scattered on the floor along with multiple pairs of boots, one of which I recognize as mine.

Oh no, I'm in a hotel room, but it definitely is not mine. Pulling the blankets down, I realize the oversized white T-shirt I'm wearing is *also* not mine.

Oh my God. I cannot believe I had a one-night stand in Vegas. How freaking cliché!

My hand flies to my face as I cover my mouth. My fingers brush against my lips, and I get the briefest cooling sensation. Metal touching skin.

Oh my fucking God. Why does it feel like there is metal on my finger? Please, God, no.

I pull my left hand away from my face and inspect the silver band on my finger... Then, I inspect the man lying next to me. He lays face down in a mess of blankets, his broad, muscled back on full display, only his lower half hidden under the blanket.

Maybe this is a joke, and we didn't actually get married. There has to be something in this room that can give me some sort of hint at what happened last night. I throw the blankets off and start looking on tabletops. Surely, they would need a marriage license even in Vegas. My hands nervously flutter through the room, flipping over the couch cushions, looking under the scattered clothing. The room is freaking huge, it must be some sort of suite. It has a whole formal sitting area with a minibar and a bed big enough to fit about five adults. It's bigger than any apartment I've lived in during my adult life.

"Can you come back and clean later?" His deep, gravelly voice makes me jump. He's either the world's biggest asshole, or he doesn't remember.

"Not a cleaner, buddy." I glare at his stretched-out form, a little extra bite coming through my words, partially from him calling me a cleaner and partially because I am freaking out.

He peeks a sleepy head up and smiles at me. His shaggy brown hair is sticking up in every direction possible. If I didn't want to throttle him right now, I would find it kind of endearing. "Uh, sorry." His grin almost looks sheepish.

His reaction tells me this is far from unusual for him. Fantastic.

"My name is Ava. I'm hoping you have more of a recollection from last night than I do." Right now, he is only looking vaguely familiar, but I'm pretty sure he was the reason I rode that mechanical bull. Unfortunately, that is where my memory runs dry.

"Ava." He mulls the name over, his eyes pinch closed. "Yes, the cowgirl. I taught you how to ride last night."

I'm not sure if that is a dirty joke or if I had ridden something other than him last night.

"Yeah, uhm, can you do me a favor and see if there is a little silver band on your left hand?" This pulls him right out of his stupor.

He sits up, the sheet falling and revealing his beautiful, chiseled chest. If this wasn't such a shit show, I would sit and admire it a little longer because he is built like a Greek God, but I see it when he does: the glinting little silver band wrapped around his finger.

"Fuuuuck." He stares at his finger with the same incredulous look as me.

The smile that comes to my face is lit with sarcasm. "Welcome to the panic party. Now, if you would like to join me, I'm searching to see if we have a copy of a marriage license lying around here or if this is all a big misunderstanding."

"Shit, sorry." He shakes his head, probably trying to shake off the pounding headache if he's anything like me right now. "And sorry for calling you a cleaner. No need to panic. I'm sure it's a misunderstanding." At least one of us has a cheery demeanor this morning.

Waving off his apology, I say, "It's fine. I've checked most surfaces." Maybe this will go a little faster now that there are two of us.

"I'll check my pockets from last night." He rolls out of bed, and I turn my head just as I get a peek at his bare ass. His very nice bare ass, but once again, we are on a mission.

That reminds me to check my purse. Running barefoot through the plush cream-colored carpet, I see it hanging on the edge of a chair. At least I didn't lose it. Trying to fly home without my ID would be a nightmare.

I hurdle over a pile of clothes. He's nice to look at, but sure is messy. Ripping open the bag, relief floods me when I see that all that's in there is my ticket stub from last night, a lip gloss, and my ID. I hold it to my chest in relief. At least that's one crisis adverted.

I wait for a response, but when I turn, I see he's put on underwear and holding a piece of paper.

Please be a paper saying literally anything else other than we are married.

"Did you find something?" I question as he reaches up and scratches the back of his head before letting out a laugh. My arms fall flat to my sides; he is quickly becoming more annoying by the second. "Please share with the group what you find so funny."

"My buddies Weston and Rhett all had a bet on which one of us would get married first." He points to the floppy, oddly long paper in his hands.

That's it. I'm going to jail today because I am going to kill him. "This is serious! We are legally married." My voice raises to an almost hysterical octave.

He rolls his eyes as a buzzing sound fills the room. "Hold on, I need to find my phone."

I throw my head back and blink up, looking at the white textured ceiling and wondering what I've done in a past life to deserve this because what we need is an annulment, but sure, finding your phone is equally important, I guess.

"Why is Doug calling?" His thick, dark eyebrows crease with confusion as he puts his phone up to his ear, and I can hear yelling.

"Maverick, where the fuck are you?" The man I am assuming is Doug, sounds pissed.

His face winces a little as he scratches the stubble on his chin. "Uhm, in my hotel?"

"Did you not see the update to your schedule? You're due for press in twenty minutes in the lobby. We've been waiting for you for an hour." The man on the other line doesn't cease yelling. Maverick has to hold the phone away from his ear to lessen the blow to his eardrums.

He covers his eyes with his hands as his head falls forward in defeat. "Shit. No, I didn't see. I'll clean up and be right there." He hangs up and starts gathering some clothes.

I know this asshole is not about to walk out of here in the middle of this crisis. I stand with my hand on my hip and let out a frustrated breath. "Where do you think you are going? We need to get this figured out. We need an annulment."

"Yeah, I know that. Let me do this meeting." He tosses his phone at me. "Put your number in there, and I will call you as soon as I'm done with media today."

My anger flares, but I put in my number and call myself so I can have his number too, as he slides on a pair of Wranglers and buttons up a baby blue plaid shirt.

"Here." I hand his phone back, and he slides it into his pocket. He grabs his hat, and a little bit of memory starts to lag back to me. A brief flash of me stealing a hat from his head and placing it on mine. The start of the shit show we're now in.

He slides on a boot as he half-walks and half-hops to the door as he pulls the other one on. As he makes his way to the door, he turns to me. "Sorry, but I have to run. Take your time. I'll see you later." And with that, he is out the door and I'm going out of my mother freaking mind.

"I have a bone to pick with you," I say to Erin as I walk through my hotel door. The purse slips off my shoulder and lands on the floor with a thunk, not bothering to put it on the bed. Everything has gone to shit anyway.

Erin pops her head up from where she lays on her bed. Mine still sits littered with clothes and hair supplies from last night. Excitement lights up her face when she sees me. "Hey! You're alive."

I skip over her pleasantries, my hands going to my hips so she knows I am serious. "What made you think it was a good idea to let me leave with him?"

She scrunches her face the same way she does every time something smartass-y is about to come out of her mouth. Her eyes roll as she says, "Yeah, how dare I let you live your best life and hook up with an insanely hot, famous bull rider. You needed to have fun."

Balling my hands up in fists, I drop them to my sides. My voice comes out more of a shout, "I was wasted!"

She gives a look that lets me know she isn't taking this as seriously as she should. "Babe, we all were wasted. Plus, hooking up with a guy from a bar is a rite of passage. You're just tardy to the inauguration. It's fun. Live a little." She waves her hand at me and sits up more in bed.

"Oh well, I didn't just live a little. I lived so much that I got *married*. Drunk me decided marrying the cowboy we know next to nothing about was a grand idea." I hold up my hand as her face pales, staring at the silver band encircling my finger.

She flies out of the bed so fast, her whole body looks like a blur. "You're joking."

The smile on my face is the farthest thing from happy, it's a blaring signal that I'm one millisecond away from losing it. "Oh no, you're looking at the brand-new Mrs. Ryder. And we didn't even get a chance to talk about getting an annulment because he's famous and got called away to do media this morning. I have to wait until he's done before we can do anything about it." Taking a breath after my rant, I rip the ring off my finger and throw it in the trash can next to the entertainment center.

She paces for half a second before replying, "I'm sure it will be fine. This happens to people in Vegas all the time." She stops in front of me, and a sly grin spreads across her face. "Soooo, how was it?" I'm assuming she is talking about the sex. Which, unfortunately, was probably awesome, but I have no recollection of it. I haven't had the time to date, which means other areas of my life have been lacking. Broke the dry spell and probably had the ride of my life, and I don't even get to remember it.

"I remember literally nothing. The last recollection I have of the night is stealing his hat. Which led to me stealing his name."

Her nose wrinkles as disappointment floods her features. "Well, that's a bummer. Maybe before you get annulled, you can have fun one more time."

"I've had enough fun for a lifetime, thank you. I don't have time for this. I need to get a job. A real job." I knew Vegas was a bad idea.

"Okay, before you have a complete mental breakdown, go take a shower. Wash off the night and see if you can keep the panic attack at bay. We'll figure this out. I promise!"

I nod, grab a spare change of clothes, and try to shower off a night full of poor decisions.

My phone rings as I get out of the shower. I quickly wrap myself in a towel, and the steam from the shower encases me. Looking down at my phone, I see it's my new husband, wanting to figure out how to do the divorce.

My wet hands fumble the phone, but I manage to answer before it goes to voicemail. "Hello?"

"Is this Ava? It's Mav." His voice no longer has the freshly woken timber but is still deep and slightly raspy.

Oh, thank God. "Yes. This is she."

"Hey, listen, I have to catch a flight to Dallas." My jaw nearly hits the floor when I register what he is saying. Is he joking? Surely, he means after we get this figured out. I can't stay his wife.

"No, we need to get together and figure out how to get this thing annulled. I'm fairly certain we both need to be there." My feet nervously drag me back and forth across the tiled floor.

"I'll come to you as soon as I can. I'm sorry, but he's literally putting me in a car right now. I have to go. It's not like waiting a couple weeks to get this thing annulled will be a big deal. I'll text you when I get a chance."

I angrily press end on the call. How in the world can he not understand how big of a deal this is? We're legally married, and he's just going to circle back when he has time? And just like that, my super fun girl's weekend is now the opposite of fun. I guess I learned the hard way that what happens in Vegas doesn't always stay there.

Chapter 5
MAVERICK

Well shit. I'm a man who can admit when he's wrong, and I was wrong. Apparently, waiting three weeks was too long. I guess I didn't factor in the time it would take to get the paperwork filed and actually get a court date, so now it's been more like six weeks. Too bad throwing away the ring didn't throw away this marriage; if it did, we wouldn't be here right now.

The judge peers at us over her cat eyeglasses. If the look in her eye, judgment, is any indication, this is going to be a rough morning. "With the pictures supplied to us by the Media, we cannot rule out that you two didn't knowingly enter into this marriage. Vegas or not. Especially with the delay you had in filing. Job or not, one could argue that you two had second thoughts, and that's why you waited to file. I'm denying the annulment until you two can prove you've given it a fair shot. We can revisit the issue in six months."

Ava's eyes widen at the news. "But your honor, there's nothing to reconcile. I don't even know him." Her voice comes out more pleading than anything else.

I don't miss the glare she shoots me when she looks my way. Can't blame the girl, but in my defense, it takes two to tango. And get married.

The judge folds her arms over her chest, resting them against her bench. "Be that as it may, there is evidence blocking the proceeding today. Let's move on to the terms of this arrangement."

Shit, maybe I should have brought a lawyer to this shindig, but I kind of assumed it would be easier than this.

"Miss Davis, do you feel safe with Mr. Ryder?"

"Yes, your honor," Ava mumbles. She tucks a strand of her long blonde hair behind her ear, and I catch a glimpse of the red on her cheeks.

Even mad as hell, the girl is gorgeous. I have to force myself to tear my eyes from her.

The judge looks at us both as she says, "Perfect. I am ordering you to live together until you are deemed divorced. We'll do check-ins to make sure you both are safe. Do either of you have a dwelling where you can reside?"

Ava's jaw drops open before she tries and fails to recover. She looks nervously at me before responding, "I do not, your honor. I am currently living with a friend. I just graduated from nursing school. I have to live here, in Wyoming, though, if at all possible."

Pursing her lips, as if annoyed, the judge moves on to me. "What about you, Mr. Ryder? Do you have a home in which you could live?" She is very much not impressed with our situation.

"Uh, yeah. It's not really meant for two people. But it is in Windy Peaks, Wyoming."

Lucky for Ava, I've lived in Wyoming my whole life. It's going to be a tight fit and not one I want to make. My little cabin is my solitude away from the hustle and bustle of traveling. And sharing that space will take all that away.

Clearly not giving a shit that neither of us are happy about this whole ordeal, she goes on. "Well, I am sure you two can make it work." She looks down at the papers gathered in her hand before looking back at us. If you two can keep to the terms of this agreement, I'll grant the divorce. Mr. Ryder, I've taken into account your finances, and those will be kept separate for the duration of this trial of marriage."

"I don't care about his money. I really just need this to go away." Her voice cracks, almost like she's on the edge of tears, making me feel like the world's biggest jackass. She tried to make me handle this earlier, and I brushed it off, putting us both in a bind.

"I understand, Miss Davis. However, the annulment should have been filed earlier. My decision stands." She picks up her papers and lines them together as she taps them against the stand. "I'll give you both two weeks to get your affairs in order, and you'll have six months together after that. I am setting the next court date for August 18th."

Damn it, right at the end of Cowboy Christmas. My biggest money-making season. My manager is going to love this. He's really going to love the fact that I have a whole ass wife I've failed to tell him about. That'll be a media nightmare. A one-night stand turned into a marriage isn't exactly his idea of a "squeaky-clean" image. How the hell did I manage to make a shitty situation a hundred times worse?

Stepping out of the courtroom together, Ava and I walk in front of the courthouse in her hometown. I pull my coat tighter around my body to keep the chill of the wintery Wyoming wind off me. I'm glad I happened to have this particular day off. It's been one of the busiest years yet. It's like the closer I get to retirement, the more Doug wants to push me. Competing in both the Professional Rodeo Cowboys Association and Professional Bull Riders has my schedule packed to the brim most months.

We walk down the steps in silence before I clear my throat and say, "Listen, I'm going to get my lawyers to look into this. Maybe we can find a way out."

"The way out was the day you left me hanging. Two months ago. I won't be holding my breath."

If her voice didn't ice me out, her tense shoulders and refusal to look at me would do the trick. Fuck, I feel like absolute shit about the whole thing.

A little frustration rises in me because she clearly has no clue about the amount of time and work that goes into riding bulls for a living. "Sorry that my job called me away. There was nothing I could do about that."

"Yes, well, now I am going to have to figure out what I am going to do for a job for the next six months in your little podunk town."

It's not like the town we're standing in is much different. There's only three little shops in the city center and judging by the amount of cars I see, it's not heavily populated either. It's another small town in the middle of nowhere, Wyoming.

Ava moves to angrily stomp away from me, and she actually looks kind of cute when she is all pissed off, but I keep that thought to myself. I am pretty sure I am walking on paper-thin ice with her.

Grabbing her elbow, I swing her around to look at me. "One, you only have to work if you want to. I can float you since I'm partially to blame for this mess. Two, don't insult a town you've never been to. It's a great town, and if you spend enough time there, I bet you won't want to leave." Windy Peaks has always been home. No matter how many cities I've been to, nothing tops it.

She looks like I've gravely insulted her by the way her face pinches, and sarcasm drips from her tone as she shoots me a stiff smile. "Yeah, one, I am not taking a dime from you. Thank you very much. I'm going to have to cross my fingers and toes that there's a hospital within driving distance. Two, I'm sorry." Something about her tone leads me to think she is anything but sorry and that she is about three seconds away from spontaneous combustion due to rage, "I'm mad at you, not your town."

Unsure of how to diffuse the situation, I choose honesty. "Well, if it makes you feel better, I am mad at me too. And when I leave here, I have to tell my whole team about this, so there are going to be a whole lot more people joining the Mad at Maverick Club today."

I don't even want to think about that right now. My ass will never be the same after the chewing it's about to get.

The tense rise in her shoulders seems to let go as she takes a deep breath, her rage goes from a boiling over to a dull simmer. "Okay, well that does make me feel better. I'm sorry for the part I played in this, too," she props a hand on her hip, laying the attitude on thick, "but maybe next time, listen to me?"

I raise my hand in promise. "I swear I have learned my lesson."

"Well, I guess I will call you next week and figure out a good time to move. I need to go." She doesn't give me a second glance. But I can't help but stare as she walks away.

Maybe by the end of this, she won't hate me. But I've got bigger fish to fry today. There's a chance I'll be dead next week once I tell Doug, so she might be in luck.

Chapter 6
Ava

My head is still swimming with the ways today went incredibly wrong. How the hell am I supposed to start my career if I'm being forced to move for the next six months? Walking into the apartment I share with Erin, I find her sitting on our plush grey couch.

"How did it go?" she asks, turning off the TV and angling herself toward me.

"Oh, about as bad as it could have." I drop my purse on the small end table and let out a groan.

"Uh-oh, tell me more." She pats the seat next to her, and I slowly drag myself over.

My feet trudge against the floor as the realization of what is happening sinks in. "I'm still married, and you're going to need a roommate because I'm being forced to move for the next six months."

Her eyes widen as she kicks the plush blanket off her legs and shoots to a standing position. "You're joking? Where are you moving to?"

I sit down, hoping she will join me because I do not have the energy for this. "Oh no, I am quite serious. Windy Peaks." I'm just grateful he lives in the same state. It does make finding a job out there a little easier. Hopefully, I'll find a hospital willing to take a chance on a new grad.

She shakes her head as if this isn't quite computing. "How is that even possible?"

"We have to prove effort of reconciliation, because technically, we've been married for a couple months. I'm pretty sure the judge is making an example out of us." She took zero pity on us being young and dumb. Then again, we aren't that young. I'm twenty-eight and Maverick is... Actually, I don't know how old he is. I don't know anything about him at all except that he's a damn good bull rider with a pretty face.

She slaps her hands down next to her. "Well, that's the dumbest shit I've ever heard. Is there any way out of it?"

My hand flies up dismissively. "I don't know. Maverick's team is looking into it. I feel like it's pretty doubtful. The judge didn't seem to be too impressed with the way we got into our situation." Which makes two of us; I know better. I never do anything reckless or stupid.

I bury my face in my hands. Just when I thought life was finally going to get a touch less stressful, this happened.

"I'm so sorry. I really shouldn't have let you leave with him." She rubs my back, trying to keep me from dropping off the edge.

A deep sigh rattles through me as I sit back up. "It's okay, no one could have predicted I'd pull a Carrie Underwood card and get married to a man I'd known for all of seven minutes." However, after looking at him today, I can see why drunk me thought that was a good idea. I'm still mad as hell, but there is no denying he is one good looking man. His face is sharp in all the right places, and even though I want to throttle him right now, he has kind, warm eyes that draw you in. Makes me wonder what's under the Pro Bull Rider facade.

"Yeah, when I told you to quit being a grandma, this isn't quite what I meant. Show off," Erin jokes. Picking up the pillow to my left, I whack her with it until her laughter fills the air and the dread in my chest lessens a little.

Well, at least someone can find some humor in this.

"Yeah, I'm literally never going out with you again. You can get Cami or Jos married off next time." Hopefully, they marry someone who takes getting an annulment as fast as possible seriously.

"Let's look at the bright side. You get to be a hot bull rider's wife for the next six months. You should take advantage of it. Did you know he won like, six million dollars recently?"

Shaking my head, I reply, "No, I did not know. But I don't want his money. Or any of the benefits of being his wife. I just want to start my career, and I don't know, maybe relax a little." I feel like I've been spinning my wheels for years between school, work, and trying to keep the bills paid. At some point, life has to get a little bit easier, right?

Erin shrugs, "Well, I think that maybe you should consider using that time to relax. When do you have to move by?"

"I need to be there in two weeks. Our time won't start until I step into his apartment." Complete and utter dread fills my system. I don't want to do this.

"Well then, I think we need to dive headfirst into researching the man you married. No way in hell am I going to let my best friend go live with a man without doing a basic Google search."

"It sounds like you already got a head start on that," I say as she hops off the couch and walks over to our little desk nook in the corner. She unplugs the laptop from its charger and saunters back over to me. It's four in the afternoon, and she's still wearing her pink striped PJ shorts and button-up top.

"I may have briefly looked into his name. But now is not the time for brief research. Now is the time for an FBI-style deep dive. We need to know his family by name. His exes. His high school. The whole thing." Sometimes, I forget Erin is borderline crazy. But having a crazy lady in your corner is never a bad thing.

"With how deeply you research your Tinder matches, I bet you have really developed the skill." She has a knack for finding every little detail out about a person with only a first and last name to go off.

She looks over at me, beaming with pride. "And you thought Tinder was pointless. I mean, maybe it is, because you did meet someone the old-fashioned way." She winks at me and I roll my eyes at her innuendo. Meeting someone at a bar should not count as the old-fashioned way, maybe the dumb fashioned way or the too drunk for my own good fashioned way.

Erin opens up her computer and after it powers on, she rubs her hands together in glee before she gets to typing. Her fingers fly across the keyboard as she goes full investigator mode on my freshly acquired husband.

"Alright, obviously, he's a badass rodeo star. Never married. No kids, so you won't be playing stepmom. Let's keep digging." She clicks on another news article with an interview about him.

Erin's face falls as she reads on. "Oh, how sad. It looks like his dad died in a rodeo accident. He was a bull rider, too."

My eyebrows knit together; the pain of losing a parent isn't something that I would wish on my worst enemy. "Oh my God, that's awful." My hand goes to the ache in my chest. "I can't believe he continued to ride after that." I lean into the glow of the computer screen, reading the article myself.

Maverick Ryder, rising star in the circuit. If his name sounds familiar, it is because his dad, Bruce Ryder, was the best during his time. He paved the way for the next generation, generating higher payouts and filling arenas. Many wonder how Maverick will compare to his senior. They are big boots to fill.'

Yikes. Talk about pressure.

More articles pop up, some of them are brutal. Stating he only got his boot in the door because of his dad's tragic accident and the legacy he left behind. Who knew rodeo could be so soap-opera-y?

"Well, the good news is it doesn't look like you have any past girlfriends to contend with. There's no public pictures of him with any girls on social media." I find that almost hard to believe because even if he is absolutely on my shit list right now, he's not exactly terrible to look at. In fact, quite the opposite.

"I'm not trying to contend with anyone. I'm doing my six months and then coming right back." The idea sparks a thought in my head, and I snap my fingers. "Speaking of, what do you want to do about the rent situation?"

She waves her dainty hand at me. "Don't worry about it. If I get in a pickle, I'll temporarily sublease it out. You've got plenty on your plate right now. I'll have your room ready for you when you come back."

Six months has never seemed that long, but I have a feeling I am about to change my tune about that.

Chapter 7
Maverick

You could cut the tension in this room with a knife. I knew this wouldn't be fun, but damn. This is downright miserable. There's nowhere to run in this tiny little conference room either.

"You have got to be fucking kidding me, Maverick." Coach Sully spins in his office chair as he yells at me. He's pushing sixty now, the hair underneath his cowboy hat more salt than pepper these days. His round face is turning that slightly scary shade of red. I'm almost worried he will have a stroke. The giant vein in his forehead pops out and makes direct eye contact with me. I almost forget I should be listening to him as I look at it. You can see it pulse with his heartbeat. "Are you even listening to me?"

My eyes move from the vein to his hazel eyes. "Yes, Coach."

"You are at the height of your career. This is not the time to be shitting the bed with bad choices. We need you to look like you are as on top of your personal life game as you are your riding game." Doug's words come out in an angry snarl as I fight the urge to roll my eyes.

Bull riders are characteristically rowdy. Yes, I do need to be a little better than most, being the back-to-back champ. And yes, the sponsorships are important. They pay a lot. The fancy trailer I have, the nice truck I drive. I know exactly how important the whole thing is.

"Okay, here's what we are going to do," Doug starts, spreading his hands as if painting an imaginary picture. "We aren't going to say anything. We are going to continue on as normal while your new little wife stays hidden at the ranch. I have to ask how the hell you even got yourself in this predicament?"

How do I say, "I don't remember a single thing from that night?" without making this ass-chewing even worse? Clearing my throat, preparing to pull an entirely made up, bullshit story out my ass, Sully jumps in before I can piece together my story.

"Because he recalls nothing," my coach says, crossing his arms. He couldn't just try and let me soften the blow.

"So do you think my lawyers can help with this or not?" I ask, trying to direct the conversation away from my transgressions. I think we all know good and well I fucked up real good this time.

"Well, if you would've told us about this before the court date, maybe. But the judge has ruled. We're going to have to play defense now," Doug says.

"What do you need me to do?" I say, resting my hands on my knees, fully prepared for all of these assholes to think I'm not going to take it seriously. I will. I take everything about my career seriously, I just don't let it make me stiff like the rest of them. My dad was the world's best rider in his prime. I've been living the cowboy life since I was born.

It's one of the most frustrating things being the reason everyone in this room is paid well. For the way I perform, for the way I do pretty much everything. But the second I mess up, it's the end of the world.

"We need to try and keep this on the down low. Don't let anyone know."

Knowing what little I do about Ava, I doubt that will be a problem.

"If we're lucky, you can be divorced and moved on before anyone really knows anything. Sponsorships are at risk here, and I don't think

I need to tell you not to get yourself dropped from those." The condescension is dripping from him, and it grates at me.

"No, Doug, you do not need to tell me."

By the look on his face, he doesn't appreciate the attitude. But my nerves are frayed, and I am exhausted.

"Good. You have a lot of riding left in you. We do not need you getting distracted by some piece of ass you found in Vegas." He spins back to face the table separating us and pulls out his phone.

"I can promise you, I am as focused as ever." Not that I know her well, but it doesn't bode well with me that he calls her some piece of ass. She's showed me more grace than I deserve and should get a little credit for that. The fucker has never respected anyone a day in his life, I don't know why I expected him to act differently now.

"Yeah, that's what worries me," he mutters under his breath.

God, I hate that. If you're going to be an ass, at least be a man about it.

And, I have no clue what the hell he means by that. I've had the best run of my life this year. His part of the check shows that.

Not bothering to look up from his phone, he asks, "Are you expecting any disruptions in your schedule?"

Shaking my head, I reply, "No, the only thing I need to be there for is her move-in day."

Doug nods, and it looks like the majority of his anger has faded. "Good. We've got lots of rides lined up. With any luck, you will walk out a double world champ."

We're going to need more than luck, but I'm ready to put in the work. Even sitting here, my shoulder throbs, still recovering from the last beating it took while riding. That's going to be the real challenge this year: keeping myself uninjured. My body feels more worn by the day, and bouncing back after a ride gets harder every time. Staying healthy is going to be a lot harder to do than having Ava live with me for six months.

"That's the goal. Anything else you need to share with the group?" Sully's anger appears to be running out as well; like most people, he can only tolerate Doug in small amounts, and I get the feeling he is at his max and ready to adjourn this meeting.

"Nope, just the one wife." Holding up my index finger, I try to make a joke out of it, but for a rare moment, they agree with one another and glare at me. Too soon to joke about it I guess. They act like they're the ones legally married for the next six months.

"Great, well then I think we can call this meeting to a close. I'll see you both soon." Sully spins out of his chair, not waiting for Doug to give his approval of dismissing himself, and leaves.

"Well, I guess that means we are done here. This better be the worst hiccup of the season, Maverick, I mean it." He stomps out of the room, and like the complete emotionally developed man I am, when he turns his back, I flip him off.

Now that they're both gone, I let my weight sink into the chair. My hands rub my face as I think long and hard about the shit show I've created for myself.

Chapter 8
Ava

The tires of my Toyota Corolla crunch against the lightly snow-coated gravel of the road. We really are in the middle of nowhere. Mav sent me the address last week, but I've been in denial, so I didn't check it out until right before I had to leave. Denial that this whole thing happened and that I am the root cause behind it. My hands anxiously grip the steering wheel harder the more I think about it. I hate myself sometimes.

The fields and pastures to my right are all coated with a thin veil of snow. Towering pine trees covered in a fresh dusting line the road. All of this would look more peaceful if I wasn't having a complete and total internal mental breakdown. Erin offered to come with me, but I didn't want her to have to make the drive back in the dark just in case another random snowstorm moved in. And I need to face this by myself.

Six months isn't that long in the grand scheme of things. I already have a job interview for the hospital closest to here. Which means, I'll probably be stuck working there for at least a year to gain some experience, but the hour commute when I move back home will be worth it. This is totally fine. So fine. Like really, really fine.

My GPS dings, letting me know it's time to turn left onto the property. A large metal cutout sign with the name "Windy Peaks Ranch" hangs over what looks to be a freshly plowed drive. Little pieces of dead grass poke up above the blanket of snow. I bet this place is really pretty in the spring when all its colors come to life.

I was expecting certain things when coming to a ranch. For one, cows, obviously. What I was not expecting was a whole family compound. As I drive, I see barely visible peeps of cabins with pitched, black roofs. At the end of the long road, I can vaguely see a large house with a massive barn beside it. The cabins have their privacy, tucked behind scattered trees and bushes. They're quite a ways off the main drive, tucked away and hidden from the rest of the world. It's all actually really cute. They seem a whole lot less cute when I remember why I'm here.

"Okay, now let's see if we can figure out which one of these lovely stick houses I'll be calling home." Stopping on the road, I pull out my phone to reread the directions. "Second turn on the right." Okay. Easy enough. Hearing a rumble, I peer into my rearview mirror and see a large truck pulling up behind me. Its lights shine right into the mirror, momentarily blinding me. A honk on the horn of the truck has my frustration boiling over. Impatient freaking rednecks. Hitting the gas, I speed up and turn, a little disgruntled to see Mr. Impatient pulling in behind me. Parking my car in front of the cabin, I swing my door open with a little too much force.

Lo and behold, my betrothed hops out of the ridiculously large, shiny silver Ford truck. A cowboy hat sits on top of his dark hair, which peeps out around the bottom. His black Carhartt jacket makes his tall frame look even larger. Amusement shines in his grey eyes. Well, it might be something else causing those eyes to shine. Like pure mischief.

His lips turn up in a shit-eating grin. "Damn, now I know why all your friends call you Grandma, you act and drive like one." A flush blooms across my cheeks from the embarrassment. He doesn't remember anything about that night, but he remembers my friends calling me grandma. Just my luck.

Rolling my eyes, I put a hand on my hip and snap out, "And do you know what they say about men with large trucks?" My eyes narrow at him as I spit out, "They're compensating."

He puts his hands up at his chest as he shrugs. "Hey now, you seemed to like it enough to want to marry me and my 'overcompensation' after only one ride." The wink he shoots me sends a bolt of both pure rage and heat through me; I hate that he is so attractive and that I can't stop noticing. I cannot believe this is who I will be spending the next six months with.

"You're the worst." Turning on my heel, I reach for the back seat door handle.

Not at all bothered with how freaking annoying I find him, his voice comes out chipper. "I know. Do you need help carrying that stuff in?" Turning to face him, he adds, "I wouldn't want you to fall and break a hip with all that grandma fragility." I know he's joking. His smile stretches across his face, and he's got a little twinkle in his eye like he enjoys getting a rise out of me. Which is fine. I'm sure I'll figure out how to get under his skin and pay him back. See how he likes it.

"No, thank you," I bite out. He, of course, ignores me, and comes up and opens my back seat door anyway, grabbing the first thing he sees and walks it to the door.

The cabin looks small, and a little rise of anxiety comes over me at the fact that I am going to be stuck sharing this small of a space for the next six months. Good thing I didn't bring everything with me. I have a sneaking suspicion it wouldn't fit here.

He opens the door, and I want to throw up. It's basically a studio apartment. I take a step in and run an eye over the place, keenly aware of Mav's gaze on me. I try to school my features because I may not be happy we're in this situation, but I don't want to be rude. "So, where is my room?" I look to him, a little bit of my fear laced in my words.

"Uh, you're looking at it. The cabin doesn't have rooms. Those doors are either to the bathroom or closets." He anxiously scratches the back of his head. Isn't he some sort of rodeo god? I know they make money. The judge even mentioned keeping his money safe, so why does he live in a toybox-sized house?

"I beg your pardon? Where am I going to sleep?" I know this man is not about to suggest we share a bed. My eyes dart over the room, inspecting the place I will be calling home and trying to find a respectable place to sleep. The kitchenette is at the very back of the cabin, the bed is a few feet away from the breakfast bar, and the living room is closest to the door. A TV sits on the opposite side of the wall, in front of the bed, on a small TV stand. The space is long and pretty narrow, but somehow, it doesn't feel crowded. Then again, I haven't even gotten any of my stuff in here yet.

"Well, I have a bed we can share. And if that doesn't fancy you, the futon can be yours." He nods to a sad-looking couch that looks like a backache waiting to happen.

Aren't country boys supposed to be chivalrous? I cock my head to the side giving him an extra dose of sass. "Shouldn't you be the gentleman and take the couch?"

He flashes me that mega-watt smile, and I just know I'm going to hate his next words. "Sweetheart, I spend half the year on the road. If I'm home, I'm sleeping in my bed. You're welcome to join me." A full rush of heat douses me with those words and the implications that could come with them.

"Yes, and I'm the one who had to uproot her whole life and move. I'm not sharing a bed with you." I've slept on worse than a futon, I can make it work. It's only six months, after all. "The futon will work. Thank you." My thanks lacks sincerity, but it's the best I can do. I turn away, plopping my bag on the futon with more force than necessary.

"I'll help you bring in the rest of your things and then I have to get back to work."

Surprise fills me. It's almost the end of the day, the sun is almost completely set. "Do you have another ride today?"

He looks almost confused at my train of thought. "No, on the ranch. I work here on my off time and in exchange, I get the cabin to live in."

I can't fight the curiosity that flies out of me. "Why don't you just buy a house?"

"I love this ranch and the people that run it. Plus, I wouldn't have the time to keep up with my own house. At least here, there is someone around when I'm gone. Three, this is the most beautiful place in the world come spring. I wouldn't want to be anywhere else." He says it with such conviction that I can't help but believe him.

I figured he would be living some grandiose life. Not spending his free time being a ranch hand. Maybe I don't have him pegged quite as well as I thought. "Oh." My brow furrows as I try to reassess the man in front of me.

"Yeah, oh. Well, I'll bring your stuff in. I cleaned out a closet for you. I know it's a tight fit and I'm sorry for that. That's why I told the judge it wasn't really meant for two."

"It'll work. Thank you for making me some space." He nods and heads out the door. And I'm left feeling a little off-kilter. And staring at his ass in wranglers, which unfortunately he could be a model for. I have got to quit staring at this man.

Shaking my head to clear it, I get to work unpacking. I need to focus on my job interview next week. I'll need something to do, or I will go downright mad being cramped up in this house. Not working doesn't sit well with me or my student loans. Or my car payment. I don't just want this job, I need this job.

Chapter 9
Ava

My fist pounds on the bathroom door. "Maverick, hurry up. I am going to be late."

Perfect. I am going to miss my first job interview because I married a beauty queen. The last week has been filled with the worst sleep of my life. Partially because the futon is about as comfortable as sleeping on a boulder and partially because I've been making myself sick over this interview. This is the closest hospital and I really, really need this job.

"Calm down, sweetheart. I'll be out in a minute." I can barely hear his voice over the shower water hitting the tub. He's the worst. Just because he hasn't had to worry about anything in his life doesn't mean the rest of us don't.

You know what? It's fine. I will just skip the shower and do a low bun. I can use my makeup palette's mirror to try and put some eyeliner and mascara on, and concealer to hide the eyebags. That reminds me that I need to eventually go to town, I need to buy another mirror because the bull-riding bathroom hog takes an hour shower and I don't need to be running late every day of my life.

The shower finally turns off as I slip on my shoes. My hair and makeup are as good as they're going to get, but at least I look put together. My black slacks perfectly hug my hips and match my blazer. The bathroom door opens, and a rush of steam billows out behind

Maverick. At least he is mostly clothed. Water droplets drip off his wet hair that hangs just above his eyes. My mind becomes a little fried because, like this, he looks like a walking billboard for a body spray commercial, which makes me wish he wasn't wearing a shirt so I could sneak another peek. Unfortunately for me and my desire to gawk, he's been nothing but respectful since I moved in, minus the absurdly long showers.

"Bathroom's all yours," he says as he dries his hair with a towel.

"It's a little late for that. I have to go."

"Where are you going?" I don't miss the way his eyes catch on the curve of my hips. His eyes come back to mine, and I can see something that looks a lot like desire. But I don't have time to dissect that right now.

"Remember the seventy-five times I told you about my job interview? That's today." Walking over to the kitchen, I grab my water bottle and purse from the counter and walk to the door.

"Oh yeah. Sorry about that. You'll do great. You look..." He looks me up and down, eyes catching on hips, and clears his throat before speaking. "Professional. Gotta say, I like you better in boots though." I look down at my black dress shoes and try to remember a time he would have ever even seen me in boots. But then my NFR outfit comes to mind and I shake my head.

"If that is how you compliment a woman, I have serious reservations about how I ended up in your bed. Now seriously, I have to go. I am already running late."

"Try to use your gas pedal this time when you drive down the road," he hollers from behind me.

I'm going to find some payback for him. Would putting laxatives in his protein shakes before a long drive to a ride be too far? Pretty sure that's a criminal offense, but they'd have to prove it first.

"At this moment, we don't have any full-time openings, but if you are interested, we would love to offer you a PRN position, so we will call you as we need you or if someone calls out, and if something more permanent opens up, you will be our first choice." Since I don't have many options right now, I'm obviously not going to turn that down. And that might work out for my benefit; it's easier to cut ties if I'm not full-time staff and can still get the experience I need.

"That will work great for me. Thank you for the opportunity." The palms of my hands feel sweaty as I fidget with them in my lap. The office they have us in is small and quaint, I am glad it wasn't a large panel interview. Those scare the daylights out of me. One-on-one is a lot easier to handle.

She shuffles the stack of papers in her hands before looking up and giving me a warm smile. "Wonderful. I'll follow up with your new hire paperwork. It does take a little while to get the background check cleared. Usually, about four weeks or so, and then we can schedule orientation. We will probably have you work thirty-six hours the first couple of weeks with your preceptor to make sure you learn the hospital and our procedures, and then we will start calling you as needed."

I nod, grateful that the hours will be longer the first few weeks. Not getting paid for a month is going to obliterate my savings. Lucky for me, student loans don't start repayment for a couple more months, so I have a small cushion before I need to panic.

"Do you have any questions for me?" she asks.

"Nope, I think you have answered them all. Thank you for the opportunity. I'm excited to be on your team." Reaching over the table, I hold my hand out to shake hers. Because this really is a good opportunity, even if it's not full-time, I'm grateful I was able to find something.

"Great. I will show you the way out."

Making it back to the cabin just before dark, I walk into an empty house. A bit of relief hits me. While it hasn't been entirely unpleasant living with him, after his little stunt this morning, I don't exactly want to see him. Plus, I can shower in peace and be assured of having hot water since Maverick likes to use all of it. I should probably give him a break; he's been a bachelor all his life, and sharing a space all of a sudden probably isn't easy. But moving isn't easy either. I have no one here. The thought makes me send a check-in text to Erin. She's checked in every day and offered to come visit, but since the space is so small, that really isn't an option.

Once I get out of the shower and dressed, I start drying my hair when I hear a knock at the front door. As long as I've been here, I haven't seen anyone. Maverick hangs out at Lord knows where until nighttime, then comes home and crashes. So, it's been just me here so far.

Swinging the wooden door open, I see an older lady. A long grey braid hangs over her shoulder, and a cowboy hat sits atop her head. Her denim overalls peek out from underneath her jacket. You can tell she has spent most of her days in the sun, with all the sunspots and freckles across her face. The smile on her face is warm and kind. "Oh! I thought Mav would be here. Are you the lady friend of his?"

Her question has me a bit stumped on how to answer. Do I tell her the truth? Sensing my hesitation, she jumps back in, "Oh, I'm sorry. I didn't mean to make you uncomfortable. I'm assuming you're his, um... Ava. Right?" She stumbles over her words, and I laugh a little, not at her struggle but at the fact that she must feel as uncomfortable as I do.

"Yes, I am Ava. Maverick hasn't made it home yet." Calling this place home still feels odd.

"I'm Mabel. Me and my husband own the ranch. Maverick's friend, Weston, is our son. Well, I am sorry to bother you. Can you give this to him when he gets back? I can bring you a plate, too, if you're hungry?"

An idea comes to mind, and I answer, "No worries, and don't worry about me, I've got my dinner already figured out."

"Great, well if you get lonely, feel free to come down to the big house anytime. I can use some company that isn't rowdy cowboys." She shoots me a wink, and I can't fight the smile that stretches across my face.

I decide right now that I like her. I may not like this situation, but she seems really nice, and I could use a friend out here.

"You can count on it." The smile on my face and the promise are genuine.

"Alright, well have a good night, honey." Her thin lips stretch out in a smile as she backs away from the door and heads to the truck sitting idle in front of the cabin.

"Thank you." I wave and close the door behind her.

Walking to the kitchen, I pull a fork out of the drawer and dig in. If he wants to ruin my morning, I will ruin his night by eating his dinner.

Taking my first bite of meatloaf, I nearly moan. It's been so long since I've had a good home-cooked meal like this. I can cook, but I didn't have two pennies to rub together through college, so it was ramen noodles and boxed mac and cheese a lot of the time. This is amazing. The fluffy mashed potatoes smothered in gravy melt in my mouth. A pang of guilt flashes through me for eating his dinner, especially because this is so good. Not enough to stop eating, but enough to feel bad about it.

I sit the empty plate in the sink as Maverick's headlights shine through the front windows. My feet sprint across the floor to my futon, and I pull the book off the back of it just as he walks through the door.

He walks in, pulls off his Carhartt jacket, and slides off his boots. I pretend to be very interested in my book while watching him from the corner of my eye.

Turning to look at me, he gives me a grin and says, "Hey, how did your interview go?"

"It went great, and I wasn't even late." Another small wave of guilt hits me because he is being nice and caring enough to ask how my interview went.

He laughs at that. "What a shocker. If you use your gas pedal, you can get to places faster." He shoots me a wink, and I can't help but want to blush. His sharp jaw is covered with just enough stubble to add a rugged, sexy look. I can try and deny how attractive he is all day, but now that I'm living with him, I spend half my time being annoyed by his perky and carefree demeanor and the other half trying to hide my ogling.

He walks to the kitchen, swings open the refrigerator door, and spends a good two minutes shuffling through it. There's not a whole lot in there, so I'm not sure where he thinks a plate would hide itself.

He stands up, scratches his head, and searches the lone countertop, seeing it completely cleaned off. "Hey, did Mabel bring by a plate of food?"

"The sweet lady from the big house down the road? Yeah, she came by and dropped off a plate."

A confused look washes over his face, and he looks around the room. I bet he feels like he is going crazy or blind, which makes this even funnier. "Where is it?"

"In the sink." I try to hide my snicker behind my book, unable to keep my face straight.

He looks at me like I'm borderline crazy. "You put a plate full of food in the sink?"

I drop the book from my face so he can see the look of pure, smug satisfaction on my face. "No, but I did put an empty plate in the sink. She makes the best meatloaf I've ever had. I've always thought it was a little on the gross side, but hers," I widen my eyes for dramatics, "wow."

His face falls as his jaw drops. His tone turns accusatory. "You ate *my* dinner."

"Oops." I shrug my shoulders and bring my book back up, discreetly peering at him over it. Yeah, this is worth the guilt I feel.

"You ate my *favorite* dinner." He says it more as a statement as he stares at me in disbelief. He slowly blinks like he can't believe it.

"And you almost made me late for my first job interview. Now we are even." I'm sure he doesn't know what it's like to have to interview for jobs. Or what it's like to care about things like that.

He presses his tongue to the inside of his cheek and purses his lips. "Oh, so that's how it's going to be? You sure you want to play this game, sweetheart?"

It didn't really occur to me that he would want to retaliate. I thought we would call it a wash. "I'm not playing a game. You ruined my morning, so I decided it was only fair if I ruined your night." I mean, I wasn't really sure if it would ruin his night, but I'm sure having your dinner snuck out from underneath you would at least be a damper on the evening.

"You're lucky I'm going to be gone next week, but when I'm back, it's game on."

"I'm shaking in my boots. You're leaving again?" I feel like the championship just ended? Wouldn't that mean it's at least time for a break?

"Yup, bull riding is pretty much year-round. The more I ride, the better chance I have at earning big and securing my spot for championships." It quickly becomes clear to me that I don't know as much about his job as I thought. "Well, since you stole my dinner, I am going to head up to the house and see if there are any leftovers stashed anywhere."

He turns and walks out the door, leaving me with my thoughts, which is a dangerous thing to be left alone with as a chronic over-thinker. I can't help but wonder what other things about him I'm wrong about.

Chapter 10
MAVERICK

I hop out of my truck as soon as I put it in park. Exhaustion is eating at me, but sleeping the day away will only get me on a fucked up sleep schedule, and besides that, they need help with the fence and moving a few cows.

My best friends, Rhett and Weston's trucks are already at the house. Mabel always cooks us a hot breakfast, even if it's the crack ass of dawn. She somehow became a stand-in mom for all of us. Rhett's parents divorced, and his mom moved to the other side of the country. Mine took one look at me and decided she had better things to do. Having a mom who bailed on you makes life hard, but Mabel did a great job filling in the gaps. Her husband filled in the gaps of a father figure when my dad passed.

The bitter wind glides across my cheeks as I climb up the stairs of their wrap-around porch and head to the large double doors of their cabin. Jack had done really well for himself and gave his wife Mabel the house of her dreams about ten years ago. Though the outside looks rugged, the interior has fresh finishes while keeping the mountain feel. Makes me want to buy a chunk of land and put my own house up. Jack always told me to let him know when I'm ready and he would sell me off a chunk. But the time isn't right yet. Maybe someday, when I'm not on the road touring most of the year.

The smell of coffee and maple fills the air as I push open the door, making sure to wipe my boots on the rug. Lord knows Mable will have my ass if I drag mud through it.

"Morning," I holler out. The house is nice and open. The living room sits in front of the door, the kitchen to the back right and dining room to the back left. It makes their house the perfect place for us all to gather.

I nod to Jack, who sits on the couch, going through the paper, his cup of coffee on the end table next to him. He barely peeks his head up at me, completely engulfed in the riveting events written in our small-town paper. Rhett already has his bearded face stuffed with pancakes, and I'm grateful he waves to me instead of trying to answer.

"About time you show up," Weston says, bringing his cup of coffee to his lips. The rest of us have started to show our age, with smile lines around our eyes, but not Weston; he still looks exactly like he did when he turned twenty-one.

I pull my jacket off and hang it on the coat rack next to the door as I reply, "Hey, I got home five hours ago. You're lucky I showed up to help you ungrateful shitheads."

My nose follows the smell, and I walk into the kitchen. Grabbing a plate from the counter, I pile it high, full of eggs, bacon, and pancakes. The worst part about being on the road is that I'm always eating out. This fresh cooked food is half the reason why I dragged my ass out of bed this morning.

I sit down at the table next to Weston, and Mabel comes up behind me. "Here ya go, honey." She pecks my cheek as she sets down a piping hot cup of black coffee—my lifeline at this point.

"Thanks, Mabel." As usual, she has her long grey hair braided down her shoulder. Her blue eyes crinkle around the edges as she smiles at me before walking back to the kitchen.

I reposition in my chair, wincing as the muscles and bones in my back feel like they are on fire. My back has been screaming at me ever since my ride on Saturday. My first bull ran me right into the siding, probably would have crushed me to death if I hadn't been able to get the fuck out of there. I'm lucky I got a re-ride out of that, but it cost me. Every day, something hurts a little worse than the day before. Some days, I wonder why the hell I still choose to get bucked off a bull for a living. But I'm chasing that double title. I can rest when the work is done and the title is won.

"How's life over there with your new roomie?" Rhett asks as he takes a sip of coffee.

Really, it hasn't been bad. She sticks to herself and has her nose in a book half the time. I should probably try to make her feel a little more comfortable. It's still early spring, so it's not warm enough for her to get a whole lot of fresh air, so the cabin fever is warranted.

"It's alright. We don't really talk a whole lot."

"You too busy doing other things?" Rhett wags his bushy eyebrows at me and I roll my eyes.

"No, you fucking perv." The comment doesn't sit well with me, but I can't put my finger on why. Probably because I'm wildly attracted to her and can't do anything about it for a multitude of reasons.

His eyes widen at the bite in my tone. I'm usually the one making the jokes, but this whole situation has me all turned around. It doesn't help that I can't keep my damn eyes off her which makes living with her that much harder. I've never met anyone with a natural beauty like hers. I can absolutely see how I locked onto her the night of the NFR. I would have been crazy not to. But then again, look where it got us.

"Sorry," he mutters, almost looking guilty, and now I feel like an ass.

Blowing out a breath, I shake my head, knowing the bite to my tone was unnecessary. "You're fine. What do we have to get done today?"

Jack, who usually silently watches us be dipshits, chimes in, "We've got to fix a couple holes in the fence on the west pasture, and then bring some of the herd over that way. I want to have them all moved by the end of the month."

The beginning of spring is always a busy time, moving cows, fixing shit that winter tore apart. But I love it. I can see how Jack devoted his whole life to this land. To his kids, Weston and Aspen. Shit, even Rhett and I, we aren't his kids but you'd never know by how good he's been to us while growing up. He's always busted his ass to put food on the table and make sure everyone is taken care of. Running this place for so long has taken a toll on him. He's always been tall and lean like Weston, but he's thinned out more and more. His signature mustache has gone white, along with all his hair. Even with all that, the man is still tough as nails.

I scarf down every bite on my plate, knowing I am going to need as much energy as possible to get through this day. Plus, Mabels food is almost impossible to not inhale. She could probably make cardboard edible.

After finishing breakfast, Weston says, "Well, we better get to getting if we want to get that all done before the sun sets." He pops out of his chair and heads to the door. We stop by our trucks to throw on our winter gear before we head out. Long johns hide under my Wranglers to keep my balls from freezing off. Not really sure if I want kids, but I'd like the opportunity to cross that bridge should the opportunity arise. I pull a gator over my face to protect me from the Wyoming wind and keep my ears from frostbite. Once my jacket and gloves are on, we make our way to the stalls. Walking into the covered barn area, each of our horses perks their heads up from their stalls.

My horse, Lucy, swishes her tail as I greet her. "Hey, girl. You ready to go to work?"

She responds with a whinny, letting me know she's always ready. She's been the best horse of my life, and I love days like today when we get to work together.

It takes us about twenty minutes of trotting before we find the broken fence. It will need a new post when it fully thaws out, but for now, we fix the hole and rerun the barbed wire to the next steady post. Even with all these layers, the wind racks through my coat, making my bones chill. I'm going to need a hot bath and heating pad tonight if I'm planning on walking tomorrow.

By three in the afternoon, we are loading up the last set of cattle. My mind has drifted to the pretty little blonde thing waiting for me at home more times than I care to admit. Something about her draws me in, it has since the second I laid eyes on her. She isn't just pretty, she's got a fire to her I can't help but be enticed by. Spurring her on is far too fun and seeing the flush that creeps up her cheeks every time I've gotten under her skin, it's addicting. But I've got to keep my head because our time will be over before I know it. Weston rides with Jack, just in case something should go wrong, but Rhett and I are officially relieved of duties.

"Alright, man, I will see you tomorrow," I say, eager to get out of here and into the warmth of the cabin. I've got three ibuprofen and a heating pad with my name on them.

"Sounds good, Mav."

My eyes start to feel heavy, and the day fully catches up to me by the time I make it back to my place. Lights stream out the covered window, reminding me I'm not walking into a quiet dark house. Even though we haven't said a lot, having someone there when I get home has been nice. It takes off the loneliness of the silence. Makes it more comfortable.

I lose all sense of what I am supposed to be doing when I swing the door open and see Ava's ass up in the air. A yoga video plays on the flatscreen, but all I can see is her perfect round ass. The way her little shorts hug her curves has my cock straining against the zipper. Not that I didn't notice how hot she was before, but right now, I can see exactly how I ended up in this mess. I'd marry that ass again.

She looks through her arms and legs. "Oh, sorry. I didn't realize you would be home this early."

"No, you're okay. This is your space, too. Keep doing your thing." Plus, I really don't want her to stop.

I start walking again, my body feeling more stiff by the second. If she wasn't here, I'd probably be crawling to the bathroom to get in the bath.

She moves from her position and sits cross-legged on the floor. "Are you hurt?" she asks. Genuine concern covers her face. Guess my walk gave it away.

"No, just a rough ride this weekend. And I didn't really get a lot of sleep. I was working on the ranch today, dealing with cows and fixing one of the fence posts." I don't know why I'm rambling; she probably doesn't give a shit.

Her brow crinkles. "You got up and worked this morning? I didn't even hear you go in or out. I thought you were still on the road."

Shaking my head, I reply, "Nope, I've been working," I hike my thumb over my shoulder, pointing to the bathroom, "I'm going to go take a shower now."

"Okay. I'll be..." she looks around the room, "here." Her delicate brow furrows as she says it, like she would have anywhere else to be. I can't help but smile at her.

Once I get in the bathroom, I sit on the side of the tub. Pulling off all my clothes shouldn't be this hard. A sharp pain slices through me as I raise my hands to pull my shirt over my head. I fight to hold in the grunt that wants to come out, biting my lip instead. Fuck, this is worse than I thought.

With my clothes in a messy pile next to the tub, I rinse off in the shower before filling up the tub. The water steams, letting me know it's just the right temperature. Sinking into the water, I feel the warmth start to relieve some of the ache, but not nearly enough. I pushed myself too hard today and my body is going to be paying for it tonight.

Chapter 11
Ava

Worry starts to fill me when I haven't heard a peep from the bathroom. His shower was short, but then it sounded like he filled up the tub and took a bath. That was over an hour ago.

I don't want to be rude, but I also don't want him to drown in a tub. I bite my lip as I think over what I should do. He won't be mad at me, I know that, but I know he's tired and probably needs some time. I'll give it fifteen minutes, and if he doesn't get out by then, I'm going to check on him.

My eyes check my phone again. It's now six o'clock and I'm panicking. I hop off my little futon and head to the bathroom door. My knuckles tap against the door. "Mav, are you okay?"

I wait a few seconds and when he doesn't answer, I knock again, much louder this time. "Mav, please answer me. Are you okay?" I ask, worry evident in my tone.

The water sloshes, and I feel myself sigh out a breath of relief. "Uh, yeah. Sorry, do you need to get in here? I'll hurry and finish up."

Leaning against the door, I say, "No, I was just worried about you. You've been in there almost two hours and I was starting to think you drowned."

"There's no way in hell I would let my tombstone read, 'Drowned in bath.' I just fell asleep, sweetheart. I'm fine. I'll be out in a sec."

Warmth fills my chest. Sweetheart. I should tell him to stop calling me that, but I like it. No one ever thinks I'm sweet. Uptight? Yes. Stressed out and overstimulated? Always. Which usually leads to me feeling a little crabby and tired.

I walk back to the futon and pretend like I'm not waiting for him to come out. I know he said he's fine, but I need to see it with my own eyes before I can believe it.

When the door pops open and the steam billows out behind him, I find myself a little tongue-tied because there stands my husband in a towel. With water dripping over his very chiseled body. A body that isn't built in a gym but by years and years of work. His abs slink down into that V above his pelvis. Good lord. Maybe I don't give drunk me enough credit. She managed to bag herself one fine ass man.

"See something you like?" Mav teases, a smirk on his face. When his words finally register, I find heat filling my body for an entirely new reason. Damnit. He just caught me eye-fucking him. How the hell am I going to play this one off?

"Not particularly. It doesn't look like you're too injured from this side." Yeah, we will play the nurse card and pretend I was assessing him for injury.

"Mhmm." The way his lips tilt up lets me know he did not buy my story one bit. But it's my lie, and I'm sticking by it.

When he turns to walk away, my breath catches. Across his back are large, long, very angry bruises. They stretch across him, starting at one shoulder blade and meeting with the other. There is another along the lumbar portion of his back. Holy shit.

I stumble off my futon, rushing to him to get a closer look. "Maverick, your back. What the hell happened?"

He peers over his shoulder as if trying to assess his back for himself. I'm shocked his ribs aren't broken with the color of those bruises. No wonder he is so stiff. "What?"

"You have huge bruises all over your back. They look awful." My hands reach out to touch them, but I hesitate, not sure how he would like me touching his bare skin.

"Oh, that is probably from my ride on Saturday. It wasn't good." He says it so nonchalantly, like having blunt force trauma is normal. I guess for him, it probably is.

Sighing, I respond, "Go sit and I will warm up a rag so we can make a hot compress. We should probably rotate between heat and ice. Have you taken any ibuprofen?"

He shakes his head. "Not yet. I'll get it taken before bed. Turn around so I can put some shorts on."

I comply and turn, heading to the bathroom to grab a couple rags from the closet to run under hot water. When I walk back in, he's sitting on his bed, scrolling on his phone.

"If you lay on your stomach, I can put these on your back." I hold up the warm, damp towels.

"What?" he asks, putting down his cell phone and looking almost bewildered.

"This will help you heal faster, and hopefully, you won't hurt so bad tonight."

Shockingly, he listens, rare for a stubborn man like him. I set the warm rags over the worst spots, hoping it will soothe his sore muscles, and sit on the side of his bed. Goosebumps break out over his skin when my hand brushes against his bare back. Every little touch sends a spark through me; it's all completely innocent, but I can't help but wonder what it would be like if it weren't. I wonder if he thinks about it too, but I shut that thought down the second it enters my head. The warmth of him radiates and makes me want to curl up next to him. Wyoming mountain winters leave you chilled to the bone.

Settling myself next to him, I break the short silence. "Well, if you got beat to shit, did you at least win?" My hands fidget with washcloths, trying to get them in the right position and trying to keep my head on straight as my brain short-circuits.

He lets out a curt chuckle. "Unfortunately, no. But I did take home second. My bull wasn't that great. I actually had to do a re-ride after he rammed me into the corral side and hit his knee on the ground."

"Sure, blame it on the bull," I tease.

He shoots me a faux glare over his shoulder. "Hey, half our scoring comes from the bull."

Seriously, I need to do some research on bull riding so I don't sound like a complete idiot when I talk to him. "Really? That doesn't seem fair."

He shrugs his shoulders. "Bull riding is part skill, part gamble." Seems to me like they are gambling more than just on the bull. With the way his body is beat, it seems like they're gambling their lives.

I can't imagine not knowing if you were going to come home or wind up severely injured. Makes me wonder what the point is. "Do you really like it? Bull riding?"

"Yeah, I mean, I've been doing it forever. I think I started playing bull rider when I was six. My body is getting real sick of it, though. But my head and my heart aren't quite done. And I've still got some shit I need to prove." Part of me wants to dig deeper into that last part, but this is the first time we've really done this and I don't want to ruin it because his company is nice. It doesn't feel like this is the first time we've actually sat down and had a real conversation, it feels like we've known each other a lot longer.

"I don't know if you could pay me enough to get the crap beat out of me all the time." My hands have a hard time staying off him. I keep fiddling with his rags, telling myself it's to reposition, but I'm drawn to him, addicted to the rush I feel every time my fingers brush against him.

"The adrenaline rush is like no other. And most days, I walk away just fine."

"Yeah, you look so fine right now. You can call me grandma all you want. With the way you were walking in the door, you will need a cane by the Fourth of July."

He lets out a deep chuckle and I savor the sound of it. It's deep and raspy, and melts against me in the softest way. "Your bedside manner could use some work."

"Hey, I'm not on the clock. If you want a nice nurse, I will take no less than thirty dollars an hour." I reposition myself, getting more comfortable the longer I sit here.

He perks his head up at that. "I already told you, I'm happy to pay you. Speaking of, when does your new job start?"

"Sometime in March, but we'll see. Hiring processes at hospitals take forever. So it very well could be April."

"I know you said no, but if you need some help in the meantime, just let me know."

My head begins shaking before he can even finish his sentence. "I don't take handouts."

"I can respect that, but technically you're working right now so it wouldn't be a handout. And if you want to get really technical, I'm your husband. It's my duty to make sure you're supported." My heart thrashes a little faster at that last part.

He sure has a way of spinning things to fit his narrative. "Well, *husband*, I'm doing fine. I've been figuring it out since I was eighteen, believe me, there is no one more skilled at stretching a dollar more than me." In reality, if the hiring process gets too delayed, I'm going to have to find a part-time job around here. The thought of student loans, my car payment, and credit card payments all coming up makes me feel nauseous.

"What, did your parents give you the boot at eighteen?" His tone is light and inquisitive, like he's asking a funny question, but the feelings that come along with talking about my parents are anything but.

"Actually, they died right after I turned eighteen." I take a steadying breath, the same way I have to anytime I talk about this. I feel his body tense, then go completely still, probably a little shocked by my admission. "And I had no close relatives. So it was just me. I skimmed by on their life insurance for a while, but they didn't have a lot so I had to make up the difference."

There's a heavy pause for a couple of seconds. "Both of them?"

I hum my confirmation. That's all I want to give at the moment, all I can give. Talking about it still hurts. It took years for me to be able to blink without seeing them in the hospital. Even longer to sleep through the night.

"I'm so sorry. I'm sure you know my dad died when I was young too. So I get it. It makes you tough but in the worst of ways. If you ever need an ear to talk to, I'm here. That isn't something someone should go through alone."

We've been living together for a few weeks, but this is the first time I've seen this side to him. A side to him that makes me a little nervous because I'm finding myself not only attracted to him physically but on a level I never thought would be possible. He might be a pain in the ass, but his heart and intentions are gold.

I nod my head in agreement to what he said, but he can't see the motion. He's right. Pieces of me died that night, and I think they were all the soft, delicate parts. In their place, a darker feeling took root. Because at that moment, my childhood was over, and the reality of the world was blaring bright in my face. I was thrust into adulthood before I was really ready, but I made it. It's kind of nice being able to talk about this with someone who truly gets it.

I worked my ass off before school to have a good amount saved. I had to take some extra out from student loans for living expenses, which will inevitably come back to bite me. But I was twenty-two and doing it all on my own. The debt will be worth it someday. I'll get to have a career of saving lives. I wasn't able to save those who mattered most, but maybe I will be able to save someone else's favorite person. Maybe then my heart won't feel like it's constantly bleeding. A sore spot that never quite healed. Death will do that, linger like an unwanted pest.

"Thanks, Mav. I'm sorry, too. But you seem to be doing really well. I am sure he would be proud." My hand rests on his back; part of me doesn't want to move it and break the contact. I never thought I would like such a simple touch, but with this conversation, I find myself wanting to be even closer to him, that draw to him is just getting stronger.

I don't miss the way he grunts in response. Making me wonder what's going on in that head of his.

We sit and chat for a while; I find myself laughing more than I care to admit. I don't know if he has ever taken life super seriously, while I have taken the exact opposite approach. He seems happy, and it makes me wonder if I really have been pushing it too hard. Been too closed off for too long.

"What do you mean you've never seen The Longest Ride?" He scoffs at me like not having watched this movie was some sort of egregious crime.

"Uhm, I don't know. I was busy in school and didn't really have the time."

"We're going to fix that right now." He has to practically roll off the bed with how sore his body is, the wash rags falling to the floor as he stands.

"You need to rest." I get off the bed and grab the washcloths, putting them in the laundry hamper next.

He pays me no mind. "Nope, I need to make some popcorn." He picks up the remote from his side of the bed. "Here's the remote," he tosses it to me from his bed stand, "find the movie and put it on."

"Fine, but take the ibuprofen while you're up. I promise you will thank me for it."

"Deal," he says over from the kitchen, the crinkle of the plastic wrapper from the popcorn lets me know he was one hundred percent serious.

I go over to my futon to get comfy. He looks over at me from the kitchen with a brow quirked. "What are you doing all the way over there?"

"Going to watch the movie?"

"I promise I don't bite. You can sit on my bed, it's closer to the TV."

I nod and walk back over. Something about laying in his bed watching a movie just feels different. There's an odd little feeling coming over me. Damn, am I nervous to watch a movie with him? If I can keep my distance, I don't feel the pull to him as bad. But side by side? That's when things get fuzzy. It isn't fair that he is so damn attractive. And it turns out he isn't a complete dumbass like I originally thought. But what does it matter? In a few months, we will go our separate ways like this never happened. So I sit and lift the blankets for him to get under when he returns. We can be married and be friends. The lines don't have to get blurry. It will be easier for us both.

I wonder how many times I will have to tell myself that over time? My thoughts come to a halt when he presses play. His arm slides over my back, and I freeze.

"I can move my arm if you want, but this feels more comfortable." His voice comes out in a nervous wobble. At least I'm not the only one feeling a little bit shaken.

I all but choke on my words. "It's fine."

But it isn't fine, and the butterflies in my stomach are from the excitement of the movie. Not my roomie slash husband. And I don't lean into him because I like the feel of his presence. Nope. Denial is such a fun place to be.

Chapter 12
Ava

I'm beginning to realize living with Mav will be difficult for a slew of reasons I originally deemed impossible. Every single day, my perception of Maverick gets a little more cloudy. Ever since I went all nursemaid on him a week ago, we've been spending more time together. Every night he's home, we crawl into his bed and watch a movie together. The closer I am to him, the harder it is to fight this attraction. I'm stuck in the middle of who I thought he was and who I'm learning he is. A little piece of me is freaking out because I can't catch feelings for him, I just can't, and a large piece of me wishes Erin would freaking call me back already. I need to talk this out.

Also, I'm learning that being unemployed, hours away from your friends, and having no friends here is the most boring thing in the world. And since I don't really want to spend extra money, driving back and forth as much as I want to wouldn't be smart either. I am hoping I'll get the call soon that my background check has cleared, and I can quit lying around the cabin like a blob. My only excitement is the bimonthly check-ins the court has with us. They check in, making sure we're still living together and we're all still safe. Deep down to my bones, I know Maverick would never hurt me.

The good news about being bored out of my mind is that the place is spotless. And I'm getting in really good shape from all the walks I take up and down the road since it's the only place the snow is plowed.

Hopefully, late spring will bring more sun and less snow. Though it has been getting better, they say we are only in for a few more storms before spring blooms.

My phone rings and the screen lights up with a picture of Erin and me from college. It's my favorite of us. Goofy crooked grins, pimples, terrible hair, and all. "Took you long enough," I spit out.

"Sorry, some of us have jobs," she teases, and I can't help but laugh.

Standing up, I start pacing the house. What little of it there is. "Bitch. I technically have a job, they just won't let me work."

"Sure, blame it on that. What's your giant, very vague, life dilemma about?"

Worrying my lip, I wonder how I should word this because Erin is going to take it and run all the way to Antarctica with it. But being alone with these thoughts is even worse. So I just have to spit it out. "I think I'm attracted to Mav."

She snorts on the other end of the phone. "Oh no, you're attracted to your super hot cowboy husband. How devastating." Her sarcastic tone makes me think she isn't taking this as seriously as she should. I'm having a life crisis here.

Stopping in my tracks, I snap out, "First of all, it is devastating. How am I supposed to share a house with him for months when he comes out of the shower dripping wet and looking like..." I wave my hands around, trying to find the right words, but there are none to describe him because holy shit, it's like he isn't even from this earth. Like it's clear God has favorites because he had to put in an extra sprinkle when making him. "I don't know. Hot."

She sighs as if this whole thing is crazy. Which it is. Insane. Clinically insane. "You could always bang him. That might help, you know, take the edge off."

My eyes roll at her suggestion. "Yeah, sleeping with him worked out so well for me the first time."

"Hey, you're the one who called me, asking for advice. It's not my fault you don't like any of it." She isn't wrong. I knew this was what her advice would be, and the more I have to look at him half-naked, the more alluring it's becoming.

"Do you have a plan B suggestion?" I ask, hoping she could come up with some way for me to magically no longer feel this pull to him.

"Unfortunately, no. Because there's only one thing I would be doing if I were in your shoes, and it's that super hot husband of yours." Sometimes I wish I were as carefree as she was, because maybe then I could scratch this itch that has been building every time I see Maverick with his shirt off. But my brain is wired logic first, desires second.

"You are useless." Sighing, I let myself fall back onto my makeshift bed on the futon, which hasn't gotten any more comfortable. The second I start working and have some extra cash, I need to see a chiropractor because my back feels like I am closer to eighty than twenty-eight.

"I'm sorry, I will think of a plan B suitable to your liking. Are you at least enjoying it up there?"

"It's pretty, but he's gone a lot and I'm so bored. I'm going to have read through my entire to-be-read list by the end of this." The area is beautiful, though. I can't wait to see what happens when spring, well, less snowy spring rolls around. I am guessing up here, it doesn't bloom until summer.

"Well, that is a plus. Honestly, babe, you probably needed to slow down. Use this time to catch your breath and relax. Enjoy the mountain air and try not to plan out every second of your life for once. Just go with it. In six months, you can go back to being your neurotic but loveable self."

That's the thing with Erin, she's always blunt. Would calling someone neurotic be considered rude anywhere else? Yes. But she's my best friend and I know she says it out of love. And because I am a bit on the Type A side. She probably is right.

"Okay, I'll try."

"Good, now explain exactly how you realized you were attracted to your husband?"

A dry, unamused chuckle comes out because I knew right away. Even when I was fighting mad at him, I was half mad at myself for not being able to be an adult and think logically. But it's been a burning little ember flickering every now and then, now it's a full-on blazing fire I cannot figure out how to put out. Even worse, I can't decide if I really want to put it out. "How much time do you have?"

"For you? All the time in the world. Partly because I love you, partly because I am very nosy." There's her honesty, again.

"Okay, well, one, he's not ugly. Let's start with that. But the other day he came out of the shower, and the steam was clouding over him like a fucking cologne commercial. I couldn't peel my eyes off his abs if my life depended on it." The image flashes through my mind again and I can feel my body reacting. Heat slinks through me in a sudden rush, and my heartbeat turns from a steady beat to a quick rhythmic thump.

She gasps. "You lucky bitch. Go on."

I tuck my knees under my legs, getting more passionate as I divulge more. "Well, then he was kind of hurt, and you know me, I had to help. I held hot compresses on his back and we sat and talked. Like really talked and ugh." It would be so much easier if he were a vapid athlete or a nepo baby. But no, he has to have a work ethic. And is kind. And wants to help literally everyone around him. It's honestly the worst.

She clicks her tongue before responding. "Let me guess, it isn't just the body you are attracted to?" Her laugh almost sounds diabolical.

"He's a good person behind his go-lucky exterior. I totally had him pegged as a guy who has had everything handed to him... But he works so hard. He rode all weekend, got no sleep, and then went and worked a full day on the ranch until sunset. Who does that?"

"Oh, honey, you are in way over your head."

"I know!" I practically shout as I flop a pillow over my head. "It would be easy if he was all brawn and no brains, but he has to go and be a good person. We have more in common than anyone would have guessed."

"So what I am hearing is you're fifty shades of fucked?"

I'm leaving in six months, so getting involved would be a terrible idea for a slew of reasons. "No, I am a strong woman. I will be fine; it will just be a long, really difficult few months."

"I give you a month before you crack like an egg." For being my best friend, she has such little faith.

"Nope, it's not happening. It can't happen and we both know that."

"Whatever you say." Her tone of voice tells me she doesn't believe me, and the more I sit here and think about it, the more I don't believe myself either. But I am a damn good liar, especially to myself. So I am going to stick to my guns.

Chapter 13
MAVERICK

We walk into the big house after a long day of shitstorms. Everything that could go wrong did: the fence was down, the cattle decided it was a free-for-all and roamed two miles down the road, and my truck got a flat tire. Even if the day was total shit, it was still nice to be home and with my people. I don't have to have the perfect persona here; in this house, I can just be Maverick.

"Hello boys, how was your day?" Mabel asks as she turns her head, looking away from whatever she is whipping up on the stove. It smells so good, it makes my stomach rumble.

"Well, it's 4:30 and I already need a beer," Weston says, the dirt covering his face really enhancing the display of how shitty this day was.

"And that's different, how?" Rhett pipes in as he pulls his boots off his feet.

"Fuck off. I've settled down in my old age." Weston glares, and he has, compared to high school and college Weston, this one is practically a golden child.

"If you boys start talking about thirty being old, I'm going to have to whoop your asses," Jack says. His mostly hidden lips turn up in a smile.

"What do you boys say about staying over for dinner tonight? I'm whipping up a big pot of chili, and I've got enough cornbread to feed an army," Mabel says as she walks out from the kitchen, around the large island, and into the living room. She dusts her hands before looking at all of us, knowing good and well that we don't ever turn down her homemade meals.

"You don't have to tell us twice, Mom," Weston says as he walks into the kitchen to give Mabel a peck on the cheek. He is a giant mama's boy, even if he doesn't have the balls to admit it.

"Mav, I've got cookies in the oven for you right now." I knew I smelled chocolate chip cookies when I walked in here.

"You sure know the way to a man's heart."

"Speaking of, why don't you call your little lady friend and have her join us? I'd love to get to know her better." Mabel leans into the counter, brushing her long braid behind her.

"Oooh, me too!" Weston's sister, Aspen, walks in. Her brown hair is pulled back into her usual bun. Her oversized hoodie covers up the majority of her long legs. While Weston took after Jack, Mabel and Aspen are carbon copies of each other. Aspen did inherit her dad's sarcastic attitude, though.

"Us too. He never lets us come over anymore." Weston looks to Rhett, who has a shit-eating grin on his face. These assholes live to make me uncomfortable. I know without a doubt they will be grilling me about her the second they turn their ears. There is nothing to tell...or nothing I am willing to share with the group.

"I can see if she wants to swing by. I know for sure she likes your cooking." I'm still not over her swiping my dinner plate. The little thief may not have known meatloaf is my favorite, but I'm still salty over it. Pulling out my phone, I shoot her a text asking if she wants to come by. Can't blame her if she doesn't want to join. This is quite the crowd to throw yourself into.

I go to sit at the island in the center of the kitchen and my phone dings from my back pocket. My eyebrows shoot to my forehead when I read the message.

"Uhm, she said she will come."

"Oh yay! We need another girl around here. All this testosterone is suffocating." Aspen waves her hand around in the air to add to her dramatics. She has always had a personality that was bigger than life.

I look around the room. "Listen here, none of you better make her uncomfortable. She's new around town, and I've already put her in a shitty spot. I will whip all your asses if you make this weird."

"Do I sense some protectiveness coming off you, Mav?" Aspen leans her forearms on the marble counter and wags her eyebrows at me. Off to a real good start of not making shit weird.

"No. I just know y'all can be a lot."

Everyone in the room looks at each other and has a silent conversation like I'm not sitting here. Getting off the stool, I make my way to the fridge. I'm going to need a beer for this.

Within a few minutes, there is a knock at the front door, and my heart races with nervous energy. These are all my people, and I want her to like them. I want them to like her. Why do I need that though? I've never worried about that with any other girls before. My palms suddenly feel sweaty, so I rub them against my jeans while walking to the front door. I swing it open, and she shyly smiles.

"Come on in. I will formally introduce you to the group." She steps inside and slides off her tennis shoes. "Here, let me take your coat." I pull the coat off her shoulders and see she's dressed up a little. Her long-sleeved shirt forms perfectly against her curves, and if all eyes weren't on us right now, I'd be taking my time to look. Her jeans sit high on her hips and flare out toward the bottom.

Placing my hand on her lower back, I guide her forward. "Everyone, this is Ava. I'm sure you have all kind of met or talked to her."

"Hi, sweetheart. It's great to see you again." Weston's mom comes up and gives her a big hug. I watch some of the tension in her body melt. Her hugs have the tendency to do that. She naturally becomes everyone's mom, I don't know how she does it.

"This giant is Rhett." He dips his head as a hello; he's almost 6'5 and towers over everyone, so if she needs an identifying factor for him, giant will do it. "And this is Weston. This is his parent's house." Which I am pretty sure I have already told her, but my nerves are making me feel a little frayed. "And this is Aspen, Weston's sister." Aspen comes running over.

"I am so happy you are here!" Aspen says, and Ava's eyes light up in surprise to her warm welcome, almost as if she was startled. I shake my head, chuckling under my breath. Ava's eyes find me, and I smile in encouragement.

"Well, since we are all here, let's get to the table and dig in!" Mabel says.

"Ain't gotta tell me twice," Weston remarks, rubbing his hands together excitedly as he moves to the table.

Ava sticks close to my side as we walk to the table, and I pull out a chair for her.

"Thanks." She takes a seat and looks around the table. "Does she need help?"

"Oh no, if you try to help her, she will swat you out of the kitchen. This is her thing," Aspen says as she brings her glass of wine to her lips.

Within a few minutes, our bowls are filled up and piled high with chili, onions, cheese, and crackers. Ava stays quiet, but the smile on her face eases my anxiety about whether or not she's uncomfortable. She watches everyone around her and all the conversations.

"So, Ava, what do you do?" Mabel asks, looking up from her bowl of chili.

She sets down her spoon and clears her throat. "I am in the process of getting hired at Windy Peaks Community Hospital. I just graduated from nursing school a few months ago."

Aspen audibly gasps, slapping her brother on the arm; he winces and rubs the spot. "Shut the front door. Maverick, why didn't you tell me she was working at my hospital?" She looks at me, eyes bright with excitement, "I work as a nurse there, too!"

"Uh?" I look around, mostly because I didn't think about it, and they had never met.

"Men usually leave out the important details or ignore them entirely," Ava says, looking at me—well, it's more of a glare. I know there is little truth behind the glare Ava shoots me. We wouldn't be here if I had listened to her important details.

"So, when do you start?" Aspen leans on her elbows, resting her hand on her fist.

Ava lets out a heavy sigh, shaking her head while bringing a shoulder up to her ear. "Your guess is as good as mine. They are taking their sweet time getting my paperwork processed."

"Oh my god, I remember when I got hired there and it took over two months for them to hire me." Aspen rolls her eyes before shoving a spoonful of chili into her mouth.

Pure panic showers over Ava's eyes. "Well, I hope they've learned to be a little more efficient than that. How long have you worked there?"

"Since right after I graduated college, so about three years, I think? I was twenty-two when I got started, and I will be twenty-five in a couple of weeks." Aspen is the baby of the group. She always hated that. She tried to run with us our entire high school career, but bringing an eighth grader to corn field keggers was frowned upon, so she got left at home most of it.

"Oh, that's great. Well, I am glad there will be a familiar face."

Dinner goes on like usual. Everyone's talking over everyone. Aspen decides she wants my chair so she can talk more to her new bestie; her words, not mine. Much to my surprise, everyone behaves, and I don't have to whoop anyone's ass.

I look around the table and see how perfectly Ava fits in. A little too perfect because I am realizing I like having her around a little too much. This whole thing is temporary, and I would be smart to remind myself of that.

Only I'm not smart, and I want her alone. "Alright, well, I am ready to crash. You about ready to head home?" I ask Ava, unsure if she would want to stay here alone.

Aspen's palms hit the table with a *thud*. "Hey, you can't take my new friend away that fast!"

"Why don't you exchange numbers? You can come over and visit anytime," I say, sliding my chair back, ready to make our exit.

"You're going to regret that." Rhett pipes out. And he is one hundred percent right, but if it means we get out of here sooner, it's a risk I am willing to take.

The girls exchange numbers, and we say our goodbyes and head back to the house.

We drive the short distance separately; I wait to get out of my truck until she pulls up beside it. Swinging my door open, I step out and rush over to open Ava's door. We walk up to the cabin together, and I might be imagining things but it feels like there's a little electric charge between us.

She pulls her coat around herself a little tighter before looking up at me. "Thanks for inviting me, that was really nice."

"They're a lot. But I am glad you had a good time."

I open the door, gesturing for her to go first as she says, "You've got some good people in your circle."

"I do. Did you want to watch a movie before bed?" My voice sounds a little more eager than I had intended. In fact, it's edging on desperate.

"I thought you were tired?" She raises her eyebrow.

"A little TV before bed always helps me sleep." That might be a bit of a stretch, but telling her how much I've liked our nightly routine of watching a movie together would blur boundaries I'm not sure she is willing to cross.

"Well, alright, but I get to pick tonight. I am going to stab my eyeballs out if you make me watch another western."

"Those are classics, and you should respect them," I say in mock offense.

"Well, tonight, we will watch a classic of mine." The thought of what could be a classic of hers has me worried.

"Okay." We change into comfier clothes and climb into my bed, which is small enough that our legs touch when we spread out and I crave contact with her. I will find any excuse to get my fix, even if it means sitting through an hour and a half long chick flick.

Ava grabs the remote and presses play. She watches the movie and I watch her eyes get heavy. It doesn't take long before her head flops onto my shoulder. I gently wrap my arm around her, and in her half-sleep, she scoots closer. Fuck, I like this too much. My eyes grow heavy in seconds, calmness filling me at her touch as I hold her. My blinks get shorter and shorter apart before I find them drifting closed, the sweet smell of Ava the last thing I remember before sleep finds me.

Chapter 14
Ava

Mav hasn't even been home a couple of minutes before a knock sounds at our door. I watch his shoulders dip in resignation. He looks beat. I'm guessing the last few days away were long ones. He was on the road again, and I found myself missing him the entire week.

"You planning on getting that or are we supposed to pretend to not be home?" I say over my propped-up feet. The futon is growing on me. Though still uncomfortable, it's nice being able to have my own personal couch. Setting the book I'm reading down on my chest, I cock my head at him, waiting for an answer.

"I was debating on the second, but since they probably heard you..." He turns back to the door and takes the two short steps to grab and twist the handle.

"Yeah, because my voice is what gave it away, not the lights being on, genius." I laugh at his train of thought.

"Smartass," he bites out, but I don't miss the smirk that follows, negating the annoyance in his tone. Sparring with him is my favorite, though I would never admit it. I miss it when he's gone.

When he's on the road, the cabin feels too quiet. I've grown fond of our late-night movie sessions. It isn't lost on me that we both not-so-discreetly find excuses to touch or cuddle. His company and presence is surprisingly comforting, leaving me craving more time with him.

The door is open for no more than three seconds before Rhett and Weston bust through. "What are you guys doing here?" Mav asks.

The grin on Weston's face tells me that he is up to no good. "Well, since you've been ignoring our phone calls and refusing to hang out with us, we are taking matters into our own hands."

"Hey, Ava," Rhett says, a small grin on his face. "Sorry to interrupt, but we are taking your roomie out. We're going down to Luke's and you're going to have fun, dammit." He points to Mav, who just holds up his hands.

"Apparently, you've been rubbing off on me," Maverick says to me with a wink, a jab at my grandma-ish traits. He walks over to his side of the house and strips off his button-up shirt, leaving him in a white tee. He exchanges it for a clean blue one with a checkered pattern before pulling out a different pair of boots.

"What? Were your other ones not good enough?" I ask because to me, a pair of boots is a pair of boots.

"There's working boots, and there's show boots. These are for show." He taps his heels together like he is Dorothy.

Weston heaves out a sigh. "Wow, I expected this to be a whole lot harder."

Mav shrugs his shoulders. "A cold beer sounds nice. But we're coming home at a decent hour." Somehow, I doubt that no matter what Mav says now, he'll be out until the boys decide he's had enough fun.

"Yeah, we will be the deciders of that," Weston says.

"Have fun, boys. Call me if you need a ride," I say, shaking my head as the boys start to push Maverick out of the cabin.

The door starts to close, and I can hear Maverick's voice, "Sheesh, I'm coming!"

When the door clicks shut, I can't help but laugh to myself. Poor guy. Hopefully tomorrow, he'll be able to get some rest. But knowing him, he'll be up at dawn and working on whatever Jack needs. He really is something else. And much to my dismay, I think I like whatever that something else is. We are so different but similar at the same time.

Getting comfortable, I swing my favorite sage-green plush blanket over my legs and settle in. Three pages into my read, I am interrupted by a knock on the door, and before I can even get myself off the futon, Aspen is busting through.

Sitting up in a hurry, I ask, "Uhm, what are you doing here?"

"Sorry, I should have waited for you to open the door. But I wasn't taking any chances of you turning me down. We're going out." She shuts the door behind her and smiles at me.

This must be how Mav felt. Suddenly, I am regretting the glee I found at his turmoil. I was really looking forward to finishing my book and going to bed at the respectable hour of nine, maybe eight-thirty. When I think the words over in my head, I realize I really am a grandma. Here I am, finishing out my twenties like I'm in my sixties. I don't know what comes over me, but I find myself leaping off the couch. "Okay, I'll go."

"Really?" She looks genuinely surprised. "I never see you leave this cabin. I thought for sure I'd have to beg you for at least an hour."

"I've decided maybe I do need to live a little." Though preferably not as much as the last time I agreed to go out. But it's not like I can get any 'more' married. So, it can't get much worse.

"Great." I realize she is holding a duffle bag and feel a fresh new wave of fear wash over me. She reminds me so much of Erin, who also terrifies me. Mostly because we are different; while I enjoy laying low and blending in, she likes to live out loud and actually be seen in every room she is in. "Now we just need to get you ready. If I am bringing you on the scene with me, we are going to do it with a bang."

Lord, help me.

Forty-five minutes later, my long blonde hair is expertly curled into loose waves that cascade down my back. My blue eyes are rimmed with smudged liner and lashes so full that if I bat them fast enough, I might actually take flight.

Aspen doesn't look too bad, either. Her chocolate brown hair is tied into a high pony with the ends perfectly curled. She rocks it with her denim skirt and pink cowboy boots. She and Erin would be fast friends, if not by their personalities, then by their shared style.

She has me dressed in a red sundress that hugs my upper body. Admittedly, I like the way I look. Feminine and a little edge of sexy with the way my breasts sit high. She brought me a pair of boots, hoping we would be the same size. I didn't think to bring the boots I bought for Vegas, though, those are loosely considered cowboy boots since they were purchased from Target. Running my hands over where my red dress flares at my hips, I take one last deep breath.

"Alright, show me what a night in Windy Peaks looks like."

The front of the bar looks exactly how I imagined a country bar would. Its exterior is made up of old weathered wood and faux saloon doors. And I must admit, I really like it. The small town here was nothing like I expected, but I'm starting to wonder if it was something I needed.

Aspen's steps come to a halt and she grabs my arm just before we walk in. "So, I need to warn you. You will be the shiny new toy here tonight. It's pretty rare for a new pretty face to show up. And, well," she gestures her hand from my head to my toes, "you're hot. And they're going to notice." I almost blanch at being called hot. I've never thought of myself as ugly or unattractive per se, but kind of just there, I guess. Nothing special.

We take one step into the bar and I realize she was right. Whether my nerves are making me acutely aware of how it feels like every pair of eyes are on us, or if it's actually happening, but it causes my steps to falter. I let out a quick breath, readying myself. This will be fun.

My eyes scan the crowd, taking note of everything. The two old guys huddled next to the bar, completely unaware of what's going on around them. The two girls next to them, giving Aspen and me an apprehensive look. As if we are stepping on their turf, which we might be. The dance floor has a few couples spinning around to whatever song is playing on the speakers.

My eyes continue to search until they land on a pair of steely grey eyes. The nerves that were rising come to a quick halt. My eyes stay locked on him and the heat behind them. He doesn't spare Aspen a glance. The way his eyes stay locked on me fills my confidence right back up. His presence here gives me a certain comfort I didn't know I was searching for.

Aspen's oblivious to it all, helping me take off the denim coat and hanging it up on the old coat rack to our left. "Alright, let's go wreck the boys' party."

That's an idea I can get behind; being closer to Mav has never sounded quite so appealing. We weave our bodies through the crowd. There are more people here than I would have expected, but we soon make our way to the back, where the boys are playing pool.

"Hello, boys." Aspen's smile stretches across her face. "We'll play next."

My head whips around to look at Aspen. "Uh, I don't need to play. I've never played pool a day in my life."

She quickly dismisses my concern. "Well, being that you are a current resident of Windy Peaks, you're going to have to learn. It's basically a law."

My eyes can't help but roll because that is absurd. I look over to Maverick for confirmation. His shoulders shrug up as he responds, "She's right."

"Okay, well, just know I'm a really sore loser." Having to scrape my way through adulthood has made me a bit competitive. It's why I graduated at the top of my class. There wasn't a lot I could control, but kicking ass was one of them. So, I did.

"You and Weston both," Rhett says. Weston flips him off as he walks up to Aspen and gives her a hug.

"What brings you ladies out tonight?" Weston asks, his arm still loosely draped over his sister's shoulder.

"I thought it would be a travesty for Ava to never get to experience Luke's and, well, we were bored." She acts as if she speaks for us both because I was perfectly content with my book. Though I have to admit this might end up being more fun than I had planned for myself.

"Well then, you better get to getting." Weston gently pushes Aspen to the table. Feeling very out of my element, I look around.

"Do you want me to help you?" Maverick asks. My nose immediately scrunches up at the word help. Little does he know I'm a professional at figuring shit out on the fly.

"No, I'm pretty sure I can figure out how to hit a ball with a stick." I look at him with a little extra sass.

He holds his palms up in surrender. "Whatever you say, sweetheart." The look on his face is cute, and I find myself having a hard time looking away. But I have a point to prove.

Strutting over to the table, I grab a pool stick that hangs on the wall.

"Ava, since we're popping your pool cherry, you can go ahead and do the honor of breaking. I'll rack up and then you aim for the top of the triangle," Weston instructs.

"Seems easy enough." I shrug with mock confidence.

Fidgeting with the stick, I lean over the table. This can't be that hard. But the stick is long and awkward to control. I try and close my eyes, picturing how I've seen other people play, but that was only on TV. I've never seen a game in real life. With more effort than it should require, I finally thread the stick between my index and middle finger and aim for the white ball, which makes a satisfying clanking sound when it makes contact. Unfortunately, that's where my luck runs out. The white ball bounces around, hitting nothing.

"Weston, I think we finally found someone you can beat in pool," Maverick says, and I do my best to send visual daggers his way.

"Fuck off, Mav." Weston flips Mav the bird as he sips his beer.

My turn quickly comes back around. Heat suddenly presses behind me, and I don't even have to ask who it is, I can tell by the way my body reacts to his closeness. His deep voice whispers in my ear, "Which do you hate more, asking for help or losing?"

Closing my eyes, I try to ignore the way my body feels this close to his. With some extra bite, I respond, "Neither, cowboy. I'm just getting started. Give me a few rounds and I'll be kicking everyone's ass in no time."

Maverick chuckles against the shell of my ear and it sends goosebumps over my body. "I don't doubt that at all, sweetheart, but since you're new *and* my wife, it's my duty to help you."

My wife.

There are too many wars going on inside my head right now to fight him on this. "Okay," I say. I'm not sure if I'm more worried about losing this game of pool or losing the closeness of him in this moment.

His body is flush against mine, making it feel like my brain is full of sparking wires. I can't concentrate on anything right now. Trying to control my breathing is hard enough. I close my eyes for half a second to get a fucking grip. His woodsy smell drifts around me, filling me in a bubble entirely full of him. If we weren't in public, I wonder if this would be the final thread that would snap. But we aren't alone, and I am sure this move alone has our little friend group gawking.

"Okay, sweetheart, you can either thread the pool stick between your index finger and your middle finger or between your index finger and your thumb," he says.

"Okay, which one do you do?" I ask, not having enough brain cells left to make this choice for myself.

"I do between my finger and my thumb."

"Okay, then I'll do my index finger and my middle finger," I say, because going along with him all willy-nilly has never led to anything good. His laugh behind me brings a smile to my face, a smile I'm glad his smug ass can't see.

He helps line up the cue with the ball and then steps away. I shoot, hitting the ball, but it shoots sideways, completely missing every other ball on the table. "Son of a bitch," I mutter under my breath. I need to focus, or I'm going to end up losing a lot tonight.

Weston chuckles from beside us and Aspen gets ready to shoot her shot. She lines up and it goes straight in the pocket.

My anger starts to flare because I really hate losing. Apparently more than ever with this stupid little game. "How come it looks so easy when you do it?" My exasperated eyes land on Aspen.

"Because I've been playing pool in this bar long before I was legal. How do you think I earned my weekend shopping money?" Her sly smile has me laughing. Of course she was hustling men in pool. I tuck that away for another reason to love her.

I look over to Mav. "Okay, fine. Tell me what I'm doing wrong."

I fully expected him to tease me for it, but he doesn't, and that's the only reason I didn't whack him with my pool stick. "Alright, you are way too tight. You need to loosen up. And when you strike, you need to push through. Don't just stop because you feel the ball."

"The fact you just said tight and balls without laughing means you are more mature than I had originally thought. But okay. Loosen up and follow through, I can do that." I put on a show of stretching my neck side to side.

I lean down and get into position. My hair falls to the side as I turn to look at Mav before shooting my shot. "Is my form right?" I confirm, and a part of me wonders if he feels this heat between us too. If the look in his eyes as he stares at me, bent over this table, is any answer, I'd say I'm not the only one who feels like melting.

"You just need to move your arm a little." He slides close again, moving my arm to be better positioned on the stick. Goosebumps raise on my arm from where his hand sits on my skin. My body feels greedy for his touch. "Stagger your legs a little more," he taps the back of my thigh, and sweet Jesus, the heat that fills me could cause an inferno, "and lean forward." I do as he says. Swallowing hard, I take a deep breath to recenter myself. I notice Maverick positions himself behind me. I look down at my dress and suddenly get the feeling he doesn't like the idea of other men catching a peek. I like that. I like that way more than I should.

Okay, seriously, Ava. Focus.

Firing my shot, the ball goes gliding toward a solid and knocks it and the solid next to it into the pocket. My eyes go wide and excitement fills me as I turn to face Maverick to make sure he saw my shot.

My hands shoot in the air. "Yes! Take that, Weston. You're the only loser here now!" I surprise myself by finishing my celebratory jumps by leaping into Maverick's arms for a hug. And it's this moment, that I realize I am so very screwed because I am catching feelings for the husband I am only supposed to have for six months.

Chapter 15

MAVERICK

Ava's face gives away the shock she feels when Bertie and the Gang hit the stage. Bertie has been the headliner at Luke's for longer than I've been alive.

She looks over at me with wide eyes. "There's a band?"

"That's Bertie and the Gang. They're the most rock and roll sixty-something-year-olds you will ever see," Aspen says as she smiles over at Ava, clapping her hands and swaying to the beat. Even Ava can't help but tap her foot. There is something about 90s country; you can't help but rock with it.

Ava looks around with a genuine smile on her face. As the music picks up, people start rushing to the dance floor, two-stepping and toe-stepping all around. "I really like this place."

"Luke's is a local legend," I say as my eyes scan the crowd. With the way she drew attention when she walked in, I'm sure one of the local boys will be trying to get their hands on her. She looks like a fucking dream in that dress and pair of boots.

"I wanna dance," Aspen says as she hops off the stool, heading straight over to Rhett, who's playing pool with Weston. A risky fucking game those two are playing, and they think they are so sneaky. I think the only one who doesn't see it is Weston. Dumbass.

While my focus was on Aspen, someone managed to sneak up on us. "Excuse me, ma'am. Do you want to dance?" Jake Thompson says as he holds out his hand to Ava.

"Oh, I don't think you want to do that with me. I've got two left feet." Ava shakes her head with a polite smile on her face.

He doesn't miss a beat and looks down at his boots. "These boots are steel-toed. I think I can take it."

"Come on, Ava!" Aspen says as she drags Rhett over. Ava bites her lip before she resigns.

She puts the beer she is drinking down on the table we share before hopping off the seat. She looks at me for a second too long, but I miss the chance to take my shot because she puts on a half-smile. "Can you watch my drink for me?"

Not being able to find more than a single word, I nod my head. "Sure."

Like a hawk, I watch her take foot on the dance floor. He slips his arm around her waist and takes her hand. My anger starts to simmer, low and slow. The sight of his hands on her has mine balling up into fists. Why the fuck did I not ask her myself? She follows his lead, better than she gave herself credit for, and they begin to spin around the dance floor.

"You gonna do something about that?" Weston walks up, eyes on Ava and Jake as he takes a hearty sip of his Coors before setting it on the table.

"Do something about what?" I'm not willing to show my cards to him yet.

"Jake Thompson having his hands all over your girl." He looks at me like I'm an idiot, and to his credit, I just might be.

"She's not mine, so it doesn't matter." I stone my features over, eyes glued on Thompson. I wish I could talk shit, but he's a good guy. Actually, he's one of the best guys in town. Hard working, good family. Ava tips her head back in laughter and my teeth grind so hard I feel a pop in my jaw.

"Oh please, you look madder than that bull you rode in Cheyenne." His laughter does nothing to soothe the rage simmering in me.

"What the fuck should I do?" I look over to him, curious what his genius plan would be. She may be my wife by law, but she's not mine, and I think I'm starting to hate that more every day.

"Sitting here won't do you any good. If you want her, go get her, Ryder. Being a pussy ain't going to do nothing good."

"I'm not being a pussy." Even hearing the words come out of my mouth has me almost laughing. I can ride bulls all day, but chasing that girl is ten times scarier. And if I go dance with her right now, that means it's exactly what I'm doing.

"Alright, but if she finds someone else, and you're sad and alone, that's on you." He winks at me and finishes his beer before walking back toward the bar.

His words run through my mind, along with the vision of her with someone else, over and over and over, until the sound of my barstool scraping against the wooden floor overpowers the music. I slam the rest of my beer and move to the dance floor.

The music changes as the couples around me spin, but I've got my eye on Ava. When I approach, her eyebrows almost hit her hairline. I'm not sure if it's me out of my chair or the look in my eye, but I am one hundred percent sure she didn't think I'd come get her.

"Excuse me, if you don't mind, I'd like a spin around the floor with you." I stare her right in the eye, not even bothering Jake with a look.

"Uh, I guess." Jake thanks Ava for the dance and backs away.

"Okay, now let's really teach you to dance." My hands slip into hers like it's the most natural thing in the world.

A shy smile tugs on her lips. "I didn't think you were the dancing type." It turns out I'd be just about anything she wants me to be. Which is fucking terrifying considering this whole thing has an expiration date. My dad always told me to be tough as nails and not to let anything stand in the way of what I want. And what I want is right in front of me.

"Oh, I can dance. Let's see if you can do more than two step. Follow my lead." I twirl her around, and she spins and lands right back into my arm. Bertie and the Gang have the guitar fully twanged up today. There's a little light in Ava's eyes that I haven't noticed much before. Only when she laughs, but it's there, right now, when she looks at me as I twirl her in circles—entangling myself deeper into her with every step. My eyes get caught on her lips. Lips that are practically begging for me to kiss them. This is going to hurt like a motherfucker when it's over, but I can't bring myself to care right now.

"No more spins, or I'm going to be sick." Ava laughs as her hand lands on my chest. We've danced to song after song. Anyone who dared to try to take a step forward got a glare from me or was stepped in front of by Aspen.

"Alright, sweetheart, we can slow it down." As if Bertie could hear my thoughts, the beat changes into a slow dance. My hand wraps around Ava, and I pull her a little closer. Her sweet scent is like a siren call, beckoning me to get closer and become fully enraptured with the woman before me.

"Why do you call me that?" she asks, her words wavering a little as if she isn't sure she wants to ask.

"Would you rather I call you something else?"

"What are my options?" she toys with me.

"I've got a few, Granny," I joke as she pulls her hand out of mine and smacks my chest, a deep chuckle slipping out of me.

"Hey, I am out and it's past eleven, that means that nickname is officially out the window." The deep set in her brow makes this even better. Reaching out, I rub my thumb over it to smooth the crease.

"Okay," I clear my throat, "beautiful fits too." Her cheeks instantly flush as she tucks her head a little bit, trying to hide from me. "Let's stick with sweetheart." Because it fits her. A lot about her is sweet, especially that heart of hers.

"Okay." Her voice lacks its usual bravado, a softer side coming out. Something about that makes me feel a little proud. A girl who is hard for the world but soft for me makes me feel like I'm doing something right.

"Okay," I repeat back to her. She swings in my arms, and I let her hold on to her silence until the beat turns up, and I step back and twirl her in a circle.

The sudden change has Ava's laughter echoing around my head down to my chest, warming a piece of it I forgot existed. She twirls around, and I realize my world is going to end up spinning around her because I'm starting to fall for my wife.

Chapter 16
Ava

My boots crunch in the snow, and no matter how far I walk, the building panic doesn't ease. "Shit, shit, shit."

The bitter wind bites at my face, making my eyes water. This is good. I can blame the tears on the wind and not actually admit that my life is spiraling and I can't fix it. All this work, all this time, and I am *still* struggling. I stop walking to catch my breath and try to pull myself together. If I was sure I could break down by myself, I would. But the ranch hands take this road, and so do Jack and Mabel. I can't let them see me break.

My start date at the hospital was pushed back. It seems my recruiter forgot to turn in my background check paperwork, and now I'm delayed until that gets done. They aren't really sure when it will be done; it could be a week, or it could be a month. Fuck.

My bank account is dwindling by the second, and I have bills to pay: loans I took out for school, loans for my car, and credit cards that I would really like to start paying more than the minimum for. What the hell am I going to do? I guess I could look for a part-time job in town, but I really don't want any other commitments because I need this job at the hospital. I need to make a difference. And for once, I need to be more than just surviving. I'd like to know what it feels like to lay my head down and not do math on how I'm going to have everything paid for. To lay my head down and know it's taken care of.

Panic rises again, my gloved hands finding my knees as I hunch over and try to catch my breath.

The sound of tires plowing through the fresh snow makes me stand up straight. I blink up toward the cloud-covered sun, rapidly fluttering my lashes to bat the tears away.

"Ava, what are you doing out here?" Maverick yells out as he leans across his center console, taking in my full-blown panic attack glory. "Shit, Ava. Are you crying?" The sound of his truck door slamming shut echoes over the top of the snow.

It was that obvious, huh? Maybe I should have risked being suffocated in a snow drift.

Maverick's steps turn into a run and I turn my head as he gets close. "Ava, what's wrong?"

"It's nothing. I am fine. You can get back to work." The crack in my voice gives too much away.

"I'm not going anywhere until you tell me what is wrong." His fingers find my chin, forcing me to look up at him. "What can I do?" Concern is etched across his features. His eyes dart around my face, looking for an answer I don't want to give. Telling my super rich, oopsie husband I am flat broke is not a conversation I want to have. Telling him more than I already have divulged is terrifying. If no one else knows, I can pretend all these pieces of me don't exist. The scared, the struggling and the lonely. I have great friends, but I don't have a family. They all have places to go on the holidays and I just follow them, with nowhere to land that is really my own.

"Really, Mav, I am fine. I just need a minute." I try my best to put on my brave face, hoping he'll drop it.

"You're not fine. Please, tell me. Even if I can't help, talk to me." The desperation in his voice to make this better makes my resolve melt.

"My start date got pushed back." I turn my head out of his grasp and look out to the pine trees. They really are beautiful when they're covered in powder.

"Okay, and can you tell me why that's making you risk hypothermia?" He's trying to understand but obviously is waiting for more explanation. One that is mortifying for me.

"Because I'm out of fucking money, Mav. I know that is a hard thing for *you* to understand, but my cushion is gone. I have no job, and I'm stuck out here in butt fuck Wyoming." I throw my hands up, anger boiling up and out of me. Not at him, but at life, for never giving me a damn break.

His eyebrows shoot up in amusement; of course he would think this is funny. I don't know if he's ever had to struggle with money, counting every penny until you finally get paid again. "Butt fuck, Wyoming, huh?"

"Okay, I'm done with this conversation." The warm feeling I previously felt toward him is now as frozen as my toes. Screw this, I will just figure it out myself.

"Wait, I'm sorry. Let me help." I try to pull my wrist out of his grasp, but he is holding on to it like his life depends on it.

My tone turns to steel. I may need help, but I'll never take a handout from a man. Or from anyone, for that matter. "I've told you before, I don't want your money."

"It won't be mine. We can get you a job at the ranch. There are never enough hands for everything that needs done. You can do all the smaller projects the boys and I don't have time for."

I debate on telling him no. "This isn't a handout. I want to earn it. I don't care if it's hard."

"I know you know how to work. Jack and Mabel will be thrilled to have an extra set of hands." I search his face, trying to see if this is just a clever ploy to get me to accept my help, but I feel like he is telling the truth.

"When can I start?" I need money like yesterday.

"You can start right now if you want? I am on my way to the barn. We have a couple stalls that need cleaning and a calf that needs feeding."

"You should have led with feeding baby cows," I mutter, the last bit of my anger now evaporated, and I suddenly feel a little too tired.

"I'll remember that next time." He walks to the truck door and opens it, waiting for me to get in. "I'll show you how everything works, and then I have to help the boys drop some hay for the cows in the pasture."

"Okay. Thank you," I whisper. God, I don't want to do this, but declining help is clearly not getting me anywhere. Technically, I am still earning it myself.

Mav drives around the big house and follows the road until we get to the giant barn. Its steel sides are covered with a pitched roof. It still looks like a barn, but half of it was smooshed with a metal shop.

"I'll show you around the barn and the stables," he says, one hand lazily draped across the wheel and the other arm propped on his center console.

Gawking at the sight in front of me, I say, "That's the biggest barn I've ever seen." Obviously, I've seen it before, but from afar—never wanting to get too close to the house and feel like I'm encroaching on someone else's space. The only time I've been to the house it was was dark out, but now that I'm taking it all in I'm in awe.

"Well, there's also a practice pen. A few kids from town like to ride, but their moms won't let them compete. I like to practice there. And kids take horse riding lessons. Plus, the whole left side is the functional part, which is where you will be working." I take note, trying to remember it all.

"Wow. People come all the way out here to ride?" This part surprises me the most. The whole town is very widespread. There is obviously a town center area, but once you get out of there, houses are separated by many miles. For such a little town, it stretches far.

"When you live in a small town, everything is a bit of a drive, so you'd be surprised what people are willing to do." He shrugs it off like it is nothing new. I always thought most of Wyoming was the same. We don't really have huge cities, but I guess I never really understood true small-town life until I was here. My little town lacks quite a few things this one has, like heart and people who adore it.

We park in front of the barn; the estate fence goes around the front, making it easy to tell where to go. Good to know for future reference.

"You can come in through the main door. We try not to open the overhead door much in winter," he points to the opposite end of the barn, "keeps the inside a little warmer."

He punches a number into the keypad on the door, and it unlocks. A huge dirt pen sits to the right, and another door goes to the left.

"Here is the pen. This is where we do rides. You'll see over there," he points to the far-right side, "is a chute. We use that for practice with real bulls. We have a few that live here. They aren't as mean as the ones on the circuit, but they're great to learn from and gentle enough for the kids."

"Is this where you learned to ride?" My eyes take it all in, noting the high ceiling and the smell only livestock can bring.

He tucks his hands into his pockets as he looks around too. "Yup, this is the first place I ever rode a bull. The pen was half the size, but so was I."

"That's pretty neat. Do you like teaching kids to ride?"

"Yeah, I love it. It's fun watching their love for rodeo start. We're going through these doors; this part is for the cattle operation. We have some stalls for horses or calves that need bottle feeding. Or the occasional Couplet."

I start walking around the pin area, following Mav's footsteps as we head to the right. "That means mom and baby, right?"

"Yup." He turns the handle, and immediately, the look changes. Now this looks like a barn. There are six wooden stalls. Four of them are occupied by horses, one has a calf, and the other is empty.

I stop dead in my tracks, my eyes locked on the cute little fluff ball. Why are things always so much cuter when they're babies? "Oh my god. Is that a baby cow?"

"A calf? Yes. That will be part of your new job. She needs to be fed twice a day until she can take solids. Her mom rejected her, so she's a bottle calf." He takes a step further into the space, and I follow.

My hands reach out for one of the horses to sniff before I gently pat its nose. "I would have asked you to hire me on months ago if I knew I could pet the cows and horses."

"She's still not a pet, but I'm glad I know how to soften you up," he says, and I look over to him, unable to hide my smile.

"I'm plenty soft." My brow furrows as I take a step away from the horse and close the distance between us.

"Cuddly as a cactus." He winks at me, and I slap him with the new pair of work gloves I had shoved into my pocket he had given me in the truck. "I'm kidding. You're obviously super warm and soft."

My hand falls to my hip. Clearly, he has forgotten a few crucial details about me. "Hey, who took care of you the other night?"

"I actually don't know her. I thought you had been possessed or something?" If the smirk on his face wasn't so freaking cute, I would smack it straight off him.

"I hate you." The words lack sincerity and we both know it. I don't hate him, not even close. In fact, if the warm fuzzy feeling in my chest is any indication, it's quite the opposite. "Now show me what to do."

He turns to face me. "First things first. Are you scared of livestock?"

"Uh, no?" Should I be?" I mean, I was just petting the horse, so I feel like he should have been able to deduce that on his own.

"These are all well-trained, so no. But some people are terrified."

Maybe if it was one of the big, angry bulls I hear about him riding. But the ones in here are strangely comforting. "Then no."

"Okay. Well, you only need to deep clean out one stall a day. Jack likes to keep a super-clean stall. He loves these horses more than he loves his own children. Aspen and Weston will attest to it."

"I believe you." Looking around at their decked-out space, I can see that. I've lived in apartments less nice and way colder.

"You'll need to clean the messes out every day but only replace the bedding once a week. You'll use this pitchfork," he points to the one leaning against the far wall with other assorted things, "to grab the soiled straw and throw it into that bin over there. We will come around and dump the bin at the end of the day, so don't worry about that."

Cleaning up horseshit isn't what I had in mind, but money is money and I'm not in the position to turn down anything. "Okay, I can do that."

"For the calf, you'll use warm water and a milk substitute. I'd recommend doing this first. She'll need to feed first thing in the morning, we usually do it around five or six, and then again, around five in the afternoon. As she gets bigger, you will need more milk. For now, she gets half a bottle twice a day."

He walks to the cupboard, pulls out two clean bottles, and shows them to me. "We'll take these home with us tonight. She's already been fed this morning, but you'll come back tonight. It's best to fill it with hot water at home, so by the time you get here and get the powder substitute put in, it should be perfectly warm for her. The instructions are on the bag. I am assuming you can read?"

My eyes can't help but roll. "Yes, asshole, I can read."

"Great, I just didn't want to assume. Do you have any questions?" He props up against one of the stalls and crosses his arms.

"Where do I put the horses when cleaning out their stalls?"

"You can put two together while you clean out the stalls." He looks over to where the baby calf naps in the corner. "You'll probably have to clean the calves stall out more often, she shits a lot."

I close my eyes and let out a sigh. "Lovely. Anything else?"

"Nope." He pops the P and takes a step away from the stall.

"Well, alright. Thanks again. I really appreciate it." There is no sarcasm here because without this little bit of cash flow, I will be in a real situation I don't know how to handle.

"No problem. You're actually helping us out. The winter is hard on the pastures and fences, so this will give us more hands to fix those. Mabel serves breakfast at the house around six thirty, so if you finish feeding the calf in time, you can meet us all for breakfast."

That actually sounds great. Boredom has become my new personality trait, and having something to look forward to will be nice.

"Alright, I am going to head out. I should be back in about three hours to pick you up."

I nod my head and look around, making sure I am ready. Mav studies me for a minute and then heads out the door.

"Alrighty, guys, I am new so please be nice." The horses let out a huff, and I take that as acceptance.

Chapter 17
Ava

There has never been anyone more bored than me. For the second time, my start date has been pushed back. Some hospitals are notoriously slow at the hiring process, and this one is no exception because what was supposed to be four weeks is almost eight weeks now. Erin has been busy for the last month, and Mav has been a rodeoing machine. So, it's just been me and breakfast with Mabel, which I thoroughly enjoy. The boys are usually gone when I make it to the house. And the horses. I didn't ever think cleaning horse shit would be my idea of fun, but it's better than sitting alone in the house.

I'm used to being busy. I've worked multiple jobs and gone to school most of my life. Sitting at home, alone, with nowhere to be is killing me. Cleaning stalls and feeding doesn't take up enough of my day. This cabin feels smaller and smaller every day. I seriously need to get out of here and off this ranch, even if only for a day.

An idea pops into my head, one I am sure will get turned down, but it's worth a try. And though I hold myself in very high regard, I am even willing to knock myself down a few pegs by begging.

I throw on a hoodie and a pair of shoes to sit with Mav on the front porch. He drinks his coffee there most mornings, and when it's not too cold, he spends some downtime out there, too. I think he likes the quiet and time to himself more than he realizes.

Swinging the front door open, I feel the chill seep in through my hoodie. Maybe I should have thrown on a coat instead. Mav sits on the rocking chair, and I go sit on the one next to him. He smiles at me as he waits for me to say something, but now that I'm here, I am not sure how to ask. I hate asking for things. This isn't a big thing, but it's still something.

"Your rodeo this weekend, is it one that's close by or far away?" I keep my eyes off him, looking at the pine trees. April showers aren't a thing here, but April blizzards are. It's almost May, and you would never know spring was in sight if you looked around.

"It's about two hours from here. Why?" When I look at him, he looks at me suspiciously, mostly because I don't usually ask a whole lot of questions. I just ask if he's okay when he walks through the front door, and then follow that up with a 'well, did you win?' Most times, the answer is yes. He's damn good at what he does. It occurs to me that maybe I should tell him that, but then again, his ego is the size of the state of Texas. I'm sure people tell him all the time how amazing he is.

"Well, I was wondering if I could tag along?" I ask, my voice not quite sounding as confident as I had hoped.

His rocking halts. "You want to come with me and the team to a rodeo?"

With a shrug of my shoulders, I say, "Sure, I've only seen the one, but that was pretty fun. You know, the cows and the horses and stuff."

"You've lived with me for almost three months and you still don't know jack shit about the rodeo."

"I know you ride the bull for eight seconds. So I do know some things, thank you very much."

"Well, I'd love to teach you more, but I don't think it's a good idea."

My face falls with his quick dismissal. "What? Why not?"

"With all my endorsements, we're trying to hide the fact I married a girl I met in Vegas. My manager is worried it will damper my image."

I scoff. "I think your playboy antics dampened your image long before I arrived."

"If this is how you convince me to let you come, you're doing a piss poor job at it."

"Look, I'll stay completely out of sight. They won't even know who I am. I'll stay in the background with your team. I need to get out of this cabin, Mav. I am going to lose my freaking mind. I had a whole conversation with a cow the last time you were gone, a freaking cow!" My chest is almost heaving by the time I get my rant out, and Mav is loving every second. His cheeks, rosy from the cold, pull up as he smiles.

"Did the cow talk back?"

"I hate you. Please, let me get out of here. All of my friends are busy. I just need a little space from the cabin and to see people."

"Are you begging me right now?"

"Yes." As much as my very sensitive pride hates it, I am begging.

"Some people even beg on their knees." The mischievous smile on his face shows exactly what image is going through his mind, and I hate that my body comes alive with it. The chill that was suddenly there is gone, replaced by the flicker of a starting fire in my core. He is the worst.

Keeping my expression neutral, I say, "I'm sure you'd love that, but I'm not quite *that* desperate. I'll find Betty again and chat her ear off."

"Betty?" He quirks an eyebrow up at me.

My head sassily tips to the side. "That's what I named the cow."

He lets out a breath. "Jesus. Okay, fine. You can come. Doug is going to have my ass for it. Lay low and try not to bring any attention to yourself, alright?"

I pop out of my chair, run over and lean down to give him a hug. Thank God. I'll finally be leaving. The ranch is beautiful, but I need some change of scenery.

Mav laughs and pats my back before I pull away. "Thank you. I promise I won't be any trouble."

"Go pack, we have to leave in an hour. Weston is coming, too. We're going to have to share a room, but I'll see if I can switch us to a double bedroom."

I share a shoebox-sized cabin with him on the regular, I am sure we can handle sharing a hotel.

I skip into the cabin, which suddenly doesn't feel so suffocating anymore, knowing I will soon be leaving it. As fast as I can, I shove everything in my bag and get ready to hit the road.

We pull up to the arena and it looks much different than the last rodeo I was at. For starters, we go straight to the back. There's trailers, trucks, and cowboys galore. Erin would love this. Maybe someday, I can talk Mav into letting both of us come, but then I wouldn't be able to promise not to find trouble. Because where Erin is, trouble follows. Or she creates it, who knows?

We walk into the building and quickly run into Mav's manager, who I am pretty sure does not like me. As if I am the sole reason we are in this mess.

"What is she doing here?" The sneer on his lips makes my anger spark.

"Calm down, Doug. She'll lay low. She needs more rodeo experience." He turns back to wink at me, and I can't hide the little bit of smile that turns up. He starts walking down the hall with a swagger that is hard to miss. He has built this confidence brick by brick. Watching him do his thing sends little butterflies in my stomach. I haven't seen him ride since the National Finals Rodeo, and then I didn't really care what happened to him. But now, I can feel a wave of nerves wash over me. He has one of the most dangerous jobs in the world. I didn't think I would feel like this when I saw him ride.

"See you when I cash out," Mav hollers before heading in a different direction to get ready. I roll my eyes but know he is probably right.

"Follow me," Weston says. "Doug is an ass, so try and stay away from him. If you have any questions tonight, just find me. We're heading over to the chute. Mav will be in his dressing room until it's his turn."

"Do they always get dressing rooms?" I figured they would all roam around until their time came.

"Just at the bigger arenas. This is one of the bigger rodeos he does. He will only be riding tonight though."

"So, he just has to ride the one tonight?" Clearly, I have no clue how any of this works, and Weston is quick to pick up on it.

"You really don't know anything about bull riding." My cheeks heat, a little bit embarrassed, and he picks up on it, "Sorry. I didn't mean that in a bad way."

"Oh, no. It's okay. I don't know a whole lot, but I'd like to learn."

"Well, we will use tonight as education night. He's only riding one bull tonight, unless he gets a re-ride, then he gets on another bull."

"And what makes him get a re-ride?" My stride matches Weston's, which takes more effort than I care to admit. He is long and tall, and my five-foot-five self is struggling to keep up.

"He gets a re-ride if the bull underperforms or doesn't come out the chute right or if his knee hits the ground." Okay, simple enough.

I nod as we move down to what feels like a backstage area, where people are mingling all over. Most of them seem to be riders in their sponsor vests, waiting for their turn.

The closer we get to the pen where they ride, the stronger the smell of livestock and kicked up dirt is. Bull riders aren't the only ones competing tonight, Mav did tell me that. He warned me that I might get bored because we arrived fairly early today, and there are at least three events before bull riding.

Time goes by fast; I find other people to chat with—girlfriends of other riders and team members. I'm definitely the only one who has no clue what is going on here, and though Weston is doing a good job of explaining things, I am going to have to do some serious research so I don't feel like an idiot if I ever come back here again.

"Alright, come on up to the chute. Mav will be riding soon." Suddenly, I feel a little sick from the nerves. I shake it off and walk up to the team.

Mav is surrounded by his team. His manager and his coach sit with serious faces, talking his ear off. But as soon as I come into view, his eyes look up from the dirt floor and find mine, and the smile he sends me makes me feel nervous for a whole other reason. I shouldn't like him. I can't. We will be going our separate ways in a few months, and I'll never see him again. I'm comfortable with loss, sure, but I try to avoid it where I can.

I give him a thumbs up, and he chuckles before Doug turns his head and glares at me. It is becoming very evident that Doug is dick, and I hate him.

Doug's haughty tone floats its way over to me. "She can't be here if you can't focus."

Maverick dramatically rolls his eyes. "Calm down, Doug. Once again, this isn't my first rodeo." His nonchalant answer does nothing to cool Doug down. If anything, it makes him madder. He turns on his heels and stomps off, glaring at me the whole time.

"When are you up?" Weston asks Maverick.

"I'll be going after Gonzales," Mav says. His eyes move to mine as his tone turns playful. "Are you getting your need for a change of scenery met?"

"Yes, thank you for bringing me." The nerves rattling inside me won't let him out of my sight without saying, "Be safe tonight."

He dramatically huffs. "Don't worry, wifey. I am always safe." My mind can't help but wander to the night I had to keep heat on his back for hours. Nothing about that felt safe.

"Ryder, come on up." The voice comes from a man I am guessing is his coach. He's older and has a big ol' cowboy hat.

Maverick gives us a nod, but not before placing his hat on my head. "Hold on to this for me, sweetheart." He turns to start walking closer to the pin, and we follow. The grin stretching across my face almost hurts as I pull the hat from my head and hold it against my chest while we walk along the dirt path.

Over the intercom, I hear, "Up next, we have Maverickkkkk Ryderrrrrr." The crowd starts hooting and hollering, and when I think I can't smile any bigger, I do. Suddenly, I feel a little proud to be a part of his entourage today.

I stand a few feet back from the chute as Maverick hops over the rails and onto the bull. They use a rope to practically strap him to the bull, which seems like a shoulder dislocation waiting to happen. I take half a step forward, wanting to see what is going on. Coach is yelling something at him, and he nods, his head angling up just enough to see me. I send him a thumbs up.

A thumbs up? Really? How lame am I?

Mav nods his head, and the bull is out of the chute. I hop up on the fence next to Weston, wanting a better view. My grip on his hat becomes deadly as the seconds tick by. I thought running on a treadmill was slow, but it's nothing compared to watching Maverick on the back of this bull. Time seems to all but stop as he rides. His free hand stays in the air as he rides the bull with grace, if it's even something that can be graceful. But he looks good doing it. Really, he looks good doing anything, and I hate that.

The eight-second buzzer goes off, and I feel a crash of relief. The bullfighters come out to distract the bull, something I also learned about today, and Mav runs to safety.

He pulls off his helmet and looks to the screen, waiting for the score. When it flashes across the screen, the team goes wild, so I take it as a good sign and join in on cheering.

He easily hops over the gate and walks over to me. A small sheen of sweat causes his tousled brown hair to stick to his forehead. The smile he gives me makes my stomach swoop. "I've got to meet with Doug and talk to Coach real quick, but I will be back in a few."

"Alright, I'll be here watching. Here, don't forget this." I get on my tiptoes and plop the cowboy hat back on his head. Our eyes stay locked a second longer than they should, and the butterflies that rush through my system have me feeling a little bit hopeful for the first time in forever.

Chapter 18
MAVERICK

The adrenaline starts to fade as I make my way back to my dressing room. Doug didn't even see the ride, but I am sure he will want to be a part of the conversation. If he hadn't been with my dad the majority of his career, I would have kicked him to the curb. But he got passed down to me when I lost my dad and has stuck around.

The hallway is brightly lit, and I smile and nod at the other contestants as I pass by, wanting to get this over with and head back to the hotel. A hot shower and a long sleep sound great. Plus, the nightly movie marathon with Ava has become something I look forward to more than I want to admit. The movies are usually not my favorite, but hearing her laugh makes tolerating two hours of trash completely worth it.

I open the door to my dressing room, seeing that Doug has Gonzales' ride streaming on the small TV. This is one of the better arenas. It's nice having space to settle down in after the rush of riding. I can still keep up with the contenders but not have to be in the public eye.

"Good ride out there today, Maverick."

"Yup." I'm still a little peeved at how he talked about Ava earlier, right in front of her. I knew he wouldn't be the biggest fan of her being there. But this is my ride, not his. If he wants more of a say, he can get his happy ass on the back of a pissed off bull and start making his own money.

"Don't tell me you're upset with me over the girl." He looks as if my frustration is completely uncalled for. Calling her "the girl" brings another round of anger in me. He knows her fucking name. She didn't do anything but show up tonight, and he's out of his God damned mind if he thinks he can disrespect her, or myself for that matter.

"You don't get to have a say in who I bring to these things, alright? If I want to bring a friend, I can. I think you are forgetting who pays who here. You manage where I am riding and who is paying to be on this vest." I tap some of the badges littering my riding vest. "I do the rest." The shock on his face could be read from outer space. I never mouth off to him, small little quips, but I usually ignore him and walk out when he gets on my last nerve, which feels like something I should be doing now.

Coach walks in, breaking up the awkward silence that has fallen over the room. "Gonzales had a good ride, but his bull wasn't nearly as good as yours, and his scores show it." He must catch on to the tension in the air. "Did I interrupt something here?"

Brushing past Doug, I say, "No, I was just leaving." Screw that. I am going to find Ava and get out of here.

Stalking out of the dressing room and down the hall, I see Ava talking to no one other than Gonzales. Fucking leech. Of course she would catch his eye. She should catch his eye. I've been knocked in the head a few times, but even I know Ava is a knockout. Everything about her is too damn good for that little fucker standing in front of her.

She seems to be making pleasant conversation, but as I get closer, I can hear bits and pieces of their conversation.

"What? Is Ryder the only rider you are willing to ride on?"

The shock on her face at what he said is front and center. "I'm just not interested. But thank you for the offer." She goes to stalk off, but he follows close on her tail.

"I didn't think buckle bunnies played hard to get. Come on, let me buy you a drink." He reaches for her arm, pulling her back to face him, and I lose it. Every ounce of control I had cracks.

"Excuse me?" She whips around at the buckle bunny insult. Between Doug and this douche, I'm seconds away from blowing a gasket.

Rushing to her side, I push her behind me with my arm. "Who the fuck do you think you are talking to my wife like that?" My voice comes out in a murderous thunder, loud enough for the whole arena to hear. Which is good. "If you want to fuck with Ava, you're going to have to get through me."

Ava grabs my arm. "It's okay, Mav, really."

My anger is still too hot and needs a place to be released. "It's not fine." Clasping Ava's hand in mine, I keep her positioned behind me. 'If you have something disrespectful to say about *my wife*, say it to my face or get the fuck out of here." I point to the door, which I would like to drag him out of and kick his ass.

Gonzales, being the pussy he is, puts his hand in the air. "I didn't know she was your girl."

"It doesn't fucking matter. Maybe you wouldn't have to beg a woman for a drink if you treated them with a little respect." He tucks his metaphorical tail between his legs and heads back to his crew.

When I look up, I see quite a crowd gathering around us, and what I just did hits me. So much for keeping this whole marriage thing under wraps. Cameras flash in our direction, and the weight of it crushes me. It's not me I'm worried about, it's Ava. She's already stressed out with everything that has been going on, and I don't want to ever add another thing for her to worry about.

"Shit, Ava, I'm sorry." But she isn't looking at me with anger; something else that looks a lot like wonder simmers behind her eyes. "Let's get out of here before this becomes a cluster fuck." Gripping her hand, I lead her out the back. I drove my own truck here, and we can head to the hotel in that. I will text Weston and Coach when I get there.

Ava's silence unnerves me. I know we were supposed to keep this thing quiet. Partially for my reputation, a super short marriage and divorce are not helpful in keeping my image squeaky clean. People will speculate and talk, they always do. The other half of it was for her. For exactly what happened tonight. I don't want anyone coming at her because she's my wife. Or my wife by name.

When we finally get to the truck, I turn toward her and take her hands in mine. "Listen, I know we were supposed to keep this under wraps, but when I heard him talking to you like that, I snap—" My words are cut off by her lips crashing into mine. God, how I have wished for this. Savoring the taste of her on my lips, I ensnare my hands around her hips, pulling her close enough to feel the rapid beat of her heart against me.

She pulls back, her voice barely a whisper. "I'm not mad, Mav."

Confusion fills me, though it shouldn't, considering the way she's reacting. "You're not."

Her hands grip the front of my vest as she shakes her head. "Not even a little. You had my back."

A piece of my heart breaks that simply standing up for her would elicit this type of reaction. "I'll always have your back, sweetheart." My palm cups her face, my thumb brushing against the soft skin on her cheek. Her lips crash back into mine, and the urgency in the kiss rises.

I reach behind me and try to find the handle, desperate to get her out of here.

Breaking the kiss, I turn around and open the door. She hops in without a word, and I hustle to the driver's seat.

I expect her to let me get the key in the ignition, but the second my ass plants in the seat, she's reaching over and kissing me over the console. I lose all sense of what I am supposed to be doing; the only thing I can think about is her lips on mine.

She takes me, pulling me closer in stride, and crawls over the center console. Her hips straddle my lap, making it impossible to hide the swell of my cock right now. Her center perfectly lines up over it, delivering the tiniest bit of friction.

My voice comes out in a rough grumble. "You better be careful, or I'm going to end up fucking you in this parking lot."

She pulls her face back; mischief and fire are written all over her features. I don't know if I've ever seen her eyes shine like they are right now. "Would that be so bad?"

"Fuck." My head is thrown back against my headrest as my resolve starts to melt away. How am I supposed to resist that? How am I supposed to resist her? The way she looks right now. My bones feel like they are on fire.

Her lips find mine again as she rolls her hips, creating the perfect amount of friction for it to feel good. I've never come in my pants in my thirty years of life, but I think Ava is on a mission to brand my cock as hers and take home the title. She rocks her hips again as she moans, and the sound causes goosebumps to erupt over my skin.

"Make that sound again," I command. I feel her smile break out against my lips as she drags herself against me again. "Ava, let me touch you, sweetheart?"

"Please," she pleads, and my lips move to her neck. My hands roam her body, cupping her ass.

When my hands eventually find her tits, I feel my grip instinctively close over them with a gentle squeeze. "Yes, Mav. More."

More. Exactly what I want from her. *More.*

Maybe six months with her won't be enough. I feel like the more I'm with her, the more I crave her.

Unable to keep my composure, I unbutton the top of her jeans and slide down the zipper. Pulling my head back, I grip my fingers under her chin, guiding her attention back to mine and silently asking for permission. She doesn't answer, but she nods her head and leans back in.

The windows begin to fog as her breath grows heavier; my hand is a tight fit between the jeans and the zipper. I want to push down her pants, but the blue jeans are glued to her figure. My hand slips down and grazes against her clit. When my fingers circle, I am met with a moan.

"Is that what you wanted, baby?" It's not nearly enough for me. I want to dive my hand between her legs and feel how wet she is for me. Maybe have a little midnight snack on her pussy. Anything she is willing to give me, I'd take it. "Let me hear you say it, Ava."

"Yes, Mav." She places her hands on my shoulders and rocks her hips, my fingers slipping just far enough to get a feel for how wet she is. I wonder how wet she gets after she comes. It becomes my personal mission to find out.

My index finger circles around her clit in small sharp movements. Her breathing grows heavy, making a dense fog cover the windows. If anyone had a question about what we were doing behind my tinted windows, they won't anymore.

"I need you to come for me, in this truck, for anyone to see." If they had any doubts about who she belongs to, they won't after hearing my name being screamed from her lips. "Let everyone know who you belong to." She may not actually belong to me, but while she's my wife, she does, and I want everyone on planet Earth to know.

Her voice comes out breathy. "If you can get me off with just a touch of your finger, I will personally deliver you a gold star." And now I'm even more motivated. Watching her unravel in my hands is one thing, but being rewarded for it? Game on.

My hand slips up her shirt and bra, my free hand circling her pebbled nipple as I pinch. My other hand focuses on her clit, speeding up and applying more pressure, circling around her clit like a fucking Oklahoma tornado. Her body begins to shake, and when her eyes peer into mine, I know she's close. She didn't think I could, but I'm about to rock her world with a touch of my finger.

Leaning in, I whisper in her ear, "Come. Now." The touch of command in my tone sends her over the edge. Her body shudders, and I fight the urge to come. If I am going to come anywhere tonight, it's going to be in her pretty little cunt.

"Now. I am going to take you back to the hotel, and this time, you're going to remember every second I spend fucking you."

Chapter 19
Ava

We crash through the hotel door as a culmination of tangled tongues and bated breaths. This is a terrible idea. I know that, but I can't stop. I need to know what it feels like to be Mav's. Really his, even if it's just this once.

The back of my knees hit our shared bed, and we tumble down. "Let me see you." Mav's voice sends a wave of lust through my body. His hands find the hem of my shirt, and he tugs it over my head. His hands slide over my body, and I feel myself come alive. The worries that usually cloud my head are suddenly gone. All of them are quieted by his touch. My head feels airy anticipating what is to come next.

"You have no idea how long I have wanted to do this. To see you like this." His breathing is as uneven as my own. Little does he know, I know exactly how bad he has wanted this because I have been fighting the same feeling. Ever since he walked out of the shower, he's been all I could think about. Every bit of what I learn about him only drives me to want to be closer. I've never wanted someone like this. It's all-consuming. Every piece feels a bit better when he touches me. The innocent touches we shared in the past are one thing, but this... This is anything but innocent.

His hot breath dances against my neck, leaving goosebumps in its wake. My hands find the back of his hair, and I comb my fingers through it. You would expect a man like him to be emotionally hardened. His job is one of the most dangerous in the world; he's been through hell, yet everything about him feels soft in a way.

His lips start to move from my breasts down my stomach. He peppers kisses along my skin, sending goosebumps over my skin. Mav takes his time, and my body feels like an engine revving up, begging for some sort of friction. When he reaches my hipbone, my breathing becomes labored. "Mav, please."

"What do you need, sweetheart?" Him. In whatever form he's willing to give me tonight.

"You. More of you."

The smile that lights up his face is nothing short of sinister. "That can be arranged." He unbuttons my pants and drags them down my body, tossing them to the side because we definitely will not be needing those tonight. His hands roam down my thighs, stopping just above my knees to spread them wider for him. His focus is trained on my thigh as if something has caught his eye.

"What?" I ask. His thumbs rub over the same spot of my inner thigh over and over again.

"I like you like this. Branded with my belt buckle." I sit up just enough to see that his belt buckle left little indents on the inside of my thighs. I've been so worked up, I didn't even notice it was digging into my skin. The only thing I've been able to think about is him. The thought of being branded by him isn't as off-putting as it should be. In fact, I think I like the sound of that a little too much. I liked being called his *wife* way too much. It wasn't so much that he stood up for me. No, it was that he claimed me as his. As untouchable. I've been on my own for so long, I almost forgot how it felt to belong to something. To have someone to count on. Sure, I have friends, but this kind of claim is different. It's making me one of his own and doing it loud enough for the world to hear.

He gets on his knees, a sight worthy of a lifelong memory, and kisses each indent. It's so close to my pussy that I buck up at the feel of his breath against my panties. My body feels wound so tightly that it will take next to nothing to make it snap.

I slip out of his touch to sit up. He stands in front of me on the bed, and I rip his clasped buttons open, one by one, until his shirt is completely open. He strips the shirt off his shoulders and chucks it in the same pile as my jeans. I begin to push the white T-shirt up, exposing pieces of his chiseled core. My hands brush against it as I pull, and I feel his body harden beneath my touch. His erection strains behind his starched jeans.

"I want to see you," I plead.

He pulls the white tee over his head, leaving him with jeans and a belt buckle. He's a walking wet dream for anyone with a cowboy fetish. Coincidentally, I was today years old when I realized I had a cowboy fetish because everything about this man is doing it for me.

My hands start to work at his belt. "I thought you dry humping me was hot as fuck. But watching you claw at me, trying to get me naked, is going to make me come in my pants."

"If looking at me undressing you is all it takes, we need to work on your stamina, cowboy."

"I have plenty of stamina, but looking at you while you look like this? That's something I couldn't have prepared for." The glint of lust in his eyes makes the moment so much more heated.

"Can I?" I ask, looking at him as I undo his belt the rest of the way and begin to unbutton his pants.

"If you don't soon, I'll probably beg."

"I'd love to see you beg for me." It's only half a joke. Seeing this man, who is afraid of nothing, on his knees for me makes me feel a whole new level of powerful.

"Speak the word, baby, and I will get on my knees for you anytime you ask."

Fuck me. My pussy throbs at his words and the implications of them.

My fingers loop around the top of his boxer briefs, and the swell of his cock makes me feel a bit of pride. I've never really felt sexy or like I'm something special, but to be the reason for a reaction like this? I suddenly feel like I am glowing in my skin.

My breath hitches when his cock springs free. His free hand immediately begins to stroke it, and I can't take my eyes away. I'm locked in on the way his hands grip around the girth.

"Do you still want to touch me?" he asks, his lids growing more hooded by the second.

Unable to speak, I nod my head, and my hand shakes a little as it circles around him. My hand, much smaller than his, can't quite grip all the way around. His hand covers mine, and as he begins to stroke, a small bead of precum makes its way to the top. I think it's my turn to come. Something about this experience feels incredibly intimate. Not just sexually. When my eyes drift up, I see his are already locked on mine.

My thighs begin rubbing together, desperate for some sort of attention on my clit—literally anything.

"I think I've got you wound a little too tight. Do you want me to take care of that?" he asks.

"Yes. Please."

He drops back to his knees and grips my panties. "Lift your hips, baby."

My body immediately responds; the rush of the air from the room tells me just how wet I am. I don't have it in me to be embarrassed. "Fuck, you're so wet for me." He holds up my no longer dry panties, and I see where I've soaked them through. "Does your pussy want me this bad? You should have asked me sooner, baby."

My thighs snap shut, the pulsing of my clit becoming too much. "Fuck, Mav."

He tosses the panties to the side, and his big, calloused hands close over my knees to spread them wide and push them up.

"I'm going to get a little taste of you now," he says, and I have to keep my gratitude to myself because if I have to go another second without him, I think I might implode.

His touch starts gentle and slow. A small kiss to my hip bone, and he works his way down. When his full lips meet my clit, a zing of pleasure shoots through me and I can't hold back the moan.

"That's it, sweetheart. Let me hear how much you want this," he murmurs against me, the heat from his breath skits against me. My hips roll, needing more.

When he kisses my pussy again, it is no longer slow. It is a man on a mission to make my body fucking explode. His tongue dives into me, and I relish the feeling, desperate to have something to fill me up. He moves back to my clit and I feel his fingers breach my slick entrance, gliding in with no resistance.

"Fuck, Mav. Yes. That's it." His fingers curl into my G-spot, and I feel the familiar tingle of an orgasm brewing—a tension building higher and higher.

"Do you want me to fill you up?" he asks, and I nod reverently. That's all I want right now. To feel full of him. "Can you be a good little wife and ask for it?"

I've loathed being called his wife, loathed the entire situation since the moment we woke up in Vegas, but at this exact moment, I can't remember why. Because when he calls me his wife? My body likes it. Loves it. It wants to comply with whatever he's asking.

"Please, fuck me. Fill me up," I beg.

"God, hearing you beg, Ava. It could make a man come undone."

"Maverick, fuck me, right now."

His answering grin sends sparks through the air. Almost like I didn't know what I was asking for. He steps away from the bed, and I have to stop myself from asking where the hell he thinks he's going. But when he walks back to his jeans and pulls out a wallet, I get it. He comes back to the bed as he rips the condom wrapper open with his teeth. His eyes look a little erratic, like he's as crazed as I am at this moment. At least I am not alone in that.

My eyes stay locked on his cock as he rolls the condom down. It's not usually something I find sexual but watching him touch himself feels inherently sexual.

"You're sober, right?" he asks. I feel a little dumbfounded because I never had a drink in my hand.

"Uhm, yeah. I didn't have anything to drink. Why?"

"Because when I fuck you this time, you're going to remember it until your last breath. Do you hear me?"

My eyes stay locked on his as I nod slowly. "Yes." My heart hammers beneath my ribs. I've never felt so turned on in all my life; I've never been so desperate. All I want right now is for Maverick to make me his.

He grabs my waist and scoots me back just far enough for his knee to get on the bed. Then his hands move us both up until we're in the center.

His lips find mine, slowing the moment down. I taste myself on him, and it sends a fire through me. I feel the head of his cock brush against me, and my knees fall open around him. His lips never leave mine as he begins to thrust forward. Filling me. Stretching me. The feel of him has me moaning against his lips. His hips snap forward as he seats himself fully inside me.

"Look at me," he says as another thrust racks my body. He props himself up on one hand, and starts circling my clit with the other. My back bows off the bed as the sensation of him filling me and playing with my clit becomes almost too much. Almost. My eyes stay locked on his.

The moment feels like much more than it should be. Part of me wonders if he feels it too. The connection. I've felt it so many times with him: opening up about our pasts and him forcing help upon me when I'm too stubborn to ask. It's like a piece of me has known him long before we met.

"God, you feel good, Ava." Hearing my name on his lips feels sinful. Too good. He repositions himself and grips his hands behind my knees, angling me in a way that has him perfectly hitting my G-spot.

"Right there, Mav." A bead of sweat drips off his brow. This man is putting in his best work, and my body loves it. My hands reach for him, wanting to be closer because I am seconds from falling over the edge.

"Come for me, Ava," he says as his hand works my clit in perfect synchrony with his thrusts. My body starts to tighten and I can feel the scorching flame start to burn through me as I reach up to drag Mav's face back down with me. Tangling his tongue with mine, I come hard for him. His release finds him seconds after. Our chests heave together as we catch our breath, and his forehead rests on mine.

I've been sure of a lot of things in my life, but right now? I'm not so sure I'll ever have enough of Maverick Ryder.

Chapter 20
MAVERICK

M y mind reels as I walk from my truck to the barn. Things are changing. After my little rendezvous with Ava two days ago, I woke up to an empty bed. And she was practically mute on the ride home. Did I do something wrong? Did it mean something entirely different to her? Because for me, that was life changing. I will never be the same man I was before her. Even in my small one-bedroom cabin, she's been making herself scarce whenever I'm home—either faking being asleep or being distracted on her phone. It's been the longest forty-eight hours of my life.

Is she mad at me? I can't figure it out. I pull my hat off my head to run my hand through my hair in frustration, determined to figure out what's going on in that beautiful head of hers.

I enter the code for the barn and, once granted access, open the door. Weston and Rhett stop in their tracks, and I know the day is going to be long from the no-good looks on their faces. "Wipe those smug grins off, we got shit to do." We need to reweld some pins and rake through the dirt floor today so we can work the horses a bit and drop hay.

"Oh no, the first bit of business today is to ask you what's got you all riled up?" Weston says.

"Sorry man, got to agree with the dumbass today." Rhett crosses his arms and leans against the metal wall.

"Fuck you," Weston says to Rhett before turning back to me. "How's your *wife*?" His eyebrows wag at the last word.

I drop my head back, closing my eyes and taking a deep breath. Awe fuck, that means people for sure heard if Weston did. "So you heard that, huh?"

"The whole arena heard. I thought you were supposed to be lying low about that."

"Oh, I was. Doug has already left me three voicemails ripping my ass." Have I responded? Absolutely not. Doug is getting on my last nerve quicker and quicker these days.

"Well, you gonna tell us or do we have to beat it out of you?" When Rhett joins in, I know I'm not getting away with it. He's usually the more reserved one of our bunch, so if he's invested, I ain't getting out of here scot-free.

"There is nothing to tell." Turning my head, I walk over to the pile of supplies.

"Rhett, is it just me, or is someone avoiding the conversation?" I hear from behind me. Fuck, I'm not getting out of this. When Weston is on a mission, there's nothing that will stop him.

Rhett's deep chuckle doesn't help me feel better. "Oh, someone for sure has some information to share."

"There is nothing to tell because we haven't really even talked about it."

"Well, do you like her, or is this just a phase you're going to go through?" I stretch my neck to the side, unsure exactly how much I want to tell them because this can quickly turn into ammunition for the rest of my damn life.

"It's not a fling." I grab a rake. Apparently, I am the only one who's planning on getting any work done today. "At least I hope not."

Weston probes further. "Is she not interested? That's a first for you, Ryder." Oh, he is going to love watching my wife humble my ass.

"I don't know." She's at least physically attracted to me, I know that.

"How can you not know?" Weston walks over to grab another rake, closing the distance I am trying to put between us.

"She hasn't been around to talk about it. I don't know?"

"You live together in the world's smallest cabin. Where has she been hiding? Better yet, what did you do?" Rhett joins in on the questioning.

"Fuck if I know, man." Women are complicated, and I am quickly learning I may be way in over my head in this marriage.

"You gonna tell us what happened after you went all caveman and claimed her as your woman in front of everyone?" Weston asks, but I'm pretty sure he knows exactly what happened.

I put on a nice, tight smile and look at him. "Sure, we went to our hotel and had a nice quiet night."

"If she was quiet, that tells me everything I need to know." They can make jokes at my leisure, but over my dead body am I going to air out what goes on between us when the lights are off.

"Can we get to work now? I have some shit I need to do this afternoon. Unless you dumb fucks want to do all of it by yourself."

"Fine," Weston rumbles out, "but your silence speaks volumes."

"Real original, dipshits." I shake my head and get to work.

The lights are on at the cabin when I come through the line of trees and pull up to the side of the house. Maybe she isn't avoiding me and has just been busy all day.

The house is filled with the scent of mahogany and vanilla, her favorite candle. I stomp my feet on the rug, trying to get the leftover dirt from the barn off my boots.

Ava leans over the kitchen counter, wiping it down. Looking around, I see the whole place is clean. Like really clean.

"You go on a cleaning kick today?" I ask.

She practically jumps out of her skin, whirling around with her hand on her chest. Her sweatpants sit low on her hips, exposing a bit of skin below her belly button. I've seen that skin, touched that skin. My eyes stay glued on it, no matter how hard I try to drag them up.

"Uhm, yeah, I guess." The tone in her voice has my hackles rising; something is wrong.

"Where were you this morning?" I step out of my boots and set them off to the side. Part of me wants to ask why she was so quiet on the drive while I'm at it.

She goes back to wiping down the already spotless counter. "Oh, I got up early to feed the baby cow, clean out the stalls, and then go for a walk."

"Okay, well, I've been wanting to talk to you." I take a few steps closer, and she stops in her tracks at my words.

She hangs her head for a second before looking up at me. "Listen, Mav, I don't want you to feel any pressure. If you don't want anything else to happen, that's okay. I kind of jumped your bones. And I—"

Closing the gap between us, I cup her face in my palms. "I made a mistake by not being perfectly clear with you. I got a little overly excited about having you in my bed and forgot the most important part." I study her face for a few seconds. "That wasn't just sex for me, and I hope it wasn't for you, either. Because I want to give this a go, for real." Her eyes go wide as saucers and grow a little glossy.

Her voice wavers as she speaks, "Are you sure? You're on the road a lot, and I'm sure there are other girls out there."

Rubbing my thumb across her cheek, I look her in the eyes, wanting her to feel the sincerity in my words. "There are no other girls out there for me if you're in the picture, and I hope you are." She sucks her lips in as her eyes water. Unable to handle the silence, I press on, "So are you? It's okay if you don't want this. I will back off, and we can go back to how we were." I would hate every single second of it, but at the end of the day, I will always respect her and her decisions.

Her hands cover mine, and her voice is so quiet I have to strain to hear her. "No, I don't want to go back."

The smile that stretches over my face feels foreign because I don't know if I've ever been this happy. The smile she sends me in return melts every piece of me. "Are you just going to stare at me, or are you going to kiss me, cowboy?"

I shake my head as I lean in, and my lips start as a whisper against hers. My pounding heart thunders in my ears.

This kiss isn't heated like our previous one, it's slow. An exploration of each other. The little sigh she lets out makes my blood heat. But I don't want to push it, I want to slow this down and do it right because I think I could spend forever kissing her.

Chapter 21
Ava

The day has come, freaking finally. The hospital finally cleared me, and I get to start working. I still woke up at the crack of dawn to feed my baby cow. I've decided it's a pet, and though she's down to one bottle a day, she's now my baby. Rhett and Weston will have to go back to being the stall bitches. But really, the work wasn't that bad, I really enjoyed it. On my days off from the hospital, I still plan on helping because I've become slightly attached to all the furry critters.

Pulling into the hospital parking lot, I try to settle my rumbling nerves. First days are always scary. Add in the first day as a fresh nursing graduate, and it's even worse. On the plus side, I'm decked out in a new pair of scrubs and shoes, leaving me feeling slightly more confident going into my first big day.

The outside of the hospital is all brick and stone. Being that we are in a rural area, it's pretty small. I was told that HR or whoever would be training me would meet me in the front lobby at eight to do the paperwork, and then it's go time. The sliding glass doors automatically open in front of me and I walk through. I've noticed that all hospitals smell the same: sterile. Like the air and everything around it is a little too clean.

Lucky for me, I was provided a tour during my interviews, so I have a pretty good idea of where I'm headed. Of course I showed up embarrassingly early. The roads were clear, but I didn't want to be the girl who was late on her first day, so I left thirty minutes earlier than I needed to. The drive was uneventful, so I made it even faster than I thought.

Time passes slower than molasses as I tap my shoe, looking around. The front area has nice little plants here and there, and pictures of local scenery hanging on the wall. There's a charm about small towns; all the little finishing touches make even the hospital feel just a little bit cozier.

"Ava?" Aspen says, practically skipping toward me with her pony-tail swishing from side to side.

"Aspen, hi!" I hop off my seat and pull her into a hug.

She pulls back, keeping a grip on my forearms. "Guess who gets to train you?" She wags her eyebrows, clearly trying her best and failing to contain her excitement.

"No way?" My hands squeeze onto her forearm.

"Well, they mentioned a new hire, and I rolled the dice, thinking it would be you, and volunteered." She smiles and wiggles her whole body at the same time. I love her energy. She reminds me so much of Erin, it almost soothes the little piece of me that misses home.

"Alright, so for the first part of the day, we'll have you complete computer orientation and take a lunch break, and after lunch, we will work on seeing where your skills are. Let me take you to the computer room." I follow her down hallways of white tile and fluorescent lights.

She leads me into a breakroom with two computers in the back corner, facing a large window. The sunlight will be a nice reprieve from staring at the computer screen all day.

"Let's see if you can get logged in. I have a folder here for you, it should have all the info you need."

The setup goes easy, and she gets me logged into my charting train-ing. "Okay, babe, this is where I leave you. You will be dying of bore-dom. So, stay strong. I'll swing by and grab you for lunch, and then we can get started on the fun stuff."

Aspen was absolutely correct. These video trainings make me want to melt into a puddle on the floor in the worst way. My brain feels like complete and total mush and I can feel the oncoming headache from the computer's constant light starting to buzz in the back of my head.

The door to the room swings open. "I am here to rescue you from your misery."

"Thank God," I say, ripping the cheap headset off my ears.

She walks up to where I sit huddled in the corner and hops on the desk. "You want to stab your eyeballs out yet?"

That is putting it lightly. "Yes. That was the longest five hours of my life."

"And just think. You have a whole week of that to look forward to." Her pointer finger boops me on the nose, and she laughs.

Deadpanning at her, I reply, "This is the worst pep talk I have ever received."

"Truth hurts, baby. Let's go eat." I log off the computer, and we head down to the lunchroom.

The cafeteria, if you can really call it that, is just a small order win-dow with some well-worn metal tables and chairs scattered around. The menu list is even smaller, but the woman taking the orders offers me a kind smile, and suddenly I feel bad for judging this place too soon because I get a whiff of the food and my mouth starts to water.

Aspen wastes no time and starts prying the second we take a seat. "So, how are things with Maverick?"

I eye her suspiciously. "What do you know?"

"Literally nothing but my spidey senses are tingling." She wiggles both her fingers at me, and I can't help but laugh.

I quickly debate in my head how much I want to divulge. But she's the only girl I know that knows him. And I think she's trustworthy enough to give me sound advice and warning if needed.

"Things are, uhm, well…" I chew on my lip, trying to figure out how to word this.

"Spit it out, or I'm going to start making assumptions." She waves her fork at me before shoveling a bite of salad into her mouth.

My words come out in a rush, anxious to talk to someone about this in person. I updated Erin immediately, but face-to-face girl time is just different. "At the rodeo, some guy called me a buckle bunny and was in my face and rude, and Mav came to the rescue. And well, I haven't had a whole lot of people in my life looking out for me. I couldn't believe someone would stand up for me like that. He's something else." I couldn't fight the smile that comes to my face if I tried.

She gives me a knowing look. "Maverick is hard not to like."

"I was one hundred percent convinced based on the way he handled our whole debacle that he was a complete moron—"

Aspen cuts me off. "Oh, he is, but he has one of the best hearts of anyone I've ever met. You'll never find anyone more genuine or loyal than Mav. His schedule is hard to deal with and he can be an annoying pain in the ass, but at his core, he's good."

"Yeah, I'm finding that out." I've also wondered why he's still single, but I guess a life on the road would make it difficult to settle down.

"He's been through a lot, and he has the weight of the world on his shoulders. His dad left quite the boots to fill, and for some reason, he's had it drilled into his brain that he isn't deserving and he has to prove himself." She shakes her head as she stabs her salad with her fork. "Which is crazy because the man has a work ethic as strong as steel."

"So you think he's a good guy?" I ask before popping a piece of cheese into my mouth.

"The best. Your heart would be safe with him. I would tell you if it wasn't. And if he breaks it I will fuck him up. And he knows I can. A swift kick in the balls renders all men useless."

"Wouldn't that be cheating?" I ask before I take a big bite of my chicken sandwich.

"All is fair in love and war," she says, and I cannot help but laugh.

"I'll remember that." And I'll also remember to stay on Aspen's good side.

The rest of the day flies by in a flash. Nursing school teaches you a lot, but there's only so much it can do until you get your hands in it. Aspen held my hand through it all day, and when it was finally time to leave, I left with a smile on my face. This is what I have been working so hard for, and I can't wait to see what it brings.

Chapter 22
Maverick

This is the longest I have been on the road in a while. A two-week stint and three different rodeos. It's funny how quickly things change, because I used to love this shit. The different people. The attention. But now there is only one person I want attention from and she's waiting at home for me.

I gather my stuff for my last ride and head out the hotel door. Sully meets me in the hallway. "You ready?" He looks me up and down as he always does, trying to find a crack in my facade.

"I'm always ready." Which is usually true, and when I'm not, I've learned how to fake it till I make it.

The sounds of boots scuffing against the ground bounce off the walls as we walk. "Alright, for you to remain the top earner, you have to win this one, or Evans will take the lead." I nod my head as we walk through the hallway. It's always a tight race to the top. There are new up-and-comers constantly coming on to the scene, hungry to make a name for themselves. That kind of desperation pushes you far. I would know; it's been my MO for my entire career.

There is an SUV waiting for us at the front. The drive to the arena takes about ten minutes.

"So how is the girl?" Sully asks. Small talk isn't his strong suit; I can tell he feels awkward just asking.

Any mention of her always causes a smile to shoot across my face. She's turned into my own little personal sunshine. "She's good."

He clears his throat. "Well, before we meet up with Doug, I want to chip in my two cents. Life is short, kid. If it gives you something good, you better hold on for dear life. Tighter than you've ever held on to any bull, ya hear me?" He looks at me, and I can see the sincerity there. While Doug is a complete fuck, Sully has always had my best interest at heart. Even when I didn't like it. If he is giving me shit, there's a good chance I deserved it.

His words ring true because now that I've got her, you'd have to pull her out of my cold, dead hands for me to give her up willingly. "I know. Trust me, I know." He nods and continues looking forward.

We get to the arena and make our way inside, where Doug is waiting by the contender's entry door.

"I had to pull some strings but I got you your own room, no locker room bullshit." I nod, not bothering to tell him that I like the locker room bullshit. The shit talking adds to the fire. It helps me focus, but Doug thinks otherwise. In his mind, it's a distraction, and he probably thinks it makes us look more important.

We head into the small room, and I start unpacking my things. My leather chaps get clipping around my thighs and my waist. I put my riding vest on and shake out the tension in my body.

Doug and Sully leave the room, giving me a few seconds of peace. My phone vibrates on top of my bag, and I pull it open.

> Good luck! If you win, I'll reward you with a special present. ;)

Well, that's one way to motivate a man.

Can I get a hint about my present?

Nope, you will just have to find out when you
get your sweet ass home.

I love that she calls my little cabin home, that it's slowly becoming hers too. God, I hope she stays.

A knock on the door pulls me out of my thoughts. "You ready?" Sully pokes his head in, and I nod.

"Yup." I grab my helmet and head out the door.

As we get closer to the arena, the cheers get louder, the energy gets higher, and I settle in. Some get spooked by the noise, I get fueled by it.

Looking up at the score, I see the numbers I have to beat. It's not bad. A few riders are after me, so I have to aim high. My bull isn't the best, but with any luck, he'll be in a mood and try extra hard to kill me. It's a weird thing to wish for, but if it makes the score higher, it's worth the risk.

Time blurs as I get myself loaded up, wrapped up, and ready to ride. We get settled into the chute, and I hear the buzzer ding as the chute gate opens. And my bull is fighting mad. My thighs are screaming for dear fucking life as he bucks around. My concentration is poured into the next second. Just one second at a time is all it takes. When the final buzzer goes off, I rip my wrist and hand loose and hop off. Darting to the corral, I hop up and swing my legs around before dropping to the other side. When the score pops up on the screen, Doug and Sully both pat my back. It would take a fucking miracle for one of the young bucks to come out and beat me tonight. All of the seasoned riders have already gone. It looks like I will be cashing in on my prize.

I end the night with another win and more cash for the bank. Doug walks beside me as we make our way to my dressing room.

"Good work out there tonight. Looks like the girl isn't too much of a distraction."

My head whips around. "What?"

"Oh, come on, most boys start to lose their itch the second they find a girl that's half decent." She's more than half decent, she's the best woman I've ever met, and I am pretty sure he knows that.

Feeling fed up with his shit, my tone comes out curt. I want this fucker to know I mean business. "Doug, I'm going to say one thing and one thing only. The only place you need to insert yourself is in my career. My personal life is none of your fucking business."

"It's my business if your personal life starts interfering with your career."

My boots scuff against the concrete floor as I come to a stop. "That is for me to decide. You seem to forget your purpose here. Unless you feel like hopping up on the back of the bull and making this money yourself, I would reconsider your next words."

He shakes his head and rolls his eyes. "You are so young and naive. I just don't want to see you make the same mistakes your dad did."

My mouth falls open for a second. If I thought I was pissed off before, he really added gasoline to the fire. "What? Have a kid. A kid who is currently employing you?"

He waves off my temper. "You know what I mean. Focus keeps you safe. I don't care if you get pissed. The girl is gone if you start slipping. You're getting that world title this year." He's right. I am getting that title and keeping the girl while I'm at it.

Not bothering with him, I shake my head and march forward because knocking Doug on his ass right now would absolutely prove his ass right. And the itch to knock his teeth in is becoming unbearable. Plus, unlike his miserable self, I have someone at home waiting for me.

Pulling up to the cabin, I feel like I can finally breathe. Life on the road isn't what it used to be. I miss these mountains—the serenity of it. Knowing what's waiting inside for me, I don't bother grabbing my stuff because I've got a girl in there I'm dying to see.

Swinging the door open, the smell of freshly baked cookies hits my nose, and I find myself hustling to get the door closed behind me—sweet mother of all things holy. There's my girl sitting on the counter in a black lace bra, eating a cookie and staring right at me. Fuck, I never want to leave this house again.

Cocking my head to the side I ask, "Is this part of my prize?"

"Depends, which one do you want first?" she asks.

"I think I can enjoy both at the same time." I don't even bother stripping out of my boots and make my way to her. My long strides eat the distance in a few short steps.

Walking up, my hands glide across her bare thighs, my eyes staying glued on her skin. I look down to where her legs are crossed. "Can you open your pretty legs up for me, sweetheart?" She uncrosses her legs as my fingers grip her warm skin and I take a step closer, now eye to eye with the most beautiful girl in the world. "Can I have a taste?" She offers me the cookie, but I shake my head. I want her lips.

She leans in and kisses me, and the sweetness from the cookie comes across. "Told you I could get both," I say between kisses, not wanting to break the contact. Everything in me feels settled when we're touching.

My hands wrap around her backside as I deepen the kiss. Fuck, I missed this. My hands rub against her bare skin and it breaks out in goosebumps against my touch. "Now this is a prize worth rushing home for."

"Glad I could provide some motivation." She smirks at me, and I love this bold side of her that comes out.

Leaning in, I kiss her neck with small little pecks. Her hands thread through the length of my hair as she pulls me closer. Kissing down her body, I make my way to her perfect tits, reveling in the sound of her whimpers and the feel of her hands pulling me closer. "God, your body is a fucking masterpiece, baby."

She tilts her head back, and my eyes catch the way she looks completely undone for me. It has me wanting to claim every inch of her body as mine. I hook my thumb into the lace of her bra and pull it down until her breasts spill out. The moan that comes out of her when my mouth sucks in her pretty pert nipple makes my cock strain against my jeans.

Moving my hand off her thigh, I slip it between us and let out a groan at what I feel. It seems I'm not the only one who missed this because her body is coming alive for me tonight.

Pushing her panties to the side, I turn my hand over and run my finger down from her clit until I am sinking it inside her. "This must be what heaven feels like. You are so fucking wet for me." Leaning in with my fingers still buried inside her, I ask, "Did you miss my cock as much as it missed you?" If her loud, boisterous moan doesn't answer the question, the way her pussy clenches around my fingers does. Her mouth parts open as I work my fingers in and out of her. My gaze moves down, watching my fingers disappear and stretch out her perfect little cunt. When my thumb starts circling her clit, her hands fly to my shoulders and grip them.

"Fuck, Mav, I need more."

Kissing her neck once more, I murmur, "Okay, sweetheart" against the crease in her neck. Whatever she wants, she gets. I spread her legs wide and drop down to my knees, ready to worship her body the way it deserves. Pushing her panties all the way to the side, I get to see just how wet she is for me. "Look at this perfect little pussy. It's fucking dripping for me, baby." My cock feels like it's seconds away from bursting through my jeans, bordering on uncomfortable, wanting so badly to sink home into her. Unable to hold back any longer, I lean in and devour the taste of her.

"Holy shit, Mav. Yes." Whimpers start to fall out of her mouth as I suck on her clit, sliding a finger in to fill her up. I could spend forever watching her fall apart for me.

Her pussy squeezes around my finger as a loud moan rips through her mouth, and it's a sound I will never get tired of. Looking over her body, I can't ignore the fact that she looks so good when she comes undone. She opens her pretty blue eyes and stares at me with such a fire, I think I feel myself taking flame. "I'm not done with you yet," I say as I slide my hands under her thighs, bringing her closer to the counters edge.

Sealing my mouth on hers, I roam my hands against her bare body, desperate not to break the contact. Fuck, I missed her when I was gone. And not just this part. All of it. Our late-night talks and waking up with her nestled into my chest. This is all good and great but having someone you can count on is worth so much more.

I should be a gentleman and take her to bed and ravish her the way I want to, but I can't fucking wait. I am a man completely undone for her.

"Baby, can you look at me?" My hand goes up to cup the side of her face, and her eyes lock on mine. "I want this pussy bare. While you're my wife, I want nothing between us. I want to feel your soaking wet little cunt swallow my dick. Is that okay?" I'd never do it without her permission, but having anything between us while I fuck her feels like a crime.

"Yes, please. I want you bare, too."

"Can I get you to beg for this cock, baby?" I rasp, wanting to tease her the way I have been these last few minutes, I unzip my jeans and let my cock free of its zipper prison.

"Maverick, I need you to fuck me. Now." The command in her tone has my cock twitching. I push her back so that she lays flat on the counter, legs spread wide around my hips. Slowly, I drag the head of my cock through her wetness. Her hips buck up to meet the friction.

"That's not quite begging, but I'm so fucking desperate for you, I'll let it slide." In more than one way, I am desperate for this woman. For her body, soul and heart. I am feeling forever famished. None of it ever feels like enough.

I keep my eyes down, notching the tip of my cock into her pussy. My eyes roll back when her pussy flutters against the head. "Has anyone ever told you that you have the most fuckable pussy?" A dangerous question because the thought of any other man touching what's mine, seeing her like this, it makes me rage.

"I don't think anyone has been this obsessed with me. It's good for my ego." She flashes a sultry smile, her eyes hooded with lust.

My smile beams down at her and the perfect response. "Good, 'cause I am about to show you just how fucking obsessed with you I can be."

My cock thrusts in, not willing to take any more delay. She's right, I am completely fucking desperate. My thrusts are anything but gentle. I watch her mouth pop open as she gasps. Her fingers search the cold countertop, looking for something to grip onto. My hands stay glued on her perfectly filled-out hips, using my grip to push her down harder on me.

The angle has me perfectly hitting her G-spot, and with the way her pussy is squeezing my cock as it glides through, I can tell she's close.

"Can you come for me? Squeeze that pretty little pussy around my cock?"

Her breathy pants fill the room, unable to speak, as she just nods her head. Thank fuck, because I am seconds from exploding inside her. Seconds later, she grips down so hard that I can't hold my orgasm back. Thrust after thrust, I fill her up, branding her as mine.

I look down as I pull out, a primal sense filling me as I watch my cum drip out of her. It's a silent claiming, fucking her like this. No one else will see it, but I'll know that she will be thinking of me all day tomorrow.

When I finally catch my breath, I look down at her perfect body, still panting and catching her breath. "Sometimes, I can't believe that you're mine." I lean down and seal her lips with a kiss, pulling her up to a seated position.

Her arms drape around my shoulders. "You know, I'm feeling pretty lucky these days, too. Did you know my husband is a hot rodeo star who's completely obsessed with me?" The teasing grin on her face makes my heart swell. This fucking woman.

"That he is, and proud of it." I shouldn't like her calling me her husband. In fact, it should terrify me, but the only scary thing about it is the looming court date. I'm hers as long as she'll have me, and I can only hope we figure out how to make that last. "Let's get you cleaned up, sweetheart."

Guess I should probably take off my pants and shoes now. I kick off my boots and pants aiming for the corner. Grabbing her legs, I wrap them around my waist and carry her to the shower.

Once we are all cleaned up, we crawl in my bed and turn on a movie. I never thought I'd look forward to simple nights like this, so accustomed to the active lifestyle on the road that leaves little time for rest. But with Ava, I want to slow it down and enjoy every single second I get with her. She's too damn good for me, and I thank the lucky stars she hasn't figured that out yet.

Chapter 23
Ava

I sit on the front porch, sipping my coffee and propping my feet against the spare chair—a book in my hand and the crisp breeze through my hair. The air out here feels different, the subtle scent of pine mixed with a certain sense of clarity. I survived my first mountain winter. Wyoming winters can be brutal anywhere, but even the short spree I had here was rough. I shouldn't hold my breath, though. Just because it's finally June doesn't mean we're free and clear from the snow. But today, the sun is out and the birds are chirping, so I can feel the seasonal depression leaving my body.

My eyes close as I lean my head back, resting my book in my lap. I can't remember the last time I felt this relaxed. My bills are paid, I finally have a steady income, and training is going well. For the first time in forever, I don't think I have anything to worry about. Well, except for Maverick getting his ass killed by a bull. The time he's away for rides always passes slowly, mostly because I'm paralyzed by the fear I'm going to get a call that he's been hurt, or worse. But he's on his way home from a week away, so even that isn't a worry. My breathing levels out, and I sink deeper into the rocker. The gentle squeak of the chair against the wooden porch lulls me to sleep.

I feel a hand running through my hair and snuggle into the touch, still halfway in dreamland. My mind slowly comes back to reality, my eyes fluttering open, and I can't help but smile.

"You're home." Sitting up, I stretch my arms over my head, taking Mav in. His T-shirt hugs his chiseled chest. He squats in front of me, gear bag still slung over his shoulder as he rests his hand on my thighs. I love that about him, his constant need to be touching me. His touch makes me feel a little bit safer than I have ever before. Grounded, steady, and seen.

The edges of his eyes crinkle with his smile. "You must be really bored if you're passed out on the front porch."

"Just comfy. How was your drive?"

"Too long. I missed you." He leans forward and presses a quick peck to my lips, leaving my heart galloping in my chest.

When my lips pull back from his, I smart off, "Of course you did. I am a delight."

He dramatically rolls his eyes. "*Ohkayyy*, well I was going to see if you wanted to go for a horseback ride around the ranch, but clearly you are too tired and I was not missed. I'll ask Weston." He winks before he saunters into the house.

I've been itching to see more than I can see while wandering around during my walks. I get a little scared I might get lost or, I don't know, find a bear or something. Death by bear is not how I plan on going out.

I launch out of the chair, quick on Mav's heels into the house. "I'm awake, and I missed you." The floorboard creaks as I come to a halt in front of the bed.

"Where do you sleep when I'm gone?"

"What?" My brain takes a few seconds to understand what he is asking. My cheeks instantly blush when he asks because I sleep in his bed. It smells like him and makes it feel like he's still here even when he's gone. I don't care if it's weird. We sleep together when he's here, so I guess I never thought much of it when I officially broke up with the futon.

The smile that stretches across his lips tells me he hears all the words I'm not saying. "Yeah, you missed me alright." He walks to me, slowly, as his hands encircle my waist, wrapping his arms around me. Contentment fills my body. I get on my tiptoes and throw my arms around the back of his neck.

"Maybe just a little."

"I like the thought of you warming my bed when I'm gone." He leans down until his forehead rests against mine.

"Well, in that case, I may have slept in it a time or two." More like every single night, but he doesn't need to know how down bad I am.

"The messy sheets gave you away, sweetheart." Damn, the one time I forgot to make the bed. He leans down to kiss my lips, and I melt into his embrace. I've been so tough for so long, but finding someone I can be soft for feels safer than anything else ever has. He pulls away and studies me for a second. "So you want to go?"

"Yes!"

"Alright, it might get a little chilly, so throw on a sweater and we can head to the barn."

We start the trot up a trail that cuts through trees. Without the sun, it does feel a bit colder. I lean back into Maverick's warmth as the horse trots below us. Taking it all in, with the snow gone, the grass has started to green and leaves are growing back on the aspen trees. The sound of the horse's hooves hitting the ground is the only sound around. It's a different kind of peace. Serene.

"This is my favorite trail to ride when it finally gets warm enough. It gets even better a little bit ahead." My eye catches what looks like a cabin. I saw another one but figured it was some sort of outhouse.

"What are all the half-crumpled cabins for?" Curiosity gets the better of me, and I have to ask.

"Those used to be occupied by those who owned the land before Jack and Mabel. They've kind of just slowly deteriorated over the years."

The view expands when we pass the trees, showcasing the valleys, pine, and aspen trees covering the mountainside. "Holy cow."

"You haven't even seen the best part yet." We keep trotting down the road, and a little stream comes into view. With the bright blooming flowers coming up, contrasting the wild grass beneath it and the flowing water, it could pass as a postcard. My eyes close as I take a deep breath in, feeling a sense of home like I've never felt before. I get why Maverick is so obsessed with this land. It's like nothing I've seen before. I've been into the mountains, yes, but getting into the brush and diving deep into the ranch is different. It's a whole other world, where life isn't crushing down on you.

"You were right. Windy Peaks isn't what I expected." It's a town so small, you're likely to be related to someone in a ten-mile radius. But the freedom up here is worth being an hour away from a fully stocked grocery store.

"Hold on, let me get my phone out so I can record you saying that." His chest shakes with laughter behind me.

"I might have been wrong about the town, but I was right about you. You're an asshole."

"Hey now, I can leave you here." As beautiful as this place is, I don't think I am built to bear the elements without electricity. That is my limit. So I change my tone real quick.

"But you're my asshole," I reassure him.

He grabs at my waist, tickling my ribs.

"Damn right I am." He leans his head into my neck, planting a kiss on my bare skin as his forearm wraps around me. My body curls into the touch. The feeling leaves goosebumps across my skin. "How do you feel about learning how to ride by yourself?"

"The horse?"

"Unless you're scared?" The taunt is obvious but still does its intended job.

"No, I want to learn." He wastes no time, I feel his body slip off the horse, and my eyes go wide, realizing I'm on top of this giant beast without him.

"Alright, you're going to take those reins. If you pull back, she'll stop, but if you pull too hard, she will walk backward. If you pull right, she'll go right. Same with left." He looks to me to make sure I am absorbing it all. So far, it seems pretty straightforward. "Alright, to get her moving, you will use your heel and give her a little kick. It doesn't have to be hard, just enough for her to feel. Want to walk her in a circle?"

I nod. Gripping the reins like my life depends on it, I kick my heel lightly, and sure enough, she takes off. Not fast, but a good little trot. I pull my reins to the right, trot a little, and then take us back to Maverick.

I couldn't stop the smile that stretched across my face if I tried. Pulling on the reins, I bring her to a stop as elation runs through me.

"Way to show off, sweetheart. You're looking like a real cowgirl."

"Before you know it, I'll be out-riding you on a bull." I raise my eyebrows in challenge, and a crisp bit of laughter shoots out of him.

"I'd love to see you try." He crosses his arms with far too much confidence.

"You do it. How hard can it be?" I wink at him, and he shakes his head at me, tongue in cheek.

"Well, do you want to put your money where your mouth is and ride us home?"

"The whole trail?"

He quirks a brow up at me, "I thought you were a professional?"

And now he's made me a woman with a point to prove. A dangerous position he's put himself in. "Get on the damn horse, Mav."

With far too much ease, he hops back up on the horse. Thank God we didn't have a full lesson on that, because he had to hike my little ass up on this horse.

His hands land on my thighs, and I turn the horse around, keenly aware of all the places his body is touching mine. "Alright, show me what ya got."

Turning the horse around, I direct us back on the trail and back toward the ranch.

When we get back to the barn, Mav hops off to open up the stables, and I guide Lucy in.

"Alright," He claps his hands, and rubs them together, "now let's see you dismount."

"Uh, I don't know if that is a good idea." Over my dead body am I about to crawl into the very ER I work in with a broken ankle. Talk about embarrassing. Especially if they find out it was from riding a damn horse. I would never hear the end of it. You can't live in Windy Peaks and not know how to ride a horse.

"You can do it, sweetheart." He puts his hand on my thigh, giving it a little reassuring rub. "Plant your foot in the stirrup, swing your free foot around, and hop off." He removes his hand and gestures for me to get going.

My burning desire to rise to every task in front of me is fighting with the very reason that has kept me alive all these years. But if I have a weakness, it will always be my damn pride. Maverick stands close with a hand out, ready to catch me just in case.

Planting my foot firmly in the stirrup, I swing my free leg around, keeping a grip on the saddle tip pommel. Three incredibly scary seconds later, I'm landing on the dirt floor, both feet on the ground.

Well, it looks like my pride will remain intact another day. Smiling, I turn around and look at Mav, ready to mouth off, but the look in his eyes makes me stop dead in my tracks. They burn into mine with an emotion too strong to put words to.

"What?"

"Nothing, just proud of you. That's all." My brow furrows in confusion, but before I can ask what he means, he reaches his hand out. I push mine forward and lace our fingers together.

My mind reels for more than one reason, mostly because I can see myself here. I can see myself with him. Life here is so much easier, I feel like I can breathe. And that scares me because that makes this just another thing I stand to lose.

Chapter 24
MAVERICK

I drive to the big house to pick up the picnic basket Mabel made for my first official date with Ava. We kind of skipped right over the whole normal start to dating, and it hasn't sat right with me, so I'm fixing to remedy that. It'll be full of all the things I have learned Ava loves and a few of my favorites, like chocolate chip cookies. Maybe if I show her all my favorite things about out here on the ranch, she'll learn to love it as much as I do. I can see her here, and I hope she can too.

My hands feel sweaty. Why do my hands feel sweaty? I wipe them against my jeans before regripping the steering wheel. And why the fuck am I nervous? I mean, sure, it's been a while since I've gone on a date. I can't remember the last time I cared this much about how a date went. But this is different because it's her. It's Ava.

I park my truck and walk into the house. Mabel stands on the other side of the counter, arms crossed, with a smile on her face that makes me feel like I'm going to regret having asked her for help.

"So you really like her, huh?" The pure glee on her face makes me want to retreat slowly out the door. How can someone who looks so sweet be such a menace?

Heavily sighing, I reply, "Whatever happened to hello?"

She rolls her eyes and plants her hands on the counter, leaning closer to me as I walk up to grab the basket. "Hello's stopped when you stopped knocking on my door."

I throw my hands up in the air. "That was like twenty years ago."

"And it only took you twenty years to notice." The smile on her face has her eyes crinkling at the corners. Sometimes, I forget how much she's aged over the years. I forget her grey hair used to be brown. I've spent a lot of time in this kitchen with her and her family, and that's time I will always cherish, even if I don't say it enough. She pushes the basket to the edge of the counter, and I reach for it.

"Alright, give me the basket. I'm already nervous. Don't need you making me feel like a complete idiot on top of that." I hide my eyes from hers, snatching the basket and ready to retreat, but she grabs it before I can.

"Oh, honey, I'm sorry." She walks over and gives me a quick peck on the cheek as she pats my back. The wicker basket is covered with a red plaid towel and stuffed to the brim with enough food to feed us for a week.

"No, you're not." I smile at her, unable to hold on to my faux anger. "But thanks for the food anyway." With some extra pep in my step, I make my way toward the door.

Leaving everything but the flowers in the truck, I take a deep, settling breath before I knock on the front door. The front door of my own damn house, but if we're going on a real first date, I'm going to go through all motions and make this her best first date ever. And if I'm lucky, her last first date ever.

Ava opens the front door; her cheeks have a rosy tint to them, and her long blonde hair falls in waves down to her waist. Fuck, she's pretty. So pretty that I find myself completely tongue-tied right now. I've seen her a million times, but right now, I feel like I am seeing her for the first time. Like I would have if we would've done this whole thing the right way.

"Mav, what are you doing?" Her brows scrunch in confusion with a small smile causing her lips to lift.

"Ava, not legally Ryder, but Ryder in my eyes, I am taking you on a date today." Earlier today, I had texted her to be ready when I got home, but I left out what to be ready for.

She looks me up and down. "You're serious."

"If I'm going to have you be mine, we're doing this the right way. Now, if you can go ahead and put your shoes on, sweetheart, I have some plans for you and me." I hand the flowers to her and kiss her cheek. "These are for you."

She immediately sniffs the bouquet of bluebells, daisies, and sunflowers. I picked the flowers from the fields around the cabin while getting ready for today. I don't get a lot of downtime and will be gone a lot, but I want her to always know she's worth the extra time and effort.

"These are beautiful. I'll go put them in a vase and then be right back." Her smile turns shy before turning back around. The sun is just setting, so we should have the perfect background. There's nothing more beautiful than a Wyoming mountain sunset.

When Ava returns to the front door, I take her small hand in mine, intertwining our fingers, and walk us to the truck. I open the passenger door for her, and she hops in. We back out of the drive, and I can't help but notice how much better my truck looks when she's in it.

Reaching my hand across the console, I lace our fingers together, desperate to always be in contact with her soft skin. "Alright, where are you taking me?" she asks.

Giving her hand a quick squeeze, I shoot her a smile. "You'll see when we get there. You just sit pretty, and I'll take the rest."

She rolls her eyes but relaxes back into the seat. "Whatever you say, cowboy."

When we pull up to the entrance of the meadow, she straightens in her seat and looks around. I can't blame her for perking up at the sight. It's beautiful. The flowers have bloomed, leaving little bits of color all around, and the wild grass is growing green and tall, but not so long that we can't enjoy a picnic. She looks over at me, the furrow in her delicate features tells me she's trying to figure out what I've planned.

"Because I know the anticipation is killing you, I packed us a little picnic and have some Wyoming stargazing planned."

"Seriously?" I almost feel a bit offended at the look of utter shock on her face.

"What are you saying? That you didn't think I could be romantic?" The look she sends me before I even finish my sentence answers my question. "Baby, I could romance you all day long."

Her eyes brighten as a playful smile dances on her lips. "Oh, so you packed this whole thing yourself?" She nods to the picnic basket sitting between us.

"Okay, small confession," I hold up my finger, "I did outsource the picnic portion, but the original idea was mine. Give a man some credit."

We arrive at the center of the meadow that overlooks the mountainside. It's one of my favorite places on earth with its views. The snow-crested mountain peaks never get old. I set up a dining station as the sun starts to set. Wanting this to be the best picnic ever, I went a little overboard. A blow-up mattress covered in blankets so we don't have to lay on my hard, metal truck bed and a lantern for some extra light just in case.

We take our seats and dive into the food. Ava has her legs tucked under her. She dips a strawberry into the whipped cream as she looks around, wisps of her blonde hair blowing over her shoulder. The summer breeze spreads hints of the sweet smell of bluebells. The sun starts to dip down beneath the mountain peaks. Everything about this night is perfect, especially who I am spending it with. Seeing that gentle smile on her face, free of worry and stress—this is exactly what our first date should have been. Night falls quickly up here, the stars start shining their light down on us.

As we look up at the stars, I can't remember a time when I felt like this. So completely enraptured with someone. Happy and truly content. I've chased this feeling my whole life, thinking I would find it in rodeo. But no, I found it in her. I turn my head to look at Ava, and she's completely transfixed by how beautiful a clear Wyoming sky is, while I'm completely transfixed by her.

She must feel my stare because she turns her head toward me. I study her beautiful face, the moon providing just enough light to see the details of her features. From the smattering of freckles across her nose to the dark spot in her left iris, she is exquisite. A flush rises in her cheeks the longer I watch her. My eyes drop to the fullness of her pouty mouth, and I'm overcome with the need to taste her lips.

Cupping my hand under her chin, I bring her face a little closer. I lean down and capture her lips with mine, kissing her slowly and savoring the taste of strawberries and cream that comes off her lips. My hands thread in the back of her hair. Her hand fists at my button-up shirt.

The air mattress underneath us dips as she rolls over and straddles me. God, she looks perfect from this view. My hands glide up and grab her waist; she leans back down, and her kiss is instantly demanding. My hands wander down to her tight ass, and I squeeze the second I get a handful. Her hips start grinding against me, no doubt feeling the evidence of what she does to me. All intentions I had of a sweet evening come to an end because when it comes to Ava, I have no control. I never have.

My hands pull at the hem of her blue shirt, and I lift it over her head. The view of her tits in the thin lace bra snap my composure. My hands roam up and she meets them halfway as she guides them to her tits. I squeeze and the moan that escapes her has my cock throbbing. My hands wrap under her and I roll, pinning her underneath me.

"Fuck, did you wear that for me?" My thumb grazes against the soft lace, causing her to arch into my touch.

"Do you like it?" she asks, looking up at me with doe eyes, and fuck, if she isn't the sexiest thing I've ever laid eyes on.

"I like you in anything, sweetheart." Or nothing. I really enjoy her in nothing.

"Then you're really going to like your next surprise," she taunts.

Ava gently pushes my chest, causing me to sit back on my heels as she unbuttons her jeans. Feeling too damn wound up to sit here and not touch her, I grab the top of them and help pull them down her legs. I sit perfectly in front of her bent knees, and as she drops them to each side, I let out a hoarse breath.

"Holy fuck." Between her sweet little thighs is a sexy, tiny pair of crotchless panties. Providing me with a front row seat to admire her dripping wet little cunt. I could die right now and be a happy man.

All of the ways I want to fuck her roll through my head, I wish I could do it all at once because I feel like I am going to explode out of my damn skin.

"Are you just going to sit there and stare?" she challenges.

Her words snap me back. The sass in her tone makes me want to remind her who's in charge of her pleasure.

With my eyes locked on hers, I drag my finger across her open slit and lean in, her scent enveloping me and I find myself salivating, ready to devour her.

"Why, baby? Do you need me to stretch this tight little cunt?" I plunge one finger in, and my eyes roll, feeling the wetness coating my finger. Pulling my finger out just to add another, I plunge again until her wordless moans echo through the mountainside. I love hearing her get loud for me. When her mind finally lets go and gives in to me and the pleasure only I can provide.

"Fuck me, Mav." Her wildly lit eyes meet mine, pupils dilated. She holds onto my shoulders, her grip tight enough to leave a bruise.

Leaning forward, I whisper into her ear, "Not until you beg for it." She snaps her legs together in defiance.

"Then it's going to be a long night." She levels me a look full of bravado.

Fuck, there's that attitude again. I feel my cock twitch at her disregard to my request. She's too damn perfect for her own good.

"A man can hope." Shooting her a wink, I spread her legs back open. Her mind may want to defy me, but her body doesn't. It answers to my every touch as if it belongs to me.

Grabbing her waist, I scoot her up until my breath flows over her sweet little pussy. My mouth finds her clit and her hips buck up underneath me. My hand hovers over her body, pushing her hips back down.

Gliding across her silky-smooth skin, I reach up until I can palm her tit with my mouth still glued to her sweet center. Grabbing her nipple, I pinch and dive my tongue inside her just in time to feel her start to clench down.

Stopping my movements, I release her pebbled nipple and lift up to look at her. "Are you going to come for me already? I thought you wanted my cock?"

"I do." Her brow pinches and her face contorts as my fingers tease her clit.

"Ask me like a good wife."

Ava's blue eyes light up with fire as she looks me straight in the eyes and responds, "Fuck your wife, or I'm going to do it myself and make you watch." Just like that, she is back in control, and I'm a man on my knees for her—ready to worship every inch of her.

"Yes, mine. *Only mine.*" My eyes stay glued on her, unable to look away until I hear her say it. "Tell me," I demand as I unbutton my shirt and strip it off. Not bothering to take off my pants, I push them down to where I kneel on my knees.

"I'm yours, Mav. Only yours."

A groan claws its way out of my throat. I love the sound of that. "I am going to fuck this sweet little cunt raw. You're going to feel me dripping out of you for days. I want you to think about who you belong to." Pulling down my boxers, my cock springs free, and I run my hand up and down it twice. Nothing will ever compare to how it feels having her wrapped around me.

My cock glides in, her arousal coating me, and I bite my lip hard enough to draw blood. The pain is the only thing stopping me from coming right now. I need to make this last.

As I slide in and out of her tight little pussy, I watch as ecstasy takes over her face, making my cock swell.

"Do you want to feel how your pussy drips for me, baby?" I ask as I pull myself out of her, not recognizing the rasp in my voice.

She nods her head yes, and I guide her hand down to her center, watching her little fingers glide in. Wetness drips off her finger when she pulls it back, and her eyes widen.

"Now, put it in your mouth. I want you to taste how good I fuck you." She keeps her eyes trained on me as she sucks her fingers clean. My cock slides back in and I press my hand down on her pelvis until I feel where my cock thrusts inside of her.

She always looks beautiful, but there's no comparison to the way she looks under the stars, the mountains behind her and my cock filling her up. Her hand drops from her mouth and lands on my forearm.

"Kiss me." She pulls me closer, and I know there's no way in hell I can deny her. Not of this, not of anything.

"Do you want to taste yourself on my lips?"

"Yes. I need you." Being needed by a woman as independent as Ava is the most humbling feeling in the world.

Her every wish will be my command. I was a goner from the second I laid eyes on her. She will be my undoing. If I can spend the rest of my days loving her sweet and fucking her hard, I'll die a happy man.

The breeze brushes across the sweat on my bare back. My fingers start circling her clit and her pussy pulses around me. There's no way I can last another minute. She feels too damn good.

My thrusts quicken; all of me is addicted to the feel of her. "Ava, baby, I need you to come for me. Let go."

She lets go with my hands all over, pulsing around me. I feel my cock swell, and I explode, burying myself deep in her until my cum starts to run out. God damn. I collapse on my forearms, feeling like a teenager with my pants around my fucking ankles.

Her hands come up to each side of my face, and she kisses me slowly. Soft. Fuck, I love this. My chest feels like it could explode every time her lips are on mine.

With a heaving chest, messy hair, and rosy cheeks, she smiles up at me. "I was wrong. You do romance real good."

"If this is your idea of romance, I can arrange something every day." And I plan to. I never imagined a life like this but I'll be damned if I let it slip out of my grip.

"I'm counting on it." My eyes catch her lazy smile, and I love that I put it there. I lean down and kiss the tip of her nose. Her eyes close as she takes in a big, deep sigh.

"You gonna leave your pants at your ankles all night?" My chest shakes with laughter as I shake my head before kissing her once more and pull my pants back on. Grabbing her discarded clothes, I help her slip back into hers. She slides her shirt back on and we relax into the bed of the truck. She curls up into my side, and my arms instinctively curl around her, holding her close. My eyelids feel heavy, and the last words off my lips before sleep finds me are, "I love you."

Chapter 25
Ava

The ER has been absolutely slammed today, with everything from sore throats to borderline severed fingers. I figured being such a small hospital, they wouldn't get the crazy stuff. But it turns out farmers and ranchers know how to keep things interesting. And we're the only hospital within a fifty-mile radius.

"CODE BLUE ROOM 2, CODE BLUE ROOM 2," blares over the intercom.

"Do we need to go?" I look over to Aspen, who's charting away at her computer as we sit in the nurse's station. We're waiting on labs, and then the doctor will provide the patient we've been monitoring with results so we can finally start their discharge.

"No, the on-call team and the floor nurses cover med-surg. We stay here. You never ever leave the ER with only one person on duty. If you ever end up with a violent patient, you'll learn why."

I shake my head, not wanting to ever learn that lesson. "I can only imagine what you've seen."

"The good news about working in a rural hospital is you get pretty seasoned quickly."

"So I won't always feel dumb as a doorknob?"

"Oh no, you will pretty much always second-guess yourself. But once you learn policy and procedures and get a few traumas under your belt, you won't feel so terrified."

"That's good to hear." Because right now, I still get a rush of nerves every time I drive into the hospital, and I've already been working for a couple of weeks. I figured the nerves would have died off, but the job is rewarding, even if I'm handing out sandwiches and tissues.

The radio on the desk goes off. "Windy Peaks Community Hospital, we have an incoming trauma via ambulance—head-on collision. Prepare a full trauma team. Two incoming." The adrenaline rushes through my system. I ball my hands into fists to hide my shaking hands. I've somehow avoided seeing hands-on trauma in clinicals. Some of my classmates did, but I never had the opportunity to dip my toes into that water. I knew this day would come, yet it still feels too soon. But this is the reason I became a nurse: to help people. To make a difference and hopefully get someone's mom and dad home, even though mine didn't get to do that. If I can do that for even just one person, I think that would help heal that little piece of me that aches. That wants to help others never experience life without your two favorite people.

Aspen pops out of her chair, tightening her ponytail as if preparing for battle. "Alright, time to shine, Ava! What do we do in traumas?" Her eyes look to me for an answer, and my mind blanks.

"We... We, uhm, we RAP." The words stutter out, but it starts coming back to me.

She nods encouragingly. "Good, and what does that entail?" She opens the trauma bay curtain as I follow behind.

This answer comes quicker. "Ready the rooms, complete an across-the-room assessment, and gown up."

"Good! You're going to do great. If you get queasy or nervous, take a step back. It gets easier with time, I promise. You can learn a lot by watching. Can you make sure the ultrasound is in the room?"

I nod my head, words failing to find me. I locate the ultrasound in the storage room and bring it into the room. "Alright, what will we use this for?" she quizzes me.

This answer comes to mind even quicker. "To check for blood in the abdomen after palpations."

"Very good. It's about to get very busy. You're going to see a lot of new faces. Respiratory therapy will be here, and the general surgeon will probably pop their heads in if they're not in surgery."

Clair, the house supervisor, comes flying into the ER. "Are the bays ready? I informed the rest of the team. They should be here any second."

"Thanks, Clair. You mind sticking around? Ava's a new hire, and having more hands on board wouldn't hurt."

"Nope, I wasn't planning on leaving. It's not every day we get to have a trauma party." Her enthusiasm is a stark difference to my crippling fear. She walks over to the PPE cabinet and gowns up, putting goggles and gloves on too. I follow her lead and get gowned up and ready. My heart races, and my thoughts feel all sorts of scattered. Taking a few deep breaths, I try to get it together. I watch as the doctor gowns up and prepares himself. He's a newer doctor but sharp as a tack, always knowing how to get us out of a bind. If I have to do this, I'm glad it's on his shift.

Within a few seconds, the roar of sirens blares outside the sliding glass doors, and two medics come running into the room.

"Male, airway was stable on transport, tachy at one hundred forty-seven, blood pressure is slightly low."

At that moment, it's like I'm eighteen again and in the ER with my parents. Blood everywhere. Seeing the ones I love slowly die in front of me. My breathing becomes more rapid, and I can't differentiate between then and now. When I look at the table, all I see is my mom. Hear my dad screaming for her, and not knowing that in a few short hours, I would lose both of them. My body starts to shake as I slowly back up against the wall and squeeze my eyes closed, but that doesn't stop the memories from flooding my mind. I never wanted to relive that day. I wanted to be a nurse to save someone, but I can't do that when I feel like my heart is breaking all over again.

I watch Aspen work; for such a carefree person, she handles the chaos with ease. "We need to intubate and get the ultrasound over here. NOW!"

I can't do a lot, but this I can do. I bring the ultrasound closer, and the doctor drops a glob of gel on the patient's belly, grabbing the head of the ultrasound wand.

"Free fluid in the abdomen, page general surgery now. If he can't get down here in the next five minutes, we need to stabilize and ship. Clair, call the flight team just in case," the doctor orders.

"Yes, sir." She darts out of the bay and off to her next mission.

The hour flies by, and I never kick the feeling of Deja vu. The general surgeon recommended we stabilize and ship since she doesn't have a second surgeon on staff tonight.

The room empties as the team gets ready to load the patient onto the chopper. Time passes, but I feel frozen, stuck in a memory I've never been able to forget.

Aspen rips off her disposable gown and looks over to me. "You did great!"

"All I did was grab the ultrasound machine." My weight shifts from foot to foot as guilt fills me because I did not do great. I locked up and froze.

"This was your first trauma. It'll be hard to know what to do until you get your feet wet." She taps my arm, completely oblivious to the war going on in my head. She has no clue this wasn't my first trauma bay. But it was my first time being on the other side, and now that I've been there, I'm not sure if I can do this.

I sit in my car for a few minutes. My head feels too loud and too quiet all at once. It feels like static. My glossy eyes stare at the front door, needing to move but not seeming to be able to. My body feels useless and heavy.

I take a deep breath, steeling myself. It's days like today I wish I had my own room so I could fall apart with no one to see.

Pulling open the front door, I hope Mav will be out with the boys or something so I can take a shower and sleep off this day. When I swing the door open, I realize I have no such luck because he locks eyes with me the second I step through the door frame. One look at me, and he knows. I don't know how he does it, but he sees right through me.

"Ava, baby, what's wrong?" Those words are my demise because the second I hear them, I break into a million tiny shards. Reliving all of the pain I've pushed down for years. A sob racks through me, and in seconds, I'm wrapped up in Mav, his scent covering my body like a soothing balm and moving to his bed.

"Shhh, it's okay. Tell me how I can help?" But there is no help because he can't bring them back.

"I had to do it again today, relive that day." It takes no more words for him to figure it out. He knows exactly what day because he's had his own day like that. A day you never want to live through again. "There was an accident, and all I could see was my parents. It was like being there again on that day; all I could see were their last moments. And I was supposed to help this time, but I couldn't." My voice shakes from the tears clogging my throat.

His voice comes out in a gentle timber. "That's okay. The first time will be the worst, it'll get better."

"What if I can't do it? What if I make a mistake?" My voice wobbles as another sob creeps up.

He pulls away and puts my head between his warm palms. He stares at me the way he does when I swear he can see a bit of my soul. "Do you want to help people?"

Without any hesitation, I nod my head. "Yes. Of course."

"Then you didn't make a mistake. Give yourself time. Grieve and mourn as many times as you need. Eventually, you'll be able to tell the difference between that day and what's in front of you."

My head shakes with denial as more tears stream down my face.

"It's okay, baby. Cry. I'm right here." My hands grip his arm like it's my anchor, keeping me here. My body shakes with silent sobs as he rocks us back and forth until my eyes close and my body finally gets tired enough to shut down the thoughts.

When I wake up, I'm wrapped up in Maverick, and for the first time ever, I don't feel alone. I had to lose my parents by myself. Watch it all, make all the decisions, and come home to an empty house. This time, when I had to relive that terrible day, I had someone waiting for me. Ready to pick up the pieces and hold me until they were put back together. And that makes me more terrified than I can even comprehend.

Chapter 26
MAVERICK

Sunday dinners at Jack and Mabel's house have become a routine. I was gone last Sunday, but Ava came down by herself and hung out with Aspen and the rest of the family. She fits in so perfectly here. She's the puzzle piece I didn't know was missing but just snapped into place. Now I can see the big picture, and it's the best damn thing I've ever seen.

Buttoning the top of my jeans, I look over as Ava comes out of the bathroom, putting an earring in. God, she's so fucking beautiful it hurts. Her blue jeans perfectly conform to her curves, sitting low and leaving a sliver of skin showing. My gaze feels heated, and when her eyes meet mine, it's as if she can read my thoughts.

"Don't even think about it, cowboy. I am starving."

Not bothering putting on a shirt, I stalk over to her. I'm unable to take my eyes off her, and my hands are itching to get a touch. "Hey, I'm starving too." Burying my face into the crook of her neck, I get a whiff of her perfume and feel my cock instantly harden behind my zipper. I can't get enough of her. I feel like a desperate teenager, greedily taking anything she gives me.

My hands slide under the back of her tight T-shirt, and I feel the warmth of her skin against my rough palms. Her arms wrap around my neck, and I mentally calculate how long I can spend with her.

"Mav, we're supposed to go to dinner."

"I know, baby, but I can be quick. I just want a little taste."

She pats my chest twice and slowly backs away. "I just finished my hair. You can mess it up when we get home. Maybe that'll be the motivation you need to not eat yourself into a food coma."

"You're killing me, sweetheart." My voice comes out as more of a whine.

"I can promise you, no man has ever died from blue balls. Now let's go eat. The sooner that's done, the sooner you can have dessert." She winks at me, and I slide my shirt and hoodie on in record time.

We walk in the doors and are greeted with the smell of garlic and basil. The kitchen bar is surrounded by its usual people. I always love walking into this house because the first thing you hear is laughter.

"Hey guys! We're glad you made it," Mabel greets us as she waves from the kitchen, busy whipping up dinner at the stove.

"Thanks for having us," Ava responds as she slips off her shoes. She's really warmed up to Mabel, but she has a way of making everyone feel welcome. Don't get me wrong, she'll beat your ass if you step out and need corrected. Plus, you have to be one strong woman to be married to Jack for so long.

"I see you got a little lady with you," Tommy, our new farrier, says as he walks toward us. He's almost as tall as I am but a little leaner. He took over for his dad when he retired last year. I haven't quite warmed up to him like the others have.

"Yeah, I do, this is my—uh—my..." I struggle to find what to call her. We've decided we're together, but introducing her as my girlfriend feels wrong—not quite enough—which causes a whole other round of thoughts to barrel through me. What would she say to that? If I told her I was all in?

"Hi, I'm Ava." She puts her small hand out to shake Tommy's. He gives her a strong shake and looks over to me with eyebrows raised.

"This is Maverick's new wife," Weston says, all too happy to butt in. If I could deck him right now, I would. He somehow always knows when I'm having inner turmoil and relishes bringing it to everyone else's attention.

"Oh! I didn't even know you were seeing anyone," Tommy says as his eyes bounce from Ava to me, the look of disappointment a little too obvious on his face.

"Uh, what can I say? When you know, you know." I look over to Ava and realize those words are one hundred percent true.

I do know.

I've never met someone like her who works as hard as she does. Most girls I've met have known my name and always expected something, but she's the opposite.

She refuses my help even when I wish she wouldn't. She wants to work for everything she's got, and I respect that more than I can say.

I get her, and she gets me.

The scars on her soul look really similar to mine. I guess they were right when they said like calls to like. You wouldn't get that from looking at us, but I guess that's what I love most.

That I am the only one who knows that dark little corner of her and I like even more that she's let me in there. That's a privilege I never plan to take for granted.

"Yup," Ava says, the edges of her lips curving up into a smile, showing off her perfect full lips as she tries to hide the smile begging to pop out.

"Well, I am happy for you. It looks like you married up," he appraises her, eyeing her up and down, his eyes lingering a little too long.

"Sure did." I'm not sure if I need to tell him to stop eyeballing my wife like that. He has about one more second of staring at her before eating his own balls for dinner.

My hand slips around her waist, giving him a gentle reminder that she's mine. This woman has turned me into a fucking caveman.

He seems to notice the gesture and smiles warmly at both of us before turning back and walking to the center island.

"Do you also need to pee on me?" She cocks her eyebrow up at me.

I can't help but laugh as I lean over and kiss her cheek, whispering in her ear, "Well, if you wouldn't have left me all wound up, I would have already marked my territory. My cum would've been dripping out of you as we speak."

"Jesus, Mav." A blush rises up from her exposed chest all the way to her cheeks. Pulling her closer, I kiss her cheek once more for good measure. When I lift my head, I see everyone in the kitchen staring at us—big ol' smiles on all their faces.

"I think I can speak for the group that we're glad you two wised up and noticed how good you are for each other," Mabel says. "Now, for the rest of you, head to the table. Rhett and West, can you help me out?" They both nod and push off the granite counter.

I'm used to all eyes on me, so I laugh it off, but Ava tucks her head, hiding her blush. My hand finds her lower back as I guide her to the right and head straight for the large table. On an average night, there are a lot of us. But with the addition of Tommy, the table is packed to the brim.

"So, Ava, are you from this area?" Tommy asks from across the table.

"No, I actually was born and raised about two hours from here." She takes a sip of her wine, and my hand instinctively lands on her thigh. Following the stitching pattern on her inner thigh, my hand moves higher and higher. She squeezes her thighs, trapping my hand between them, which is fine with me.

"She's adjusted to ranch life like a pro," Weston says, tipping back in his chair. I wasn't sure how she'd like it out here, but if you didn't know better, you'd have thought she was born into it.

"I don't know about that, but I do love it out here. It's much more peaceful than being in town."

"And she's made some great friends. Tell them about your best friend, Betty," I joke with her. She's still way too attached to some of our cows. Now we'll never be able to sell them because they're her pasture puppies.

"I'm going to tell Betty to run your ass over next time your back is turned to her," Ava says, narrowing her eyes at me with a little bit of an embarrassed flush to her cheeks.

"So I take it, I won't be taking Betty or her calf to the sale barn?" Jack raises his grey bushy eyebrows at me. I shake my head no, and he just chuckles under his breath. Somehow, I get the feeling Mabel has done this exact thing to him. He exchanges a look with her, and her sheepish smile confirms my suspicions.

After we finish eating, the chatter of voices fills the room, each one of us having our own conversations and laughs. My hand still firmly planted on Ava's leg, I give it a squeeze, hoping now that dinner is done, we can leave. I was promised dessert, and I'm ready to cash in on that reward. My thumb moves in slow, tortuous circles on the inside of her thigh, causing her to squirm in her seat. It appears I'm not the only one who's all hot and bothered tonight.

"Well, I picked up a shift in the morning, so I am going to head out," Aspen says.

"Yeah, all this wonderful food made me pretty tired. I am going to head out," Rhett says, rising out of his chair. "Are we still going to pick up a load of hay tomorrow?" He looks to Weston, who nods his head, shoving a bit of his second helping of lasagna into his mouth. Honestly, how that guy is the skinniest of all of us is a mystery.

Taking advantage of Aspen and Rhett leaving at the same time, as always, I force my hand out of Ava's thighs and say, "Yeah, we are probably going to head out too."

"I'll see you at work tomorrow, Ava!" Aspen says as she makes her way to her boots and slides them on.

"Hopefully, you two can have a nice, quiet day tomorrow," Tommy says.

"You're an asshole," Aspen says, her eyes shooting daggers toward Tommy.

"What?"

"The Q word is banned in healthcare. You pretty much just cursed us to have the worst day ever," Ava says, clearly feeling a little less reserved than normal. She's either comfortable or pissed off. Either way, I like it.

"Well, in that case, I hope you have a busy day."

"You can't reverse Uno the Q word. But nice try. Goodbye, every-one!" Aspen says as she swings open the door. Rhett waves as he closely follows her out. We make our way to the door and say our goodbyes. My pace is picked up the second I hear the click of the door. Heading home has never sounded as good as it does right now because I have plans for me and my woman. Plans that will take the entire night.

Chapter 27
Ava

I've barely closed the passenger door to the truck before Maverick has slung me over his shoulder, walking us to the front door. My laughter bounces off the pine trees as I admire how good Maverick's ass looks from this view.

"You promised me dessert, and I'm fully planning on cashing in on that," Maverick says as he swats my ass, earning another hearty laugh from me.

We move through the door, and I quickly find myself landing on the mattress, looking up at Maverick. The look in his eyes has my heart stilling. There's no hiding the pure adoration painted all over his face. I've dreamed up a lot of things I never thought would be possible, but never in my wildest dreams would I have dreamed up a man like Maverick. He hears me even when I don't say a word. He knows my heart on a level that doesn't seem possible for how long we've known each other.

Somehow, our pasts have perfectly prepared us to be just right for each other. I've never believed in fate. Life has done me dirty far too many times for me to think fate could be real, and if it was, my fate was a shit show. But *somehow*, Maverick and I ended up exactly where we needed to be, at just the right time. That sounds a whole lot like divine intervention, if you ask me.

"So, what sounds good for dessert?" I playfully quirk an eyebrow up at him.

His muscled arms frame my body, and I can't look away from his face. His sharp jawline, the little bit of scruff peeking through, and the way his nose is slightly crooked, either by a mishap with the boys or a riding incident, I suppose. I'd ask him about it, but his steely grey eyes are burning for me, and I love that. "I think I would rather show you."

His hands go to work on my zipper, quickly working my clothes off my body, which seems so unfair, considering how damn good he looks with his shirt off. I have a desperate need to get my hands on his skin, to feel him against me. He sits me up enough to pull off my shirt, leaving me in my matching red bra and panties.

"Ava, baby, you're killing me," Mav says as he runs his hands across my ribs and slowly moves up until his thumbs are against the underside of my breast. "This has to go. I want to see all of you." He wraps his arms around me, and I feel my bra slip off, leaving my top half bare to him as I sit on the edge of the bed.

He leans down, kissing the side of my neck, causing a fire to erupt in my core. "You know, I think you deserve some payback for making me wait." His voice comes out husky, and it has me squeezing my eyes closed at the rush I feel. His lips graze over further down until he meets my neck. His teeth gently bite into me, and a moan tumbles out of me as my hands fly to the back of his head, desperate to keep his touch.

He pushes my shoulders back until I'm flat on the bed. "Scoot up, baby." Digging my heels in, I push back until my head hits the pillows. He strips off his shirt, and I get the view I've been waiting for; his chiseled chest rises and falls quickly as desire starts to overcome him. The lust in his eyes is hot enough to catch this whole damn cabin on fire. His body crawls over mine, and I strongly debate begging him to touch me to relieve some of the need twisting tight in my core.

His lips roam up from my belly button all the way up to my breasts. He looks up at me as he sucks one of my nipples into his mouth. It becomes too much and not enough all at once. "Maverick, please, for the love of god, fuck me."

"Sorry, sweetheart, we aren't playing by your rules. You made me wait, and now you can get a taste of your own medicine."

"If I say I'm sorry, will that speed things along?" There's a rasp to my voice I don't recognize.

He shakes his head as he slowly works his way back down, my thighs rub together trying to get some friction—literally anything to ease the tension building inside me. My pussy feels like it's aching, dying for something to fill it up.

My eyes stay locked on him as he stops right above my panties. I roll my hips up, hoping he will put me out of my misery.

"Are you that desperate for me, sweetheart?" The glee in his eyes is infuriating. He's loving this, watching me practically beg for even a sliver of a touch.

"I hate you."

"You won't be saying that later when you come all over my cock."

I go to fire off a smartass retort, but it gets stuck on my lips when he pulls my panties to the side and glides a finger through my core. The brief movement sends shivers up my body. *Finally.*

"Ava, baby, you are making a fucking mess down here. Look how wet you are for me. I should tease you more often." Propping up on one elbow, he swipes his fingers through me and brings his fingers to his lips. "Sweetest dessert I've ever tasted." If I thought desire had sparked before, it's full-on flaming after that. I watch him intently as he licks each finger clean, like my dripping wet pussy is the finest delicacy he's ever tasted. His eyes close with the movement, and I feel like I'm going to combust from the heat within.

His eyes land back on me, as he brings his mouth down to my clit. When he sucks it into his mouth, my hips jerk. He tsks, "You're going to stay nice and still while I eat my dessert." His forearm splays across my hips, holding them down as he dives in. His tongue dives as deep in as it can, and I relish the relief it brings.

When he slips a finger in, I feel the edges of an orgasm building. My breathing becomes more rapid as my pussy grips on to his fingers. I feel myself getting wetter, and the sounds that come out of my mouth don't even sound like myself. It would be embarrassing if I weren't so lost in it all.

"Oh my God, Mav. I'm going to come." The second the words are out of my mouth, he halts, withdrawing his fingers from my pussy and pulling his mouth back. I swear I whimper at the sight of it. "What the fuck?"

"Oh, you thought I was done teasing you? Not yet, baby." His lips glisten with my wetness smeared across his face. That shouldn't be so fucking hot, but it is—seeing myself all over him. He wipes off his mouth with the back of his hand as he scoots off the bed and unbuttons his pants. "The only place you're going to be coming tonight is on my cock."

My head nods without my permission. I think at this point, I'll go along with anything he says as long as it ends with me finally getting to come.

When his cock springs free, my pussy clenches down again. There are a lot of things I love about Maverick. He's genuinely the best person I have ever met, and some days, I can't believe that he's mine.

But good lord, my husband's cock ranks way too high on the things I love about him. I've never been fucked like this. He makes my loud mind shut off and be at his mercy, and I love it.

He grabs a pillow from beside me. "Lift your hips," he says as he slides the pillow under me. His large hands grip my knees, spreading them wider. My eyes are locked on him, and his are locked on my pussy. I've never felt more confident in my life than the moments this man looks at me with this level of hunger.

He drags the head of his cock up and down, gathering my wetness on the tip, while his hands hold my knees up almost to my chest. He slides in me with one swift thrust, taking me by surprise. My eyes roll back at the sensation of being so fucking full. My hands grab his, and I lock eyes with him.

Thrust after thrust, he digs deeper, leaning forward and hitting areas I've never felt before. A feeling comes over me, and I feel a flood rush out.

"Fuck yes, Ava. Squirt on my cock, drown it." He throws his head back as his fingertips dig into me. I feel the sensation over and over again as it trickles down to the pillow beneath me. His pace gets quicker, and with every stroke to my G-spot, I feel the flicker of another orgasm. Building, building, building until it feels so fragile that I shatter.

Mav's pace stays steady until he stills, filling me up until his breathing is the only sound in the room. He collapses down on my chest, and we take a second to gather ourselves. When he lifts his head, he leans in, kissing me deeper and with more emotion than I was anticipating. Leaving me feeling cherished and loved.

"I need to get you cleaned up." He pecks my nose, and I let out a small laugh.

I've known for a while how screwed I was, because there was no other way. No matter how hard I fought, no matter what I told myself and others, I was never going to win this fight. Being with Maverick feels as natural as breathing. Like this is where I was always meant to be. I can no longer deny he's stolen my heart. There's a sense of calm that comes with his presence, and after a life of being constantly on edge, I want to sneak in closer and hang on to that feeling for dear life.

Maverick slips out of the bed and starts the shower for us. It feels better than it should, having someone take care of me like this, and I think I'm done fighting it. If he wants to love me, then I'm going to let him because I love him too.

Chapter 28
MAVERICK

Leaving for rodeos has become harder and harder. In my twenties, it was great; there were new towns, new people, and new girls. But the latter hasn't mattered in a while; after a few years of meaningless sex, it grows old. The spotlight, the attention from women, and the never being home all seem so superficial. Even worse now, leaving Ava feels like a crime. Even if I'm only on the road for a few days. I've always missed the ranch when I was gone. There is something about the air here that makes you feel free. I love working side by side with those who choose to be my family. I find myself looking forward to the days when I get to do that, and only that, more and more.

Staring at Ava, which I find myself doing more of every day, I'm completely transfixed by her. She blew into my world and is somehow changing everything. Life is better with her. I bet life on the road would be better too, which gives me an idea.

"Hey, are you working this weekend?" I ask.

Lifting her head from scrolling on her phone, she responds with, "Nope, I'm off until next Thursday, actually. It's the longest stretch I've had in a while, but training has gone quicker than they thought, and they haven't had any callouts."

"Good. Want to go on the road with me this time?"

"Really? Are you sure? Doug didn't seem so thrilled the last time I tagged along."

"Doug could use a firm reminder of who the boss really is. It would be fun having you with me again."

"Is this your way of saying you miss me when you're gone?" She gives me a look with pursed lips and amusement filling her eyes.

"Baby, I miss you even when you're at work, so yes." I've always been tough, bound tight and impossible to unravel. Especially when it came to my heart. I didn't think I would ever want to give it to anyone, but somehow, this beautiful little thing in front of me stole it without me noticing. I don't know if she even noticed herself. A happy home life and a life on the road is why I never went for anything serious. I never thought I could have both. And now, I find myself being the problem. I am the one who never wants to leave her sight. Joke is on me, I guess.

She sighs dramatically before getting off the makeshift futon/couch and comes to sit next to me on the bed. "Well, we can't have you being sad on the road, so I guess I can pencil you in. You're turning out to be a stage five clinger, you know that?"

My laughter rumbles through my chest. "What can I say? I'm a man obsessed with his woman." Grabbing the back of her head, I pull her into a kiss. And with every movement of my lips, I show her how much I care for, love, and adore her. I haven't said it yet, partly out of fear that saying them out loud will suddenly make this too much for her, and partly because it's a first for me, and I don't know how.

Ava and I hop out of my truck and head toward the arena. We've got three nights of riding this weekend, and I intend to earn big money

tonight. Having my own little good luck charm will make that even easier.

Ava helps me carry in my lighter riding gear. I won't get my own dressing room here, but that's alright. Some of the fun is shit talking to the boys in the dressing room anyway.

Doug comes around the corner with Sully, who's sporting a smile when he sees who I dragged with me. Although, I don't know why.

"Maverick, are you headed to the dressing room now?"

"Yes, but only to drop off my stuff. I am going to show Ava around and then get dressed out." I walk away before he can tell me what he had planned for me and how I need to 'focus'. He hasn't even said anything yet and I can already feel myself getting pissed off.

We walk through the back of the building and through painted cement hallways until we reach the rodeo attender's spot. "Alright, I will be right back. I just need to throw this in my locker." I lean down and kiss her pink cheek before heading in.

We arrived early enough that the locker room is pretty empty. I keep my head down and throw my stuff in my assigned locker before heading back out. With Doug sulking around, I feel anxious to get back to Ava. The last thing I need is him getting her alone.

Walking back out, I find Ava and capture her hand in mine as I begin showing her behind the scenes of the rodeo. The last time she joined me, it was a busy day, and I wasn't able to provide her with a full tour, but I'm correcting that now.

"Can I see the animals?" she asks, already scanning for where they might be.

"You won't be able to see them until we're in the arena. They're pretty well guarded beforehand. No one cares more about those animals than those of us who rodeo. They do their job, and our job is to keep them safe."

She nods as she takes in the new information. "I guess I never thought of that. Well, cowboy, what else is there?"

"You want to see the inside of the chute?" I ask, and judging by the way her eyes light up, I am taking that as a yes.

The smell of dirt and livestock permeates the air, the bright lights shine on the arena as we walk through huddles of teams and attendees. The media is out with force tonight, and I make a strong effort to dodge them as we walk to the chute.

"Alright, over there behind that tarp is where they lead in the bull. Here in a little while, the riders will all draw their bulls. Then they will get led up here when it's time to ride."

"So how do you stay on? Just by holding on to the pummel on the rope?"

"Well, I use rosin to make my rope and glove sticky, and we wrap our rope around the bull so it stays secure. Plus, my legs have a death grip on whatever beast I am riding."

"What happens if you fall off?"

I don't know how to tell her I just hope like hell I can get my hand loose. Most times, it comes off fine at the end of the ride, but I have had a couple of broken arms and hands in my day from being unable to get loose. "I know how to get my arm out, it just takes the right angle." Kind of the truth, but mostly not. I don't need her to worry about me when I'm out here.

I walk her around for about fifteen more minutes. When I start cutting it down to the wire, I walk with her to the shopping level. "Alright, I have to go, but if you come down in about an hour or so, it should be riding time. You're always welcome by the corrals, too." I gave her a lanyard with backstage access to roam wherever she wants. She's officially part of Team Ryder, and the lanyard is another indicator. I lean in, my hand cupping the side of her face and as I peck her on the cheek. When I pull back, I find myself not wanting to leave her. My thumb brushes over her cheek for a few seconds. "Alright, sweetheart, I gotta go. See you soon." She nods with the corner of her lips quirked up as I walk off.

As I make my way through the arena and back toward the dressing room, I find Doug leaning against the cement wall when I make it back.

"I was worried you were so preoccupied with your little 'wife' that you were going to miss check-in." He doesn't even bother to look at me, which pisses me off even more.

"I'm not in the mood for your passive aggressive shit today, Doug. I've been doing this for years."

"You sure seem distracted to me. Exactly like I warned." He has not the slightest idea what having her here does for me. It does the opposite of distracting me. It makes me want to perform even better for her. She grounds me in a way that his small brain could never understand. Probably why he's still alone.

"Funny, I wasn't aware you were a mind reader, Doug. Tell me, what am I thinking right now?" He levels me with a stare that says he isn't entertained, but I don't care, I am. Giving him shit back is actually a good time. I should have started doing this sooner. "I'll give you a hint: it's two words..."

"You were never like this before. I don't like what she's doing to you."

"Fuck you, Doug. That's what I was thinking. And you better think fucking twice before you start insulting the woman I love or you'll find yourself out of a job."

He lets out a curt laugh. "Love? Son, the only thing you have time to love is bull riding. Your sole focus needs to be the sport if you really want to be the best. You know why? Cause if that woman loves you, like you claim to love her, at some point, she's going to ask you to quit. And then all of this will have been for nothing."

My anger boils so hot in my blood I debate if I'd get kicked out today for knocking him on his ass, but I take a deep breath and choose a different option. "You're wrong. She's different. She supports me for me, unlike your sorry ass. Don't forget, Doug. I sign those checks you love so much. So you better watch your mouth."

My hand slams against the swinging door as I open it. His words swirl around in my head. She would never ask me to quit, would she? She's one of the few who have gotten a peek inside my head. And one of the few whose opinion actually matters to me. That's what I need to focus on. I shake my head, clearing all this out. If there's one thing I know better than, it's to go out there with your head focused on something else. That's when you get hurt. All my worst injuries have been when I wasn't mentally prepared for what I was about to do. And getting hurt in front of Ava is the last thing I want to do.

Getting my riding gear on, I strap into my chaps and get my riding vest ready; it's all decked out with sponsoring logos. I remember just how fucking lucky I am to have the freedom to do this. To have people bankrolling the whole damn thing. I hope I make them all proud and live up to the legacy. Every ride, that's what it's about. Outdoing who I was yesterday. If I do that, there's not a man on earth who will be able to compete with me. Cocky? Maybe. But it's true.

Today, I'm smack dab in the middle of the lineup. I lean against the rails, watching the others ride. The bulls today are doing their part. The air of the arena is coated with a thin veil of dust from the bucking of hooves. So far, there have only been two riders to stay on. Of course, one of them is Gonzales. Stupid prick. Bet he won't make the mistake of hitting on my wife again.

Every rodeo you see familiar faces sprinkled in with a few new ones trying to drop-kick the door open and make their way onto the scene. I think that's why the majority of them hate me; I didn't have that. But they fail to remember that being on the scene alone doesn't make you a winner. Taking home the buckle does. No matter my last name, if I can't ride worth a shit, it's over.

Ava makes her way over a few minutes before it's my turn to ride. I see her searching through the crowd, eyes scanning the groups of people until she finds me. The smile she gives me could knock me straight to my knees. She hurries over, bags in hand.

"Did a little shopping, did we?"

"Hey, I finally have more than four dollars to my name. And I need outfits for when I hang out with Aspen so she finally leaves me the hell alone."

"I don't think Aspen has ever left anyone alone. I'm pretty sure being a pain in the ass is part of her personality." The buzzer sounds, and the rider is done, leaving only one more before it's my turn. "Alright, sweetheart, it's my time to shine." I kiss her on the forehead and head over to the tent.

Her voice comes from behind me. "Go kick some ass, cowboy. Be safe." I turn to see her hands full with bags and a bright white smile. God, I love her, and I love that she's here. I don't think I can go much longer without telling her. It's on the tip of my tongue all too often.

Once I get to the chute, the team gets me ready to ride. The chatter from the stand and the announcers slowly start to fade as I get in the zone. I close my eyes, grounding myself before the gates bust open.

"Alright, Mav. It's just eight seconds," Sully says as he double-taps my helmet before stepping down from the chute rails.

When the buzzer sounds and the gates fly open, that's when it all goes wrong. My bull doesn't go forward, but he sure does buck. His snarling huffs become the only thing I can hear. I have nowhere to go and nowhere to bail to. He bucks up again, his strong back legs planted into the dirt, and turns enough that my back slams against the rails. Pain radiates through my ribs as I struggle to catch my breath.

"Get him the fuck out of there," Sully's deep voice booms, somehow louder than the beast underneath me when he realizes I'm now stuck. The bull crushes me to the rails. Fuck, this hurts.

Arms reach for me as I struggle to get my hand loose. Tying myself up extra tight is nice when I'm getting tossed around like a ragdoll, but not so much when I need to get free.

Fuck, keep your head, Maverick. You have to get home to her. Ava. Ava, Ava.

With one final pull, my hand comes loose, and I'm drug against the rails until I'm sitting at the top of them. My breathing comes out in heavy pants. It takes a few seconds to realize I'm no longer in danger of being crushed to death, and a chuckle leaves me.

"You're the only fucker I know that would laugh after a near death experience," Sully says, his voice back to normal volume.

I look down past him and see Ava. Her blue eyes are wild and filled with tears. Her breathing is ragged as her chest rises and falls rapidly. Fuck. She's too far away to even hear me say I'm okay. And I am, my back will be bruised to shit, but I don't think anything is broken, and for me, that's a win with this type of event.

The only thing I can do is wave and smile at her. She mouths, "Are you okay?" And I smile and nod, hoping that will give her enough reassurance until I'm done.

"Mav, focus," Doug says, his bushy eyebrows furrowed. I am beginning to hate this asshole more by the day.

Sully cuts in, "Alright, they're giving you a new bull. You feel okay to ride?"

"Of course he does." Doug rolls his eyes.

"Well, you heard from my mind reader directly, Sully." I hold my hand out, gesturing to Doug. "I'm good to ride." The look I give Sully tells him to get this next ride going before I punch Doug in the dick.

My ride goes as well as it could have, the buzzer sounds, and I rip my hand free from the rope and the tape before making out like a bat out of hell to the corral fence. Ava stands beside my team on the second level of the fence to get a better view. She still looks a little rattled with her smile not quite reaching her eyes. She cups her hands around her mouth and hollers anyway. I nod my head at her, patting my heart twice before I point to her. Ignoring everyone else, I make my way over to her.

She hops off the side of the fence when I get closer and throws her arms around me. "Are you okay?"

My arms wrap around her as I pull her close against my chest. "Yes, I'm totally fine. It looked worse than it was." I keep my eyes on hers, not wanting her to get a chance to let her mind run.

Her hands anxiously pat over me to confirm my words, part of me worrying she might find something because that ride did hurt like a bitch. But she comes up empty and I feel her let out a sigh of relief. I lean in and kiss her forehead, reminding myself yet again how lucky I am to have her.

"At least you got back up there and kicked everyone else's ass. But don't ever scare me like that again." A smile comes to her face, and I let out my own sigh of relief at seeing her relax.

Sarah Andrews comes up beside us, microphone and camera in hand. "Maverick, it's great to see you out here tonight. That was a spectacular performance. Can you tell us what was going through your head preparing you for the ride, or should I say rides, after that rough start?"

"Thank you, Sarah. It has been a great season so far. Even with my little mishap today, the bulls have been fantastic, so I need to give them a little credit. I'm more focused than ever. It's no secret that I'm gunning to be world champ this year, and I've been trying to keep that at the front of my mind before every ride."

"That is great. Unless there is a huge upset with later rides, you are on track to win the pot today. How does that feel?"

"It feels great," looking right at Ava, I respond, "I have special guests here today, and it feels even better to get the W with those I love so close."

"That's great. Thanks for chatting with us today." Sarah thanks me again off camera and walks away, and I have a brief moment of second thoughts. Maybe I shouldn't have said that on live TV. And even worse, what if she doesn't feel the same way yet? This has moved from nothing to something in a mere matter of months. But when you know, you know.

And I know that I love this girl more than anything. My whole life, the only thing I've been willing to lay my life down for is bull riding, but then she came around and made everything better.

"I wasn't aware you were so fond of Doug," Ava says, mischief shining in those eyes.

My hands wrap around her waist as her arms link behind my neck. "Oh, big fan. Never loved anyone more."

"Mhmm." She squints her eyes at me and grins.

"Well, maybe one person. You might know her. She's blonde. An occasional pain in my ass. Acts about forty years older than she is." The last barb will be a dead giveaway, as if the others weren't.

"She sounds great. You should probably make sure you don't let that one slip away." She winks at me, and I feel the lost piece of me snap into place.

"Never." Leaning in, pecking her lips and savoring the taste of her strawberry chapstick.

She takes a step back but keeps her hands firmly planted on my chest. Her beautiful blue eyes hold my gaze. And I can feel all of the unspoken words. All of the emotion is easy to see right there in those eyes I love so much. The chaos of the arena fades around us, and all I care about is being with her.

"Hey, cowboy?" she whispers.

"Yeah?" My voice has an extra grate to it with all of the emotion spilling out into my voice.

"I love you, too," she declares, smile lines around her eyes are filled with unshed tears. Relief hits me and I take a deep breath of her in. To be loved by this woman is the greatest honor of my life.

"That's good because I just told the whole world I love you." My lips crash back into hers, kissing her with everything I have because she is finally *mine*. She has claimed every bit of me, body and soul, and there's no part of me that regrets it. Everything I am is hers to have as long as she will have me. And if I have it my way, that'll be my dying day.

Chapter 29
MAVERICK

Summer heat has officially arrived. Sweat pours off my forehead as we move the last bit of cattle. My ass is numb from sitting in the saddle all day. I look over to Weston and Rhett and see they're in the same boat. Weston removes his ball cap and wipes the sweat off his brow.

"I think we earned a little riverside swim tonight, boys," Weston says as he puts his cap back on. This July has been hotter than Hades, and we're only a couple weeks in. Doesn't help that I've been go-go-go between rides and trying to help the guys around here.

With all that being away, if I have a chance to get Ava in a bikini, then I'm going to do it. "I'm sure Ava and Aspen would be down."

"Let's meet at the river in an hour. Bring some snacks and some brews?"

We all hop in our trucks and head to our own little cabins. Each of us has a place on this chunk of land about a quarter mile or so from each other, except for Weston's place. His is farther on the east side. The beauty of how wide this property sprawls out is that we get to keep our privacy. Pulling my truck up to the front of the house, I close the door and head inside.

Ava stands at the kitchen sink, putting away dishes from the breakfast she made us this morning. "Hey, cowboy. How was your day?"

Kicking off my boots, I hurry to the kitchen, desperate to get my hands on her. Wrapping my arms around her middle, I pull her back into my chest. "It's about to get a whole lot better," I whisper into her ear, causing little goosebumps to break out across her skin.

"Oh?" She sets down the dishrag in her hand and turns around, propping herself up against the sink.

"We're headed for the river to go for a swim. Go change into your swimsuit, and then we can head out."

"Who is we?"

"All of us. Rhett, Aspen, and Weston. It's basically a summer tradition." I'm pretty sure we'll be swimming there until one of us breaks a hip.

"Well, that sounds fun," she says. Not knowing that over the years, we've decked out our little spot. Hammocks are up, and we have a little rope swing for the spots that are deeper. Summer brings out the kids in all of us. Some of my favorite memories growing up here were times spent there cooling off. And now I get to show Ava a little piece of a country summer.

Ava digs through her small dresser in her closet, while I head to the bathroom to clean up a little. I know we're about to cool off, but sweating my balls off for the last few hours has me smelling a little too nasty, even for myself.

Within the hour, we make it up to the river. This little spot was always the best; the water doesn't move as fast here, so you don't have to be worried about ending up in the Pacific Ocean if you aren't paying enough attention.

The sound of moving water and birds chirping is the first thing I hear, immediately followed by Weston yelling at someone. "Asshole."

We walk up, me in boots and Ava in sandals. "I can't believe you don't own a single pair of sandals or even slippers."

"Hey, these boots have never led me wrong."

"Whatever you say." We step over wildflowers and grass until we clear through the trees and get to our little cove. Rocks line most of the area, with enough cleared dirt to make for a decent beach spot. The sun pokes through the aspen trees, leaving it warm, but not as hot.

"Hey, guys!" Aspen says. Her hair is already wet, and little droplets run down the end. Weston is already wet as well, still in a shirt. There's a good chance she's the reason he was cursing earlier. Those two have always been thick as thieves and a complete menace to each other.

"Who wants to be the first to jump off the rope swing?"

"I'll take that challenge." I've always loved living on the edge and pushing it. I was the first one on the swing when we built it. Only we mismeasured and I landed ass first on a giant rock. It now swings well over the water, and it feels like tradition that I get to hop off first.

Pulling my shirt over my head, I catch Ava staring. When her eyes meet mine, I expect to be met with a blush, like she usually does, only this time she smirks as if edging me on. A dangerous game to play with someone who has no fear.

Grabbing on to the rope, I look up to make sure it hasn't yet been frayed to complete shit. Grabbing on with both hands, I take off in a run and jump off the rock, letting go as I do a flip and land in a cannonball. Cold water rushes around me and immediately shakes the heat that was deep in my bones. Swimming up to the shore, I hop out of the water and shake my hair off on Ava. Usually, I keep it short, but it's gotten a little long.

She laughs before looking at me. "You're a bit of a showoff, you know that?"

"You're just jealous you can't do better," I say to her, grabbing a towel from the pile and laying it down on a rock,

Weston comes around, hearing the challenge. "Oh, it seems like Mav needs to be knocked down a level or two. I bet I can top that."

"You've been trying to outdo me for years, and if I remember right, you've failed."

"You know what, fucker? This is the year. I bet I can land a double." He points and then turns on his heels to make his way to the rope.

"If I have to take you to the ER, I swear to god, West," Aspen says, hands on her hips, shaking her head. I laugh, and she turns her head to me. "If he goes to the ER, you're the one who'll have to tell Mom why, so I don't know why you're laughing, dumbass." At that, Ava bursts out in laughter.

"Aspen, have I told you lately how glad I am that we're friends?" Ava says as she plops down next to me like she didn't just side with the enemy.

"Yes, but it doesn't hurt to hear it more often." She goes and sits down on her raggedy towel to watch the show. Rhett leans against a tree and shakes his head, a laugh already shaking his chest.

Weston takes off in a run and grips the rope a little higher than I did. He pushes off the edge of the grey rock and flips backward. He nails the first one but doesn't quite make it around for the double. Instead, he lands flat on his face.

Standing up, I give a round of applause because it takes heart and commitment to make that big of an ass of yourself in front of all your friends. His head pokes up above water, and his middle finger pokes up not even a couple seconds later.

"Fuck you, Mav," Weston says as he pulls himself up. His usually white chest is now looking a very angry shade of red. He must have hit that water even harder than I thought.

"Alright, sweetheart. I think it's your turn." I turn to Ava, whose eyes go wide. Maybe having her go after Weston is a bad idea. "Don't worry, Weston is the only one who lands on his face. The rest of us have all landed toes first."

"Here, I'll show her how it's done," Aspen says, pulling off her towel and heading to the rope. Ava gets up, and Aspen walks her through it before she demonstrates. She runs, jumps, and lands with a splash, causing the water to ripple.

"Have you never swung off a rope before?" Rhett asks, a crinkle in his brow like he is surprised by this.

"Uhm, no. If I'm being completely honest, this will be my first time even swimming in a river," Ava says as she looks toward the water warily, as if inspecting all the little places danger can be hidden. If I teach her anything, I hope it's that sometimes danger is the fun part.

"What kind of Wyoming girl are you?" Rhett asks. In his defense, we've all only known ranch life, and this was a big part of it.

"The kind that swam in a pool like a normal child," Ava responds.

Rhett laughs at that as he puts his hands up as if in defeat.

When Aspen's head comes above water, she scoots to the side and stays in. "Okay, I'll stay here. Just grab the rope, run, and jump. The most important part is to let go, or you will smack yourself against the rock. Ask me how I know." The memory of seventeen-year-old Aspen finally being allowed down here alone with us comes to mind. She got scared mid-swing and didn't let go. She had a gnarly bruise on her thigh that we had to hide from her mom for weeks.

Ava looks over to me, and I smile and nod my head in encouragement. She's got this. She seems to concentrate, taking this all too seriously, but then again, she is the type that if she is going to do something, she's going to do it right. I love that about her.

She runs, jumps, and when she gets far enough out of the water, I holler, "Let go!" She lets go, arms and long tan legs flailing around. She tucks her body just in time to land in a cannonball, splashing us all. We all cheer as she comes back up to the surface; my girl has officially completed her ranch orientation.

When she makes it to shore, the smile on her face tells me all I need to know. She may not have been born a country girl, but we're going to make one out of her.

She walks up to me, dripping wet, and shakes her head off at me. "Well, I'd say that was a fantastic cannonball."

"You outdid Weston, that's for sure," I praise as I hold out her towel, which she takes and wraps around her shoulders. She turns around and sits between my thighs as I lean back. Moments like this make me never want to leave Windy Peaks again. I let my thoughts run with that, more than I ever have. Would it really be so bad if ranch life was my only life? Getting to come home to this girl all the time? It seems like I might have a new dream brewing.

Chapter 30
Ava

Staring at myself in the mirror, I swipe some mascara over my lashes because I'm finally getting some girl time that isn't on the clock. "Alright, Aspen will be picking me up in a couple of minutes." She has a full girls' day planned.

Maverick steps into the bathroom door frame, leaning against it with his arms crossed. "What are you two going to be doing?"

Looking at him through the mirror, I say, "Well, since someone hasn't taken the time to show me around his hometown, Aspen volunteered to do it for him." I do my best to make my tone sound serious, but I know that every second he's been home, he's either working the farm or here with me.

"Hey, if you were looking for a tour guide, you should have said so." He shrugs his shoulders and sends me a toothy grin.

Faking a sigh, I dramatically say, "Too late. You'll have to go hang out with Weston and Rhett. Maybe then they'll cool their jets about how I've stolen you."

"Well, maybe if they stopped being thirty-year-olds who act like teenage boys, they could find themselves their own women." He steps into the bathroom and wraps his arms around my waist.

Turning around, I wrap my arms around his neck. "You're aware you only found your own woman by getting blacked out drunk in Vegas? Maybe you shouldn't be offering up that type of advice."

"You know what? I've decided I have zero regrets about that. There's no way my country ass would have been able to convince you to take a chance on me without extraordinary measures." My heart takes flight at his words, leaving me with a soaring feeling. He does that a lot. Makes me feel lighter than I ever have.

"Yeah, well, I also decided I don't regret it. So how about that?"

"Glad to hear it, sweetheart. If you decide you need to be rescued today, call me." He leans down and pecks me on the cheek before taking a step back.

"Please do not rescue me from the only girl time I've had since I moved here."

"You work with her every day."

That is a bit dramatic. I work with her three days a week now that I'm out of orientation. I'm still not trusted to do a lot by myself, which is fine because I'm terrified nearly every moment of my shift.

"There's no part of our job that allows for quality girl time. Especially in the ER. We're either flushing out snotty noses or going toe-to-toe with the grim reaper."

"He's tried to visit me a few times. Can't say I'm a fan," Mav jokes. His words hit a little too close to home, stirring up the anxiety I've been trying to shove down since his ride last week.

"That makes two of us, anyway. I'll be out all day. And lord knows how late. But I'll text you if I think it will be too late, so you don't have to wait up." I step out into the living room.

"You know I'd wait up for you anyway," Mav reassures me. There goes that soaring feeling again.

The knock at the door interrupts our conversation, and Aspen, being Aspen, doesn't wait to be let in. She throws open the front door and flops onto the futon. Her long brown hair cascades down her middle back, loose waves as wild as she is. Her bootcut jeans hug her long legs in a way that makes me envious.

"Sure, come in, Aspen," Mav says, shaking his head as he walks to the kitchen.

"You ready for a day of fun in Windy Peaks?" she asks as she crosses her legs.

"Yes, let's go!" I'm excited to see what else this town has to offer. Not that the ranch and all the land around it isn't enough, but it would be nice to see more than our eight-person friend group.

"See you later, loser!" Aspen hollers to Mav. I turn around to see him flipping her the finger. Shaking my head, I head out to Aspen's truck. Apparently, I'm the only one on the ranch who doesn't drive a 4x4 vehicle, and after getting a little taste of winter here, I can see why it would be beneficial.

"Alright, so I have a little lunch date for us planned. And then there's a cute boutique we can do some shopping. No offense, but your wardrobe could use some updating. Oh! And obviously, coffee."

"Obviously," I reply. I need a steady three cups a day just to function.

"And then we can see what else we have time for." She shrugs her shoulders as she rolls down the window, the summer air blowing in.

I can already tell that I'm going to need a nap when I get home, or at least another coffee, but getting out of the house is something I could stand to do a little more.

My eyes stay glued to my surroundings as we drive down the dirt road into town. Soon enough, it turns to pavement, and downtown Windy Peaks comes into view. We stay on the main road and start passing a few little stores. It almost looks like we've gone back in time. The buildings are all brick with hand-painted signs hanging over them.

Our first stop at Ruby's Cafe was a success. The place looked like a house but had the best chicken club I've ever tasted. When I get back home, I'm going to have some words with Mav for holding out on me because he was right. Windy Peaks is amazing.

"Okay, I skipped coffee, so we are going to head over to the coffee shop before we go shopping. Is that okay with you?"

"Sounds great! If it's as good as Ruby's, I think I'll be making my way into town more often."

"You're going to be putting some miles on that Toyota then because that coffee keeps me alive."

The little shop has a brick exterior, but the inside looks like a saloon and coffee shop had a baby. Wooden siding lines the walls and there's only two tables, and both of them are free, meaning we have the whole place for ourselves.

We sit down at one of the empty tables and start drinking. The pistachio flavor explodes across my tongue. Sweet Jesus, now I really am going to fight Mav when I get home. I've been drinking burned bitter bean juice from a one-hundred-year-old coffee pot when I could have been driving to town and getting this? Taking another sip, I let out a little moan.

"So, speaking of moaning, how are things with Mav?"

My hand covers my mouth as coffee flies out of my mouth. "Good lord, Aspen."

"What?" She looks at me like my reaction is crazy, not her mouth.

Shaking my head, I let a little laugh escape before replying, "They're really good. You were right."

"You're good for him. He works harder than anyone I know, right next to you. You two could outwork a horse, I swear."

"He does work hard, too hard. Do you think he will be done with bull riding soon?" I'm hoping she'll say yes, so I won't have to worry about him getting crushed to death all the time.

"Who the hell knows with him? He'll probably ride until he croaks." Her words send a new wave of anxiety through me because the chance of him living old while he constantly tempts danger aren't high. And if it doesn't kill him, it might leave him with a traumatic brain injury, which wouldn't be much better.

It's on the tip of my tongue to ask Aspen what she thinks, but I don't want them to think I don't support him. So I just shove the worry down deep until I feel like I can take a full breath again. Squeezing my eyes shut, I realize I need to change the subject before I have a full-on panic attack.

Clearing my throat, I ask, "What about you? Anyone special?" Testing the waters to see if she will spill about Rhett. That will for sure get my mind off this.

"Nope." She immediately brings her coffee to her lips. What a little liar.

"And here I thought we were friends."

"What do you mean?" she says with furrowed brows. At least I can say she does a decent acting job. If nursing doesn't work out, she can try out theatre.

"So there isn't a certain boy in the friend group that you can't keep your eyes off?"

"I have no idea what you are talking about." She shakes her head.

"Being that I have two functioning eyeballs, I can see there's something going on with you and Rhett."

Pure, unfiltered panic fills her face. Well, so much for the acting fallback. I point at her with a smug smile on my face. Finally, a crack. "And your face just confirmed it."

Her palms slam against the table. "Oh my God. How did you find out? Did you see us?"

My head whips back. "What? No. I had a feeling that night we were all out at the bar. It's the way you two move together. You're too familiar to be just friends. And you always leave dinner at the same time. You guys might want to stagger your departures if you really want to keep it a secret."

Aspen shakes her head. "It's nothing serious. We've only been messing around for a while."

My eyes narrow on her because something is off. "Define, 'a while'?" I add air quotes for emphasis.

"I don't think I want to." She once again reaches for an emotional support cup to fill the silence, but I put my hand over hers, stopping the motion.

"Hey, I spilled my guts out to you with Mav." I raise my eyebrows at her expectantly.

She lets out a deep sigh that is far too dramatic. "Okay, fine." She fidgets with her sleeve, heavily avoiding eye contact. "We've been messing around for…" she worries her lips and turns her face away before answering, "a year. Or so."

My mouth falls so far, I worry it's going to hit the table. Not serious, my ass. "That's longer than most relationships last. You know that, right?"

"He's great, and he's so good to me. But it can never happen. Weston would literally blow a gasket. They've been friends forever." She nervously flails her hands through the air, and my heart breaks a little for her. It must be painful to have someone but not actually *have* them.

My voice softens a little. "What does Rhett say?"

"Rhett just goes along with whatever I want." That answer gives it all away. "Seriously, Weston can't know. I'm sure Rhett will meet someone, and it will be in the past anyway."

Not wanting to push her anymore, I settle for, "Well, if you ever decide to make the jump, I've got your back. And so does Mav."

She drags her hands across her face before throwing her head back. "Oh my god, Mav knows?"

"I'm going to be honest with you, anyone who has eyes can tell something is going on. The fact that Weston doesn't know is a miracle. But you don't need to worry about Mav. He is good at minding his own business."

"Maybe I need to work on my stealth." I don't know how to tell her you can't hide chemistry like that. But I'll let her live in her little land of delusion. "What other juicy gossip does Mav know about?"

We continue sipping coffee while spilling the tea. My heart feels so full. I've missed having girl time. Not to mention, making friends at this phase of life is plain hard. But with Aspen, it's easy. It feels like I've known her forever, and there's something about her that feels genuine. Having a friend like her is just what I needed.

Chapter 31
MAVERICK

Walking back to the bed, I fluff the blankets for the millionth time, wanting to get this right. Ava's texted a couple times that work was a rough one, they had to fly out a patient, another one puked on her. Needless to say, she deserves a night to get her mind off it all.

I went to town earlier today and picked up a frozen pizza, and every single candy I could think of because I don't know her favorite but I wanted to have my bases covered.

Laying out all the snacks, I take a look at the spread and hope it's enough to turn her day around. I've got bowls of Reese's pieces, Swedish fish, sour patch kids, and red hots sitting in a line on the counter. An empty bowl for the popcorn I'll pop when she gets home and then let her pick out whatever movie she wants.

Walking back into the kitchen, I light her favorite candle, making the house smell like lavender. I grabbed her a bouquet of flowers when I was in town too, every pretty girl deserves some pretty flowers when the day gets the better of her. I pull them out of their packaging and into the brand-new vase I bought. Their sweet aroma fills my nose as I lean down and smell them. Pink, red and white roses, baby's breath and lillies make one hell of a smell.

Selfishly, I think I'm also looking forward to this. I love nights alone with her. The simpler the better. I've lived a busy life, and the thing I value most now is spending time with the ones I love.

Ava's headlights shine through the front windows, letting me know she's home. My heart thumps a little wildly in my chest, I get excited every time she comes home. It has me feeling like a damn dog.

The front door swings open, and I can tell it's been a day by the look on her face. There are dark circles under her eyes, and the girl just looks exhausted. Her hair sits lopsided on the top of her head, little strands of blonde hair shooting everywhere.

She looks around the room a little, her cute little brows furrowing in confusion. "What's all this?"

Walking to her, I place a peck on her full lips and grab the lunch bag and water bottle out of her hands. "Well, you said you had a rough day, and I want to make it better." I smile sheepishly, knowing that when it comes to her, I'm about as pathetic as they come, but I don't give a damn. I'm obsessed with the woman in front of me. "Go hop in the shower and I'll get dinner in the oven." I place another quick peck on her cheek before I nod my head toward the bathroom, making sure she takes the hint.

"Well alright, don't have to tell me twice. I probably reek." She looks down at herself and shakes her head.

"I'm just glad you said it so I didn't have to be the asshole." I shoot her a wink and she slaps my shoulder before rolling her eyes and walking to the bathroom.

After dropping her stuff off on the kitchen counter, I turn toward the bathroom as soon as the water starts to run to snag her towel and throw it in the dryer.

Before long, the smell of pizza overpowers her candle, and my mouth is watering. I pull open the oven to see the cheese bubbling and pull it out as the buzzer on the dryer goes off.

The dryer is probably from the 90s, and it's small as hell, but it does a good job of warming up her towel.

The water turns off as I open the bathroom door. Steam encases me as I step in and close the door behind me. The shower door whips open, and Ava practically jumps out of her skin.

She places a hand over what I can guess is her thundering heart. "Maverick, what the hell are you doing?"

With the towel still in one hand, I hold my hands up in defense. "Sorry, I didn't mean to scare you. I was just bringing your towel back." I hold it out to her, getting an eyeful of my wife. Her body flares at all the right places, my hands itch to touch her but tonight isn't about that.

"Eyes up here, cowboy." My eyes leave the sight of her perfect tits and snap up to her face, to see her smirking at me with an eyebrow quirked. "It was really nice of you to warm up my towel. And is that pizza I smell?"

"It sure is, get your PJs on, we're having a junk food and a movie night."

"Sounds perfect." The smile on her face makes me beam with pride. I'm not the most romantic guy in town; I have a tendency to think with the wrong head, but with Ava, I want to get it right. And that smile on her face says I did.

Backing out of the bathroom, I mentally catalogue the image of my smoking hot wife with water droplets running down her for a rainy day and head to get her dinner plated up.

A few minutes later, she walks out of the bathroom, looking refreshed. The smile on her face puts one on mine.

"Feeling better?" I turn my head and ask before pressing start on the microwave for the popcorn.

"Much." Her arms come around my waist and the warmth of her presses into me. I rest my hands over hers. "You've got quite the spread here. Lots of choices."

Turning around, I slip my hands around her, and she moves her hands to my chest. "Well, when I was at the store, I realized there was a lot I don't know about you. Your favorite ice cream, your favorite candy, what's your bad day pick me up, so I uh, got it all and hoped for the best."

"Well, for ice cream, I don't discriminate, but a good cherry chip can turn any bad day around. Candy, sour patch kids, or a salted nut roll. Pineapples do not belong on pizza, so you can do pretty much anything but that and I'll eat it. What about you?"

My gaze stays locked on her baby blues; if I were having a bad day, this girl is all I'd need to turn it around. "A heavy dose of you will turn a day around for me. Food-wise, cookie dough ice cream, Reese's for candy, I love chocolate, and pizza we're on the same page, so you're in no danger of having pineapple on your pizza." Leaning down, I kiss the tip of her nose. "Alright, let's get you fed."

She grabs the pizza I had plated for her and grabs a small bowl out of the cabinet, piling candy in it before hopping on the bed and tucking her legs under her. "So what movie are we watching?"

"Anything you want?" I grab the remote off the side table on my side of the bed and pass it to her. I lean against the headboard and cross my legs in front of me before passing the remote.

"You're going to regret that," she sing-songs, turning on the TV and picking out *Miss Congeniality*. Lord help me. Watching the tension ease from her shoulders as she laughs at the terrible jokes makes it all worth it.

She scarfs down her snacks and pulls the popcorn down from the counter, before she scoots between my legs and leans her back against my front, using me as her own personal pillow and I love it. This is the most relaxed I've ever felt in my life, and I can't help but wonder if maybe it is time to quit the road life. I could have nights like this every night if I did. Plus, it would take a load off Ava's shoulders. That last accident left her more shaken up than I realized. Hopefully, this will be the year I win it all, and then I can start my next chapter with Ava.

My hands run up and down her arms, her head starts nodding off to the side, and before long, it stays there as she dozes off. I reach for the bowl in her lap and move it to the side. I should change the movie, but I just can't. If she likes it, then it'll stay on.

My lips press into the top of her head, causing her to stir and hum in contentment. The mumbled words, "I love you," come out of her, and my heart swells. Fuck, am I in deep with this woman.

"I love you, too, sweetheart."

Chapter 32
Ava

My worlds have collided, and I don't know if I should be incredibly excited or scared shitless. Because introducing Erin and Aspen may have been a mistake. They would be the exact same person if their upbringings weren't so different.

The stands at today's rodeo begin to fill. The chatter fills the arena, and Maverick's name can be heard out of every other person's mouth as we walk around. Pride fills me because he's the best, but best of all, he's mine.

Normally, I stay with the team behind the pen, but with Erin here, I wanted to sit in the stands. I haven't watched him from the stands since the night we met, which feels like a lifetime ago. We did things a little backward. Apparently, you're supposed to fall in love before you get married, but I kind of like the way things worked out for us.

"So how do things work?" Erin asks as we sit watching the action start to unfold in the arena.

"They have a few events, and then it will be time for the bull riders," Aspen says. She knows more about bull riding than I do, but at this point, I've given up on trying to completely understand a sport where the goal is to hold on and not die—emphasis on the not die part. Hopefully, having Erin here will calm my nerves. Ever since seeing Mav get hurt a month ago, I've been avoiding watching him ride.

"And do we have to sit through all of them?" Erin's face immediately drops, and my worry melts away as my laughter fills our space.

"No, we can go shop and grab some food. Mav should be on around three if all stays on time."

We walk around the displays, and my fingers run through the racks of shirts. My eye catches on a sweatshirt. It has a bull rider on it. I bet Mav would like this.

"It's good to see you like this," Erin says, a small smile on her face as she shuffles through the clothing rack.

"Like what?" I grab the sweater and drape it over my arm to take to the check-out stand.

"Living." She says it so matter-of-factly, I can't help the smart-ass response that bubbles up.

"I wasn't aware I was dead before, but I am glad to be brought back to life," I tease, and she lightly slaps my arm.

She rolls her eyes at me but continues with her search. It'll be a miracle if she walks out of here with less than ten things. The girl is a shopaholic. "You know what I mean. You've been going through the motions. But there's something about you that's new. A sparkle." She brings her shoulders up to her ears and shakes them a little.

"That is the lamest thing I've ever heard," I mutter, but in reality, I know she's right. I feel more alive now than I ever have. Happy with everything in my life, which feels almost foreign.

"Glad to see you're still kind of a bitch." She winks at me, and I smush my lips together to hide the smile.

"I don't think I could ever get rid of that." I mock her and laugh as I move on to the next display, full of turquoise jewelry and flashy earrings. Not at all my style, but it's still fun to look. Erin quickly follows behind as Aspen checks out.

"Well, I am happy you're happy. Life not being so heavy lately has changed you, and I'm grateful. That's all."

I sling my arm around her shoulders, giving her a half hug. Sometimes, I forget how lucky I am to have her. I drop my arm and hold up a pair of earrings for her to check out. "Thank you. I am happy. It's weird. I feel like I'm waiting for the other shoe to drop. Life usually doesn't go this good for me."

She looks in the small mirror on the display table, holding the earrings up to her ears. They really do look cute on her. She can pull off flashy. "Or maybe you've lived through enough hurt for a lifetime, and it's finally your turn to just breathe and enjoy it all."

My heart suddenly feels a little weird; emotion causes a funny feeling to churn over in my chest. "Thanks, Erin. That means a lot coming from you."

"Hey losers, if you want to see the whole reason we're here, we might want to get back to our seats," Aspen hollers from the end of the tent, closer to the open walkway.

"Good, that sweater you were eyeing was ghastly," Erin says, snatching the sweater from my arms as we make our way to Aspen.

"It was not!" The metal hanger clanks on the rack as Erin hangs it back up.

She lets out a dramatic sigh. "We need to work on your fashion sense. If you insist on going country, you need to at least do it in style." She loops her arm through mine.

"Sorry, babe, I agree with her." Aspen shrugs. I knew I would regret introducing them.

"What's wrong with my style?" I look down at my outfit: plain blue jeans, a pair of boots Mav gave me, and a short-sleeve white tee.

"Well, to start, there isn't one," Erin says. Aspen laughs, and I plot my revenge on the both of them.

We get to our seats just in the nick of time. The rumble of the crowd makes the building feel like it is shaking. This is a much larger arena than the last rodeo I went to. The energy in the crowd feels almost electric.

"Up next, we have Maverrrrrick Ryder, riding the BEAST." The announcer's voice carries through the arena at the same time my nerves jump out of my skin.

"I hate watching him ride," I mutter under my breath. My hands fidget in my lap, pulling at the skin next to my nails—a nervous habit I picked up years ago that seems to have gotten worse lately.

"He's done this a million times." Aspen's hand pats my leg, but it doesn't calm the storm brewing inside my chest.

I keep my eye glued on Maverick as he gets ready. Our seats are high enough that I can see over the rails and have a near-perfect view. "That makes the odds worse, not better." I realize my voice comes out a little more stern. I look over to Aspen with an apologetic smile. "But thank you for the sentiment." I get her train of thought, but my anxiety doesn't want to listen.

A terrible feeling churns in my gut, but I shut it down. It has to be fine. He will be fine. He'll always come home to me. I repeat the mantra in my mind, willing it to be true.

My eyes are still on Mav, who's sitting on the bull as he wraps the rope tightly around his hand. His coach ensures his helmet is secure. He looks to the stands; somehow, he always knows where to find me. When his gaze lands on mine, I offer him a smile, hoping to mask the waves of emotion I'm feeling. He turns his attention back to the bull and gets situated before nodding to the gatekeeper to open up.

Holding my breath, I start the countdown. Eight seconds doesn't sound that long but watching the one you love holding on for literal dear life feels like an eternity. The bull whips around while bucking. Somehow, Mav stays on. Another kick, another second.

Mav spurs him on, and that is where it all goes wrong.

The bull rapidly changes directions, ripping Mav right off his back. His hand is bound too tightly, though, and he can't get loose. My hands fly to my face as a gasp escapes me, and the whole crowd by the sounds of it. The bull bucks again, and Mav's feet touch the ground for half a second before the bull's hooves come down on him.

The bullfighters swarm Mav and the bull and manage to get Mav's arm ripped free. I'm running before I can even see him walk off.

My heart beats rapidly in my chest, and my quick pace causes my lungs to burn. My feet stomp down the stairs as fast as they can go. I run down to the rider's quarters, dodging past people, not caring if I'm running into them. I need to see him.

Security tries to stop me once I hit the riders' area. "Ma'am, you can't be back here."

"Well, that is too fucking bad because I'm his *wife*. Let. Me. Through," I say as I try to shoulder past them with no luck.

"Let her through, boys," the rider from the night that Mav declared to the whole arena that I was his wife says. I can't remember his name, but I can hardly form a coherent thought right now.

"Thank you," he says to the guards as they step aside. "There's the medical setup." He points to the right side of the tent, and I dash off.

There's no hesitation when I pull back the tent's curtain. The first thing I see is Maverick getting his elbow popped back into place. His face is in a deep grimace, covered in dirt. He grits his teeth as the pop sounds echo through the tent. I squeeze my eyes shut. The hammering in my heart doesn't slow. I can see him, but the fear isn't gone.

The medical team hovers around him, giving him a look over. His lip has a pretty nasty cut, and his arm is already black and blue. The fact that he can move it at all is a freaking miracle. My heart crumples at the pain I see him in. I hate this. I hate this so fucking much because it is entirely preventable.

Trembling, I stay quiet in the corner, watching the medics work on Mav, so quiet that he doesn't even notice I'm here. Watching every rinse, every blood-stained rag be trashed, every wince at even the smallest movement. I've lived through a lot of pain in my life, but never have I watched someone I love choose self-inflicted pain.

When the medics start to clear out, I take a step away from the wall. Mav sits up, grunting in pain. He blinks a few times before looking around, and his bruised-up face finally turns to me. "Ava, baby. What are you doing in here?"

"Are you okay?" My voice breaks as I make my way closer to him.

"You know what they say, if you're gonna be dumb, you better be tough." I think he expects me to laugh, but none of this is funny to me. Tears brim in my eyes and I can feel my breathing kicking up again. The panic feels so heavy, I can't lift it off. "Ava, I'm okay." He furrows his brows and reaches out and grabs my hand.

A warm tear drips down my face as my shaking hand squeezes his uninjured one. "You're right. You are okay this time. But what about next time?" I plead. Because you can only avoid death so many times when you're dancing with the devil like he is.

"Chances are next time will be even better." He shrugs; his nonchalance causes my worry to morph into anger. How does he not see it?

"This isn't the first time I've been hurt, sweetheart. I'll bounce back and be fine."

I shake my head, not understanding any of this. "You have had an incredible career. Why not walk away while you can still walk at all?" My watery eyes stay glued onto him, my voice sounding hoarse from the onslaught of emotion running through my body.

"Because I still have a lot more to prove." My hand lets go of his and runs through my hair. I find myself completely exasperated with the man sitting in front of me.

"This again?" I shake my head as I drop my hands to my side. "Mav, everyone already thinks of you as a legend. What more could you possibly need?"

"The world title. It's the one thing my dad never had."

"And what happens when you get that? What is so important about a stupid title?"

"You wouldn't understand." He looks away like he is angry with me, and I find myself even more hurt than I was when I walked in here. How dare he be mad at me for giving a shit about him?

"You're right. I don't understand. I don't understand why you're willing to kill yourself to prove people who have no business having an opinion wrong." My hands ball into tight little fists, so tight that I can feel my fingernails cutting into the skin of my palm.

"It isn't just about me. People count on me, Ava." He gestures his hands out to beyond the tent, to his team.

"For a paycheck, Mav, that's all. You're their cash cow. Of course they want you to keep going." Everything boils up in me to the point where I feel like I'm going to burst. There is too much worry, hurt, and anger in my body, and I don't know what to do with it.

"You don't know what you are saying."

My words come out in a yell, a desperate plea for him to hear me and actually understand the meaning of my words. "No, you don't know, you don't know what it's like to watch everyone you love die right in front of you. I can't do that again. I can't watch you kill yourself." I throw my hands up in front of me, feeling more defeated than I have in my entire life.

He cocks his head back, trying to process my words. "What are you saying?"

I take a deep breath and close my eyes, trying to ground myself. "I'm saying, it's us or the rodeo. It can't be both. I can't do this, Maverick. I can't lose someone else I love."

"You're not going to lose me." His voice trembles as he brings his hands to his chest.

I shake my head, realizing he isn't going to see it my way. Not now, not ever. "I bet your dad told you the same thing. How did that work out? You can't make me promises you can't keep."

My words cut him, and his whole body shifts back like they weren't just words but were an actual hit. "That's a low blow."

I shrug. "You're mad because it's true. I can't watch this anymore, Maverick. I can't sit on the sidelines, praying to God you get to come home to me every single time you go to ride. Please, Mav. Please don't make me."

"I'm not done yet, Ava." His voice sounds final.

I nod my head, looking around the room, my heart broken into a million little slivers. A tear escapes the side of my eye because I know what's going to happen.

He isn't going to choose me.

He's going to choose the damn rodeo because he loves it more.

"Well, you made it clear what you love most. If you're not ready to be done, then I guess we are." I take a shaky breath before saying goodbye to the love of my life. "Good luck." I take two steps back physically and emotionally, preparing myself for the heartbreak I know is going to hit me.

He moves to stand as I turn on my heels. "Ava, wait."

I hold my hand up to stop him. "No, Mav. You made your choice. You didn't even hesitate to make it, actually. You chose the rodeo so damn fast." I snap my fingers. "Like I was never really a considerable option. That right there tells me all I need to know. I may love you, Maverick Ryder, but *you*, you love rodeo and your ego. There wasn't enough love left over for me."

His whole body deflates at the finality in my tone. "You know I love you."

"That's the first time you've said it this entire conversation. You may think you love me, Maverick, but I am beginning to wonder if you even know what love really is. My stuff will be out of the house by the time you get home."

"But the courts," he says, trying to grasp on to anything to slow this down. But there is no slowing this down. This was doomed to crash and burn the second we said 'I do' in Vegas because happiness just isn't something that happens to me.

"What they don't know won't hurt them."

"Ava," he pleads one final time.

I don't stop this time. I keep walking.

Because if I don't, I might back down, and I don't think my heart can take another loss.

Chapter 33
MAVERICK

For the first time in months, I walk through the front door to an empty house. An empty and eerily quiet house. The only sound filling the space is the raindrops on the roof. The dark, gloomy clouds match my mood. Ava kept true to her word, every trace of her is gone except for the lingering scent of her fucking candle. No shoes by the door, no blanket thrown over the futon, no books piled up on the back; it's all gone. Anger rises through me, not really at her, but at myself. I handled that whole thing wrong, and now she won't talk to me. My calls have been going straight to voicemail.

Luckily, it's cowboy Christmas and I'll be busy as hell working my ass off all the way until our scheduled court date. But even I wonder if that will be enough to keep her off my mind.

I throw my hat off my head and onto the empty futon. Looking over where she spent so many afternoons and nights curled up with a book makes my stomach drop. I have been through a lot of painful things, broken almost every bone in my damn body, but nothing hurts quite as much as losing her. She was too good for me from the start, but that didn't stop me from falling hard.

Tears fill my eyes as I look around the cabin, really study it. It no longer feels like home without her. Cowboys may not cry, but then what does that make me?

"FUCK!" I yell, throwing my bag onto the floor. Sinking into the futon, my head lands in my hands.

My body still feels sore from the last damn rodeo. I get to be home one night before I'm back on the road for the next week. The last one will be a hometown show, more for publicity than anything. Should have just stayed on the road and skipped this because the silence in this cabin is torture.

Three taps rattle the outside of my front door, but the last thing I want right now is company. Dragging my feet across the room, I whip open the door with more force than necessary.

"What?" I say to Weston. I love the guy, but I might punch him straight in the fucking jaw if he tries his bullshit with me today.

"Oh, just checking up on you. I heard you had a pretty tough ride." He has his classic smile on his face, and he's ditched the cowboy hat for a ballcap. Little watermarks stain the top of it from the pouring rain.

"That's all you heard?" I know good and well the news has probably spread through all of town that my wife left me in the injured tent. There's no hiding from your secrets around here.

"I mean, there was the part about you getting into it with your woman." He leans against the wooden door frame, crossing his arms. The covered porch keeps him protected from the rain, but the cool air rushes into the cabin.

Keeping my hand gripped on the door in case I need to slam it on him, I reply, "That's the real reason you're over here."

"The real reason I'm here is because it sounds like my best friend had a really shitty weekend and I wanted to make sure he was doing alright. Asshole." I do feel like an asshole. An asshole about the whole thing, not just this.

Running the hand not on the door through my hair, I shake my head, "Yeah, I'm pretty sure I blew it." My head hangs down like my mood.

"Care to tell me what the hell happened?" He pushes off the door a little to stand straight and shoves his hands into his pocket, rocking on his toes.

I open the door a little wider, inviting him in. "Yeah, you want a beer?"

"Sure." He waltzes in like he owns the place, straight to the fridge. I hear a can crack open.

"Well, she was there with your sister and her friend from her hometown. And I got stuck on a bull and kind of got my shit rocked." Meaning, I for sure got my shit rocked. "It definitely looked worse than it was. And then she walked in on me in the medic's station and...she wanted me to quit riding."

Cold beer in hand, he flops down on the futon. "And you told her no." He says it like a statement, like he has no doubt about which one I would pick.

Walking to the fridge, I grab my own beer, already knowing I'm not going to like this conversation. "I can't quit rodeo."

He looks at me like I am a complete idiot. "Why? Honestly, it seems like you enjoy the work here on the ranch more than you do being on the road all the damn time."

"It's just not my time to be done." My voice comes out with more bite than I intend. At this point, with the amount of times I've said this, I'm starting to feel like a broken record.

"What more could you possibly need to prove?" He leans forward, rests his forearms on his knees, and holds on to his can with both hands. I lean against the wall closest to him, feeling too fidgety to sit.

"You know what I need to prove." I look over to him, my voice quiet but firm.

"Mav, this can't seriously still be about the shit with your dad anymore." He rolls his head and his eyes all in one swoop motion. Clearly, annoyed with my response.

"You wouldn't fucking get it." I turn my head away from him. No one would. Dealing with this pressure, trying to beat the expectations of me. Trying to beat *my* expectations of me. It feels damn near impossible...

"Seriously?" His tone makes me look back at him. His expression looks almost hurt, and I feel like an asshole. Again. God, what the fuck is wrong with me? "Do you know how many people think the only reason I get by is because of my parents' money? Not all the work I put into this place, or all the dreams I have for it. If anyone is going to understand being the kid of a great, it's me. We may not get belt buckles, but it's all the same feelings at the end of the day."

Trying my hardest to get him to understand, I respond, "I have to beat my dad's records and get the one thing he never did. That'll be the only way people will ever believe I earned this shit."

"People, or you?" He points to me, and it feels like a shot fired. My mind recoils at it like it was a shot. "Because right now, it sounds like the only person you need to convince that this glory is yours alone is you." His voice lacks his usual lackadaisical tone, and his words sound as harsh as they feel. Grating on me and slowly wearing me down.

"It doesn't feel like just me." My bare hand taps my chest twice. "Doug likes to tell me every day how I'm only here because of my dad."

"Doug can fuck right off. The only reason he doesn't want you to retire is because you are his personal bankroller. You quit competing and he loses the big fat checks from you. He doesn't care about your career. Doug has always been out for himself. Why do you think he didn't want you getting close to Ava?" His words are an echo of what Ava said, making my heart thump in my chest, trying to fight off the reasoning because if the people closest to me can see it, it's probably true.

"Because it would be a distraction," I reason.

He shakes his head slowly, almost looking like he feels sad for me, and I hate the look of pity. "No, Mav. It's because he was worried she'd be the reason for you to leave the sport. Are you really okay with choosing something like this over a girl like that? I've seen what you two have, Mav. You'd be a fucking idiot to throw that down the drain for something that will never last you forever. At some point, you'll have to retire. And then what will you have?" He looks around my empty cabin, as if he notices how empty this place is without her too.

His questions leave me pissed off. Mad at Dad for leaving me here to deal with this shit alone, mad at my stupid fucking agent for putting shit into my head and mad at myself. Mad because I know that Weston is right. There will probably be nothing that will make it feel like it's enough until I believe it was enough before it ever turned into this grand scheme. There's now a crack in the glass of my resolve because deep down, I know he's right. Ava was right too.

Realizing just how bad I fucked up, I ask the only question I can. "Well, what the hell do I do now?" I'm feeling more lost than I ever have.

He shrugs his shoulders. "That's up to you. Have you tried talking to Ava?"

"She won't answer me. She doesn't want to talk to me." And I hate it. I hate that I put this distance between us. Hate that I ever made her think she wasn't enough because she's more than enough. She's everything.

"Since when has that ever stopped you before? You have a couple weeks off after next week, right? If you want her, you have to prove it to her. You need to figure out what will make you happy. And if we are being blunt, you need to learn how to be happy and proud of yourself without either of them, Ava or the rodeo." He keeps his eyes locked on mine. There's no cushioning his words. He's saying it exactly the way I need to hear it. And at this moment, I'm grateful for friends like him. Friends who are honest, regardless of if it's going to piss me off or hurt my feelings. He's telling me what I need to hear. "You're a good person. That's what matters at the end of the day."

A few beers later, Weston leaves after completely uprooting every thought I've ever had. I sit back in the futon that smells way too much like Ava and close my eyes. A deep, longing ache makes my heart feel like it's physically breaking.

Fuck, I wish my dad was here. He taught me how to do a lot: how to ride a bull, how to stack hay bales, and how to ride a horse. But he never got the chance to teach me how to be a man. To teach me what he learned from his failures. How to own up to the mistakes you make. That's where all the real lessons lie, in the failures and what comes after. All I ever saw was my dad, the rodeo star.

But I wonder, if he was around now, what would he say? Would he have had any regrets? Or would he have been okay with the way he went out? I've asked myself that question more times than I care to admit. Would he have put me first if he had known it would be the rodeo or me?

My eyes dart to the closet against the wall. There's a box in there—a bunch of his personal belongings. I was given all his belt buckles, and you can catch me wearing those every ride. I've never worn any buckles I've won, only my old man's. It makes it feel like a piece of him is with me during every ride.

I've never seen half of what's in that box. It hurt too much to look at it when the accident happened. And then after that, I was scared shitless of what I'd find. So I kept the box hidden on the top shelf of my closet, trying to pretend it was not there. Grief is an ugly beast; every time you think you've handled your demons, it comes back to haunt you.

Maybe it's time I exorcise some of those. Chugging down the rest of my beer, I set the empty can on the side table and walk to the front of the door.

I stand there for a second, steeling my nerves. My old man has been gone for fourteen years. What's in that box is all I have left of him. I've shoved it all down, but if I ever want to be the kind of man that deserves a girl like Ava, it's time I face what scares me the most. Grief. Loss. Being alone.

Placing my hand on the knob, I turn it and open the door. Reaching up, I pull the string to turn the light on. There it is, untouched on the top shelf. I reach up and grab it. Dust falls down like snow, so I blow the top of it off and make my way back to the living room. It looks like an old filing box. My dad never had a lot of belongings, kind of like me. He was always on the road.

Slowly, I lift things out of the box. His favorite denim jacket, straight from the 80s, sits on top. He always wore this alongside a trucker cap or a cowboy hat. I don't think I ever really saw my dad without something on top of his head.

Underneath are letters from his fans. Beneath that, I find a stack of Polaroids that capture moments of him on bulls or with his riding buddies. I can't help but smile at these. It reminds me of Rhett and Weston. Digging a little farther, I find pictures I had drawn my dad when I was little—usually of us on a horse, or somewhere here on this very ranch. I laugh when I see my horrible rendition of him riding a bull. It's a good thing I followed his footsteps because art was not in the cards for me.

There's a small box at the very bottom with a swivel closure. I pull it open and find pictures of me and my dad. There has to be at least forty pictures in here. I thumb through them and get to see myself grow up through my dad's eyes. Technology had gotten better, but he must have been partial to the Polaroid camera. When I get to the end, I see a picture of my dad holding me when I was what looks like about six. At the bottom, he wrote, 'My son, my greatest win." And that's when I know. I know exactly what he would have chosen.

My hands shake with the picture in my hands, and I swallow hard against the lump rising in my throat. Tears threaten to fall, but I clear my throat.

Suddenly, I understand everything Ava was saying. It hits me like a ton of bricks when I realize she is me. Because I wish he would have quit, I wish he was here with me now. That's what she was trying to tell me. The way I feel right now could be her if I don't make the right choice. If I don't choose her. My dad never had the chance to choose me, but I've been given the chance. This will be one lesson I can learn from my old man: knowing when to quit.

Fuck, I've learned a lot tonight, but most of all, I learned that sometimes cowboys do cry. And I was dead wrong before, but I've got a chance to make it right, and I plan on doing just that. I refuse to live a life with regrets, and letting Ava walk away is a regret I can't stand to live with.

Chapter 34
MAVERICK

It's a bittersweet moment walking into the arena tonight, knowing it will be my last. I'm announcing my retirement after my ride tonight. Getting to go out at a home show will make it that much more special. There's no fancy arena, just a local fairground and the Wyoming air. Everyone I love will be in the stands tonight. Well, not everyone. The most important person in my world still doesn't want anything to do with me, but I'm hoping there's still something there to be saved. Once this is taken care of, I'm free. Free to give everything I have to Ava if she still wants me. God, I hope she does because I love that woman more than life.

These small rodeos are my favorite. The crowds are just as loud, even without a roof over our heads. Everyone in attendance is here because they love the sport to their core. Not for a fancy show but to enjoy the sport in its most basic form. This is the exact type of place I always dreamed of ending my career at. I'm not one hundred percent sure what my next step will be, but I know my first stop will be Ava's door once I'm out of here. I've got to make this right while I still can.

Heading to the locker room, I see a lot of familiar faces. Some have been around forever, and some are up and coming. All of them are tough as nails. They'll do whatever they have to do to get under your skin and get an edge up on you. That's how they win, and that's how they become the best. Bull riding is as much mental as it is physical.

If you aren't tough as shit, they will chew you up and spit you out. Your skin better be tougher than your leather chaps. We may not be taking home a check tonight since this is a fundraiser, but with every win, you cash in something much more valuable than money. You get a fresh-cut check of respect, and to all these boys, that means more than money ever will.

The only person here who knows this is my last is Weston. He may be a giant pain in the ass, but he's a damn good friend to have. He tells me what I need to hear and not what I want to hear, and that's one of the many reasons I respect him so much.

"You ready for this?" he asks as he walks beside me. It hits me that this should feel more bittersweet than it does, but I'm ready to hang up my vest and chaps and slow down. Plus, I'm going to be taking up winning back my girl as my full-time job. If I convinced her to love me and trust me once, I can do it again.

"You know, I thought I would be a lot sadder, but I'm feeling a bit relieved. After this is over, I'm not Maverick the bull rider and son of a legend, I'm just going to be Maverick."

"Well, to most of us, you've always been just Maverick." He smacks the back of my shoulder a couple of times while giving me a tight smile. I haven't even told Rhett, my manager, or my coach. For now, it brings me a little peace to close this door by myself. "When are you planning on telling everyone?"

A heavy sigh leaves me, because I know the shit I'm going to catch for this. But I didn't want to deal with the fuss, I wanted to close the door and do it on my terms. Plus, Doug will be a fucking nightmare, and if I can get even one extra day of not having to deal with the meltdown he'll have, it's worth ruffling a few feathers over. "Probably tomorrow. I'm not wanting to hide it from them, I just want to get this door closed and then deal with the rest." They're all in the stands tonight anyway. Since this is a local show, my pieced-together little family all showed up. You know who didn't? Douchebag Doug. Because this ride doesn't count for points so he doesn't give a fuck.

We make our way to the locker room, and Weston heads over to the corral to wait until I get geared up and dressed out. My mind tunes out the noise in the locker room when I enter, fully focused on what's coming next. I can really see it now, the life I want with Ava. She was always meant to be my girl, and someday, I'm going to owe her big for giving me something worth walking away for. I never would have done it for myself, but for her, I would walk through fire, cross oceans, and kill for.

When I walk out, I take it all in: the bright lights shining down on the dirt, the packed stands, and the noise of it all. I really am going to miss this. But maybe someday I can find a different way to get myself involved. Judge or support in another capacity. Find a different way to love bull riding that won't kill me.

There won't be any long waits tonight since it is such a small show. Weston and I sit against the corral watching the barrel racers and the bronc back riders go. Before long, the other three bull riders and I are called over to the chute. With my bag on my shoulder, we head on over.

I get the honor of going last, for which I am grateful. Make this night last a little longer, and get to enjoy my last time slowly.

When my time rolls around, Weston is the only one there to help me, and I think this is the best way this could have happened. "Alright, helmet is secured," Weston says as he taps the side of it. Pulling on my hand, I double-check that I'm wrapped in tight and that my gloves are nice and sticky.

The beast under me huffs out a nasty snarl. He's going to be a mean son of a bitch. At least no one will be able to say I had an easy ride on my way out. With the way his body is already trying to slam me in the chute, this is going to be the longest eight seconds of my fucking life.

Fully strapped on and geared up, I put my hand in the air. The man running the chute looks to me, waiting for the head nod to signal I'm ready. Nerves are normal, but tonight, they are hitting me with full force. Maybe it's because my whole family is here, maybe it's my last ride, who knows? Closing my eyes for half a second, I settle down the roaring of my pulse. Being riled up is not the way you ever want to leave the chute. My thoughts drift to my old man, and this last ride is going to be for him. A silent salute to the Ryder legacy that only he and I know about.

When I'm sure I'm ready, I give a nod of my head, and we come out of the chute with force. I focus my attention on keeping my legs strong and tight. Arm up. No way in hell am I letting this arm fall on this last ride. The bull bucks with fury, and his snarling pants are the only thing I can hear. He bucks harder and harder, and with a sudden jerk, his body swings right. I lose the battle of gripping him with my thighs and feel my ass fly off of the bulls back.

Fuck. Fuck. Fuck.

I feel muscles in my shoulder tear and burn as he keeps whipping us around. There's a loud popping sound, and I don't even need to feel the pain to know something is broken. I try to rip my hand out of the rope or my glove, but it's not coming loose. Not again. I rip my arm back again, and it comes loose just as I feel myself start to fall. My back hits the dirt with a loud thud. The wind gets knocked from my lungs. The helmet only does so much when you slam on the ground at that force. I know I need to get up, but my vision is blurry. When I finally shake the stars away, I look up only to see his hoof coming straight for my face, and I don't have time to move. I know it in my bones.

Reflexively, I put my arms up and try to roll, but it's no use. I get hit hard enough to realize how fucking bad this is. My eyelids start to feel heavy, and I can't shake the feeling of everything being in slow motion. The screams from around me start to feel like they're getting quieter. As the lights go out and everything fades to black, there's only one thing on my mind. The only thing that matters. Her. Not my body, not that these might be my last breaths. When the lights go out, all I can see is her face.

Chapter 35
Ava

"You have to eat something," Aspen says as she drops a bag of gummy worms at my nurse's station. Her long brown ponytail sways as she makes her way to her chair. She crosses her legs, getting comfortable as she shakes her computer mouse, making the computer screen light back up.

"I have eaten." Nothing substantial, but what she doesn't know won't hurt her. The anxiety in my body is making it impossible to eat. Every time I think about him, it feels like the air gets caught in my lungs, so I try not to. Though that hasn't been a winning battle.

"You look like you've lost ten pounds in the last week." She angrily points to the bag. I keep eye contact with her as I open the bag and pop a gummy worm into my mouth.

"Happy?" I raise my eyebrows at her, my voice a little snappier than I intended, but I'm tired. I haven't slept since I moved all my crap out of Maverick's and started sleeping on Aspen's couch.

She rolls her brown eyes, taking my attitude in stride. "Not really, but it's a start. Have you talked to him?"

"No, and I don't want to." I turn my chair away from her, hoping she will get the hint.

"*Okay*, this is going to be a super fun night shift." I hear her chair rolling closer to me, and her hand lands back on my chair, causing me to swivel around. "Are you at least ready to tell me more of what the hell happened?" She flails her hands around. "I know you need time to process but I haven't asked at all besides you know, the two other times, and I just am curious how it all went to shit." I turn back around, not wanting her to see the tears that prick my eyes at the mere mention of him.

I don't want to talk about it because nothing has ever hurt quite like that. He had the choice, and he didn't choose me. There aren't quite enough words to describe how empty that makes me feel. I was so sure Maverick was my person, and I've never been so wrong. This is why it's easier just to work and stick to myself. It's less painful.

"He chose the rodeo," I say as I stare blankly at my bright computer screen. I'm not sure if it's the blue light from the computer or the shit storm of the last week, but the dull ache in the back of my head has become more of a pounding headache with every minute that passes.

"What do you mean he chose the rodeo?"

Turning back around, I give in. This is eating me alive, and maybe it won't if I talk about it. Maybe I'll feel better. "I told him it was me or bull riding, and he picked the massive bull."

"I know you haven't been around him long, but that boy would choose rodeo over his own life." That's the exact reason I needed him to stop. To choose a life with me over dancing with the grim reaper all the damn time.

"That's the exact reason I asked him to stop. I can't watch him kill himself, Aspen. I've lived that. I've done it, and I won't do it again." My parents didn't choose what happened to them, but Mav does. He has the chance to stay. No one can understand that kind of pain unless you've had the front-row seat to watching the ones you love most fade into the other side.

Her eyes soften, and she reaches out for me, grabbing my arm to give it a gentle squeeze. "Maybe give him some time."

"If he only comes back to me because he can't rodeo anymore, then he really doesn't love me at all. And I deserve to be the first choice. My happiness has been on the back burner my whole life. I've been struggling to just get by, I'm not going to be with someone who doesn't choose me one hundred percent." I want that, no, I *need* that. The security that comes with someone choosing you so wholly that you never have to question your love.

She nods in understanding as her eyes change, a little anger flickering in them. "You know what? You're right. I'm kicking him in the shin the next time he shows face at my parents. Actually, I think a strong kick to the balls would get the message across."

"And hurt more." It's the least he deserves for making me hurt. You know, an eye for a sack tap, or something like that.

"That too. You're amazing and he's a dumbass. I'm willing to bet my left tit he'll be coming back to you." She taps my thigh a couple times before rolling back to her side of the desk.

"Your left tit?" I cock my head. Sometimes, she says things, and I wonder where the hell she came up with them.

She looks over to me. "It's bigger than my right, so I have more to lose with it." She says it like it should be common sense, almost annoyed I didn't get it.

"You are so freaking weird," I shake my head and laugh, "but I love you." She's been the best part of this whole experience. Making friends hasn't always come easy for me, but she showed up and stuck around, and for me, that means everything.

The radio on the desk beeps "Windy Peaks Community, we have an incoming trauma. Not conscious, pupils are equal and reactive.

Airway is clear. Pressures are a bit all over and he's tachycardic. Prepare for arrival."

Adrenaline slams through me, quickly turning off our conversation.

Gosh, I hope I don't freeze up like last time. I can do this. I know I can. It's not a car accident, but even if it is, I'm ready this time. Ready to give back. Ready to serve.

"You ready?" Aspen gives me a look, she knows exactly why I freaked out last time.

I nod my head. "I..I think so." I shoot out of my chair, rolling my shoulders. Mentally running through my checklist.

"Good, prepare the room. I'll page the team."

I pull back the tan curtain, opening the trauma bay. I hang a bag of fluids, knowing we are going to use those. I double-check that all the needed supplies are out and walk over to the cabinet with our PPE and gown up. I let the adrenaline course through me, making me quicker and sharper, feeding on the rush.

The sound of sirens penetrate past the sliding glass door at the entryway, and I rush to it, finding Aspen slipping on her gown and gloves as the ambulance pulls into the drop-off bay just outside the doors.

The back of the ambulance opens, Aspen rushes toward the patient, and the paramedic hops out the back and starts talking.

"Male, approximately thirty, struck multiple times by a bull. Blunt force trauma. He hasn't regained consciousness. Vitals are somewhat stable, could be worse."

"Thank you." I nod and look down, and my whole world stops. *No.*

The man I love is lying flat on a gurney. Blood runs down his temple, and his arm is definitely broken. I blink down, trying to wrap my head around it. Nausea rolls deep in my gut from the sharp pain I feel in my heart.

Aspen's voice shakes me out of my moment. "Ava, I am going to need you to hold your shit together. Let's get him inside." With that, I am back in the action, head on straight. He needs me, and I know I can do this.

"Check his airway," Aspen says.

The sound of his heartbeat fills the room as Aspen gets him placed on monitors.

Beep..Beep..Beep..Beep.

By the sound of that alone, I know his heart is working too hard. Placing my stethoscope over his lungs, I check both sides. "The right side sounds diminished." I look over and see Doctor Thomas palpating his belly.

"Get me an ultrasound, and where the fuck is anesthesia and respiratory?" Dr. Thomas says behind me. I've been so wrapped up in what's in front of me that I didn't even see him come in. Trauma shears in hand, Aspen cuts through Maverick's shirt. Her hands shake, but her face is steadied with determination. When his shirt falls off, the sight makes my heart drop. Bruises are already blooming over him. Everywhere. He is completely and utterly broken. I take a steadying breath and refocus.

"They're on their way," I answer, grateful that Aspen was ahead of that game on that one. I swing the ultrasound machine across the room for the doc to have easier access to it.

Beep.beep.beep.beep.beep.

Fuck, why is his heart rate getting faster? My hands start to shake, and my brain feels cloudy. Fuck. This cannot be happening. I can't watch this happen. If he would have listened to me, he would have been fine.

Get it together, Ava.

"Abdomen has free fluid, page general, I need them down here now," the doctor hollers out. The charge nurse dials out on her small, blue Ascom phone. The team works together effortlessly.

Beepbeepbeepbeep.

"Guys, his blood pressure is tanking. We need to find the source of the bleeding right now or we're going to be in trouble," I say as I look up to the monitor, seeing his vitals start to crash.

The general surgeon runs in. "Prepare the OR for a laparotomy. I need extra sutures and staples up. How is his neuro exam?"

"Pupils are equal and reactive. Witnesses say the head suffered the least of it. We will get a CT as soon as possible," Dr. Thomas says without lifting his head from Mav.

"His sats are dropping, guys. We need to intubate," Dr. Thomas says. Tears fill my eyes. I've lived lots of bad days, and I do not need another bad one to contend with the worst day ever. My eyes roam over him, and I can feel my heart breaking.

Standing at his side, I take his hand, allowing myself one moment to break my professional façade. "Maverick Lee Ryder, you cannot leave me. Do you hear me? Everyone leaves me, but you can't. Please hold on. I love you. Please." I don't care who is around.

Aspen pulls me away as anesthesia comes to the head of the bed. "Pushing roc, get me the glidescope." He works for a few seconds. "I see fog, we are good. Let's get him up to the OR."

"Can our hospital handle a trauma like this?" I look over to Aspen, shocked to see the same amount of horror in her eyes I assume is in mine. She handled this whole thing so well; I know she loves Maverick too. She was calm and steady until it was finally our chance to hand the baton off. That's what this feels like, a race to save Maverick.

"Yes, the OR crew is amazing. That is a world-class surgeon right there. He only moved out here because he thought it would be an easier, quieter job. No one warned him about farm accidents or dumbass boys getting on the back of bulls." She tries to smile, but it fails to meet her eyes; only one side of her lips moves up.

The charge nurse and an OR nurse wheel Maverick out of the bay and I feel my world crack and splinter.

"What happens if something goes wrong?" Panic grips my throat. It feels too hard to breathe, too hard to think. My breaths come in ragged pants. All I can think of is the worst-case scenario, my life has trained me for that.

Aspen grabs onto me, anchoring me back to reality, and forces me to look at her. "Just like anything else when you're rural. Stabilize and ship." Aspen drops my arms and swings her arms around me, holding me for a second. My arms close around her too, holding on to her for dear life.

"I can't lose him too, Aspen," I whisper, holding on to her like she is my life raft, keeping me afloat when all I want to do is drown in despair.

"He'll be okay. He's tougher than you give him credit for." Her voice sounds so steady and sure this time that I try and believe her.

I nod my head, wishing it was Maverick holding me instead.

My eyes close, and I let out a silent plea to the universe. *Please don't take him from me.*

Chapter 36
MAVERICK

Beep... Beep... Beep.

God, that's fucking annoying. Where am I? My head feels cloudy and dingy like I did a week-long bender in Vegas, but even that was less painful. My head is screaming at me. And my eyes won't fucking open. Damn, did I die on the back of that bull and this beeping sound is my hell?

Slowly, the world starts to come to, and as my eyes finally open, I take in my surroundings. Well as much as I can considering I can't fucking move with this damn neck brace on. The bright fluorescent lights overhead do my headache no favors. I wiggle my toes to make sure they still move. They do, thank fuck. Next, I check my fingers, they also work. I let out a breath. I've been hurt a lot of times, but I can't say I've ever woken up in a hospital bed.

Now that I'm up, I know exactly what I need to do next. Absolutely no doubts. My eyes scan the room and catch on a curled-up Ava. In the world's smallest recliner in the corner.

She came.

God, I hope that still means I have a chance to fix this. I have to. This couldn't have all been for fucking nothing. I feel around the bedside table the best I can with this contraption on my neck, hopefully it's only a precaution. I find a small pen and do the most gentlemanly thing I can do: I chuck it at her.

"What the hell?" She sits up, looking around, her blonde hair a tangled mess on top of her head, pulled into a pony. When she realizes it was me who hit her, she sits straight up, eyes rapidly clearing.

"You sleep like the dead, sweetheart." A bit of anger finds her face, along with relief.

She moves out of the chair and stands next to me, looking at the monitors to my left. "You would know, since you just decided to dance with death itself. How do you feel?" Her eyes look at me, and I feel instant relief at her closeness.

"Oh, like I just got curb-stomped by a bull."

"That's putting it lightly." She crosses her arms, clearly still guarded. "You had an emergency laparotomy to control your internal bleeding that took six hours. They pulled your sedation yesterday, you've been out for four days." That explains the awful pain I'm having in my stomach. "I'll go get the doctor and your nurse so they can talk to you." She moves to turn around, but I can't let her leave this room until I get out all of what I have to say. *Need* to say.

"Ava, wait, I need to talk to you." Desperation drips in my voice. Fuck, I wish I could get out of this bed.

I see her walls trembling around her the second she stops her steps. "About what?" Her tone doesn't have the bite I would expect. It's what I deserve. I've put her through hell.

There's no hesitation in my words because even I fully believe them now, I knew it then too, but was in such deep denial and so damn stubborn I couldn't face it. "You. Me. How you were right."

"Right about what?" She's testing me; I can see it all over her face. She's great at hiding her feelings from everywhere but on her face. That furrowed little brow tells me everything I need to know.

"Can you come sit? Please?" If she doesn't think I'll get up and chase her out the door, she's dead wrong. I can't let her walk away without telling her, even if it kills me.

"Okay." She nods and takes a few steps back to the bed.

The end of the bed dips under her weight, and I find myself grateful that I'm at least propped up so I can see her and try to read her. "That rodeo was my last ride. And it wasn't because of the accident. I was planning on announcing my retirement after my ride, but, well…" scratching at my facial hair that must've grown in while I've been out of it with my only good hand, I add, "I guess I tempted fate a few too many times."

She stares blankly at me, and I realize I'm going to have to work hard to earn her trust back. If I could kick myself right now, I would.

"I'm so sorry, Ava. There was a lot of shit I hadn't dealt with and didn't know it was still bothering me until it hit me in the face. Actually, Weston helped me pull my head out of my ass. There's a lot of things I should have said differently, but the first one should have been I love you, and I choose you. If you let me, I plan to choose you every day for the rest of my life."

The war in her head is easy to read. She may be tough as nails, but that heart of hers has always been easy to see. And right now, it's at war with her head. "I don't know, Maverick. It shouldn't have taken you almost dying," she lifts her hand and points around the room, points to me, "for you to realize you can't live without me."

"I've known the whole time, Ava, baby. I swear. Rodeo has been my whole life up until you. You came in like a wrecking ball to all my plans, but more than anything, you helped me realize the only person I need to compete with is me. You loved me for me, not for being a part of my dad's legacy. I don't need to beat them to earn love. And I know that now, because of you."

It's hard to admit I had a lot of pent-up grief I had shoved down for years. I was too busy trying to become better than my dad to fully come to terms with the fact that he's gone. The fact that just being his son was enough to make him proud. That's what it was always about, doing what he never did so that piece of him could live on. If there was anyone in the world who could understand that, it's the girl looking at me.

"Mav, are you even sure you love me? You've been forced to be with me for months. Maybe the proximity to each other made this seem like something more than it is." I'm currently laying in a bed after being stomped by a bull until my lights went out, and somehow, those words hurt way more than any damage that beast did to me. They cut me to my core because they're wrong. Dead fucking wrong.

"It had nothing to do with the proximity. Somehow or someway, I would have made my way to you eventually. You were *always* meant to be mine. If you don't believe a single word I say, at least believe that. You're the first thing I've ever loved more than myself and my dreams. And that is scary as shit, but worth it. *You* are worth it."

"Alright, then tell me why you love me." She cocks her head to the side, her usual warm demeanor gone, and I can tell her walls are all the way up. She wants to know why I love her? Wants me to prove this isn't some fluke? I can do that.

"Because you work hard. You refuse to ask for help, even when you need it. You always find a way to make it happen, even if every single odd in the universe is stacked against you. It's not over till' you say it's over, and fuck, that's something so rare these days, sweetheart. I love you because I see myself in you. I see how lovable you are, which has made me realize I'm lovable. Not for the rides, not for the money. But for me. You were my missing piece. The other half of me, and I fully believe the good Lord knew exactly what he was doing when he brought you to me. I love you for your heart and everything that you are. Everything. You are what my world spins around now." I take a shaky breath after spilling my heart out to her in one single breath, scared to take a breath and have her stop me.

She stays quiet for a second, closing her eyes and shaking her head, and I feel my pulse quicken because I really might have lost her for good. I can't even blame her for leaving or not forgiving me. All I had to do was choose her. If I could go back and do that day differently, I would.

"I don't know, Mav. Those are all really nice things to say, but you hurt me. All I needed was for you to pick me and the life we could have. How do I know you won't regret it or resent me for it later on?" A tear streaks down her flushed cheek, and I hate it. Most of all, I hate myself for being the cause behind her pain.

"Ava, baby, if I could get on my knees and beg for you, I would. I will, as soon as I can get out of this bed, I will crawl on my knees to you and beg for your forgiveness. Whatever you need me to do for you to trust me again. I'll do it, I don't care how long it takes. I'm willing to put in the work and make you love me again."

Tears well up in her baby blue eyes as she looks up toward the ceiling, wanting to bat them away. God, I wish that I could hold her and pull her into my chest; maybe then this ache would ease. "I never said I didn't love you anymore. It's hard for me to count on people and I never wanted you to be someone I couldn't count on. I trusted you with my heart and it felt like you didn't care." Despite the tears in her eyes, her voice is steady and strong. Just like her.

"Believe me, baby, that heart of yours is all I care about. I know I was wrong. You're right, I should have chosen differently, but if you let me, I'll prove to you that I won't take you for granted ever again." There's no way in hell I want to put her through this twice. She will never have to doubt me again. It's my job to be her steady place to land, and I plan on being the best man I can be to do it right.

She takes a deep, shaky breath and looks at me. I feel like those eyes can see straight into my soul. I think she's always been able to do that, see right through me, and chose to love me even if it wasn't perfect. I don't dare look away from her. I don't rush her. She's got a busy brain, and I want her to make the choice she thinks is right. If that isn't me, I will respect that and spend the rest of my life missing her.

"Okay." She levels me with a stern look. "But Mav, I don't do third chances. You *ever* hurt me like that again or make me question my trust, there will be no words that you can say that will make me stay. I love you and almost losing you showed me just how much." The walls she has built around herself tumble down for me and I thank my lucky fucking stars. Because this woman is worth more than anything in the world and I was a complete jackass to have almost fucked that up.

"Never again. I'm yours until you decide otherwise. Even then, I probably won't let you go. I'm too stubborn." I'll be following her to the ends of the earth for the rest of my days.

The deep sigh that comes out of her chest washes a wave of relief over me. Her shoulders lose the tension, and I see a little bit of humor come back into her eyes. This is my Ava, my everything. "You're something, cowboy. But you're my something. And I love that. And you. So much." She scoots closer and leans down to kiss me. It soothes more than the aches and pains in my body. It soothes the broken pieces of me I had been trying to forget. I'm pretty sure her love could heal just about anything.

When her lips pull away, the look in her eyes lets me know everything will be okay. A stray long blonde hair tumbles forward, and I reach up, ignoring the way my body is screaming at me, to tuck it behind her ears. "Stay with me?"

"Always."

Chapter 37
Maverick

You know what's scarier than a bull beating the ever loving shit out of you? Telling your whole team you're done. It's been two weeks since my accident. I still feel like I got hit by a fucking truck, but I can almost take a whole breath without wanting to hit my knees, so that's an improvement.

"You sure you want to do this today?" Ava's eyes scan over me. She's constantly making sure I am not trying to actively croak on her. The warm breeze blows in through the rolled down windows. I love this time of year. Everything is green, the flowers are all bloomed, and it feels like a little piece of heaven.

"I'm sure. I can't keep them waiting." Especially since they're all going to need to find another client to add to their roster; that's the only part I feel bad about. Coach is probably about ready to retire himself; I partly wonder if he hasn't stuck around just for me. All these years, he was the only one who really had my back when it came to rodeo. If he was ever mad, I damn well deserved it.

Ava pulls the car to a stop in front of the house. She takes a deep breath as she looks at me, and that look right there is all I will ever need. All I need to do is look at her, and I know I will always have someone. "Okay, you ready to do this?"

"It's time." She opens her door, and I wince as I step out of mine. The bruises have all hit the ugly yellow phase, but fuck, do they all still hurt. I walk around the front of the car and grab Ava's hand. We walk into the house, a united front.

I invited everyone here today: Rhett, Weston, and his whole family. Well, since it's their house, it made sense. Plus, it'll be nice having their support should shit hit the fan. Knowing Doug, it might.

They all sit around the large table, but I don't bother sitting. My nerves would make it impossible to do so anyway. Plus, Ava has had me so cooped up, it's nice to be up and moving.

I look to Ava and have not a single doubt in my mind that I am making the right choice. It'll be a relief to have this off my chest and start figuring out what I am going to do next. Even if I don't know what the rest of my life holds, at least it holds her. Ava grabs my hand, bringing me back to why I'm doing this all in the first place. A life. A life with her.

"Alright, I won't keep you all long. I know we are all busy," I say, looking around the room. Weston gives me a subtle nod. The corner of his mouth tilts up in a half smile, and I can see the pride on his face, making this that much easier. "Before going into my last ride, I had made the decision it would be my last. I didn't want my last professional ride to go like that, but it proved exactly why I need to stop. You all know what happened to my dad, and I have a whole life yet to live, so I plan to do that."

Coach immediately finds his way to his feet and moves to stand in front of me. I stand strong and look him in the eye, ready to take whatever words he intends to strike me with. Only he doesn't.

I've hugged my coach one time in my life. When my dad died and we were at his service. He has been a huge piece of my success, but we've always kept it professional. He shocks the hell out of me when he pulls me in for a hug; the words he whispers in my ears will stay with me forever. "I'm proud of you, son. You did the one thing your dad never could."

"What's that?" I pull back and look at him.

"Walk away." His eyes have a bit of mist in them. Sometimes, I forget he probably misses him too.

I've tried my whole life to prove I'm something, and those words hit me right in the chest. I may not have gotten the buckle, but I did walk away with a life to live, and that is worth more than any buckle. Coach Sully pats my arm a couple times, with his face in a proud smile.

Our moment is ruined by an interruption. "Bullshit. You're in your prime. You'd have to be mad to walk away now," Doug's mouth pops off, quickly ruining the happy moment like usual.

"Doug, this decision isn't yours to make," I say, my voice even and firm.

"Well, it affects all of us." He opens his arms, looking at everyone around us as he does.

This guilt trip no longer works on me, I never should have let it in the first place. "You can find another cash cow to milk, Doug. I'm done." I know what this is really about. What it's always been about. Money. The only fucking thing Doug cares about. It makes me wonder if my dad ever wanted to walk away but stayed because of Doug's voice in his ear. God, I wish I would have pulled my head out of my ass so much sooner.

"Oh please, this is exactly why I wanted you away from that girl. She's just another buckle bunny whore." His words drip with disrespect, venom coating each one. Anger flares through me like nothing ever has. I don't know if I can even swing, but I am about to knock out a sixty-year-old man. No one talks about Ava like that.

I take one step forward, pulling Ava behind me, ready to lunge, but Rhett beats me to it. Knocking him flat on his ass.

"You're not welcome here, get the fuck out of this house," Rhett says, looking down at Doug.

Rage trembles through me. "Oh, and you're fired. Dickhead." I will need to find someone else to manage what sponsorships stick around after I announce this to the media on Monday.

He gets off the floor, looking like dog shit. A split lip and bruised ego. "I'll be pressing charges."

"Okay, there are a whole lot of witnesses who didn't see shit. Looks like you fell when the door hit you on the way out," Weston says.

I may not have blood relatives, but I do have a family. And every single one of them are standing ten toes down for me tonight. They always have. That alone is worth more than any amount of money I could make.

"You're going to regret this, Maverick, and don't come crawling back when you do," he says as he stands, wiping a trickle of blood off his split lip. Pathetic little man he is.

"Doug, I have wanted to fire you for the better part of our working relationship. I'll personally catch myself on fire before I reach out to you. You will be hearing from my lawyers at the beginning of next week."

He stomps the whole way to the front door as I silently kick myself for not firing the fucker years before. What a dumbass. He and I both.

"Well, Mav, what do you plan to do next?" Mabel asks.

"Hopefully working here full time, if you will have me." Guess I didn't really plan this part of it out, but there's no place I'd rather be than here. Bull riding never made me feel like I was doing something worthwhile like working here does. Keeping the animals safe and getting to take in the land. All of it. That's what I want to spend the rest of my days doing.

"You know we always need the help," Jack says as he pats me on the back. A flicker of pride shines in his eyes. My old man may not be around, but his best friend has done his best to fill his shoes. And for that, I will be forever in his debt.

"Alright, then I will see you all as soon as I am cleared from restrictions." Looking over to Ava, I add, "I have a very bossy nurse."

A *pft* sound leaves her lips as she props a hand on her hip and points at me. "If I wasn't bossy, you would have already busted out your stitches. It won't kill you to go a few weeks without working."

Raising my eyebrows, giving her a knowing look, I tack on, "Coming from the girl who started talking to cows because she was going so stir crazy."

She's quiet for a second, trying to find a rebuttal. "That was different!" she states defensively. Clearly, she came up empty.

"Whatever you say, sweetheart." The smile on my face comes easy, it always does when I'm looking at her.

Jack chuckles. "That bull must have knocked some sense into you, son. You're learning much quicker than I ever did."

"Learning what?" I look over at him as I drape my good arm over Ava's shoulders, pulling her body closer to mine.

"Happy wife, happy life," his Mabel says with a laugh as she elbows him in the ribs.

Ava laughs, but my thoughts start to avalanche. Will she still want to be my wife when time is up? Where do we go next?

I thought the conversation we had here today was scary as shit. Asking your wife if she still wants to be your wife? Now that is scary, but even scarier is not knowing. Not asking. If she needs time, I'll give it to her. Someday, she'll be Mrs. Ryder, and it won't be an accident. I kiss the top of her head; just thinking about it makes my heart feel relaxed. She was the best choice I ever made.

Chapter 38
Ava

If that was stressful for me, I don't even want to imagine how that felt for Maverick. I'm almost shocked he kept his cool. I thought for sure I would have had to take him into the ER and get his stitches fixed. Thank God for country men and their need never to let a lady get walked all over. Though, I would have liked to pop Doug straight in the mouth myself. What a douche.

The past few days have been an absolute whirlwind. I've had to turn down shifts to be able to stay home and take care of Mav. His stitches healed nicely, and if he could be trusted to lounge at home and not get back to work on the farm, I probably would have already gone back to work. But I trust him as far as I can throw him, which isn't very far. He's as stubborn as an ox, and I would call him out on it if it wouldn't be incredibly hypocritical of me.

"Are you doing okay? I know that was a lot." I look over to him from the driver's seat of his truck. Mav is playing passenger princess with the pain meds he's taking, well, when I can get him to take them. Apparently, he doesn't think he needs them even though he went through a trauma that probably could have killed him. It should have, looking at the injuries he had, but he must have a guardian angel looking out for him because he's recovering beautifully.

"Yeah, that went better than I thought." He nods his head, and I have to wonder if he has short-term memory loss or something.

"You're kidding. Did we just leave the same house?" I turn and give him an incredulous look. Rhett literally knocked Doug on his ass. And then Doug threatened to press charges.

"Well, besides Doug, no one was disappointed in me. And I honestly don't really care anymore. As long as you and I are good, I've come to realize that the rest is just not that important."

That stuns me a little, even though it shouldn't. He hasn't only said the nice pretty words to make me feel better, he's followed through, and tonight was proof of that. My trust may have been cracked, but he has put in the work to make sure that never happens again.

But despite his words, Mav is worked up about something. He nervously taps his fingers against his thigh as he looks out the window.

When we finally make it into the house, I flick on the living room light and lose the battle of not asking him what's wrong. "Are you sure you are okay? You seem upset or nervous." I look back to him as he braces himself against the wall, kicking off his boots by the front door.

Maybe he does regret quitting. Can't say I blame him. I warned myself that it could happen. But I meant what I said. If he goes back to the ring, then this is done. Whatever this is. But I don't want to go back home anymore. This ranch feels more like home than anywhere else ever has. The air is fresh and makes my head feel clear. Plus, I'm surrounded by a found family that's provided me more love and support than I've ever known. True, kind, and good people who I can count on during the good and bad.

"Nope, I'm perfect. What movie do you want to watch tonight?" he asks as he walks over to me.

"Isn't it your night to choose?" After more than his fair share of 2000s rom-coms, I decided to take turns picking movies so he isn't forced to watch them every night. With the exception of Westerns, he can go snuggle Jack if that's what he wants to watch.

"It's okay, you can pick. I'll go whip up some popcorn while you get comfy and get the movie started." He pecks me on the cheek before walking around to the kitchen.

Grabbing one of Mav's shirts out of the dresser under his bed, I make my way to the bathroom and wash off my face and pull my long hair into a messy bun on the top of my head. I discard my clothes into the laundry hamper and pull on Mav's T-shirt. It's comfier than any pajamas I've ever worn.

When I get out of the bathroom, the sound of popcorn popping in the microwave fills up our tiny space along with its smell. Buttery and delicious. I don't care that we do this almost every night; it's my favorite thing ever because it's *our* thing.

Mav comes around the corner. He must have changed when I did because he's now in basketball shorts and shirtless. Another reason to love our tradition, he's almost always shirtless when we watch movies in bed.

He pulls back the covers and notices what I'm wearing. "You sure make that shirt look good." He sets the popcorn down on a side table before crawling in bed and wrapping an arm around me. "Did you pick a movie yet?"

"Yup." Clicking play on *50 First Dates*, I snuggle in closer. "Get that bowl over here."

He chuckles and pulls the bowl to his lap. When I reach my hand in, it lands on something hard.

"What did you put in the bowl?" I ask, sitting up and pulling the bowl to my lap to inspect it.

He has a sheepish grin on his face, which makes my heart flutter from nerves because this very well could be a prank, and he's still too injured for me to smack him with a pillow right now. "I have no clue what you're talking about." But the tone in his voice says that he absolutely knows what I'm talking about but that he wants me to figure it out for myself.

Heaving out a dramatic sigh, I use the light from the TV to see into the bowl, and a little black box sits in the center.

"Mav, what's that?" My head stays down while my eyes move up to look at him.

"Guess you will have to open it and find out." He shrugs with his good shoulder.

Grabbing the box, I slide the top off and gasp. In the center sits a diamond ring. The TV light illuminates off of it, making it glitter. My head pops up and I find his gaze locked on mine. Mav studies me with a gentle smile that makes my heart still before he gets out of bed and walks to my side of the bed. Still frozen speechless, he moves the bowl out of my hands and swings my legs off the side of the bed.

He gets down on both knees in front of me and says, "So, I kind of messed this whole thing up and did it backward. I married you and then fell in love. But I'd like to right that wrong. Ava, I love you more than life itself. I don't think I was even truly living until you came around. You turned my world from black and white to color, and I never want to see a world where you're not by my side, making everything brighter and better. Will you do me the honor of staying my wife? I promise to love you until my very last breath. And if I'm being honest, I'll still be loving you from the other side."

Tears flood down my face. My voice comes out hoarse and shaky. "I cannot imagine a better way to spend the rest of my life than being loved by you, Maverick Ryder. It would be my honor to be your wife."

Finally looking down at the box, I see the perfect ring. It's simple, not too showy and everything I would have picked out for myself. An oval diamond sits on a gold band. Two smaller, triangle-shaped diamonds encase the center oval. He knew exactly what I would want and that makes my heart swell so much it hurts. To be known is to be loved, and damn this man does that without even trying.

"I hope you like it." He looks at the ring with a worried and nervous look on his face.

Cupping his face, making him look at me, I reply, "It's perfect."

He slides the cool band onto my finger, and I can't help but notice how right it feels. "A perfect ring for my perfect girl." He brings my hand to his lips and kisses the ring that now sits there.

I look down at the ring and the promise it brings—a life with Maverick. I look up at him, and the adoration in his eyes tells me everything I need to know. That I'll never go through a hard thing in life alone again, and that calms a piece of my soul I never thought would be soothed.

Chapter 39
MAVERICK

We hop out of my truck and stare up at the courthouse building. This place is the reason we're here today. It almost feels like a separate life since we last stood here on these very steps. Technically, it was. When I look back, my life will be divided into two. Life before Ava and life with Ava. And I don't think I really felt what living really was until I loved her.

She squeezes my hand, and I look over, smiling from ear to ear. "You ready?" Her loose waves rustle with the Wyoming breeze, and she tucks her wild locks behind her ear.

"Absolutely." I squeeze her small hand back, her fingers laced perfectly in mine.

We walk hand in hand and make our way to our separate booths. The Judge looks over to us, still not looking too impressed, and takes a seat at her podium. "Alright, you two, it has been a quick six months. I see you both survived. It appears that all court orders were followed. Should you both wish, your request for divorce will be granted."

Unsure of what the proper courtesy is in court, I raise my hand. "Your Honor?"

"Yes?" She quirks a brow, and I almost feel like I'm going to be scolded.

Clearing my throat, I say, "We have actually decided to stay married."

She stares at us both. A small fissure of her icy exterior begins to show when her lips curve up a little. She pushes her glasses back up on her nose and folds her arms over one another.

"Let me get this straight. You two, who had never met before getting married, are wishing to stay married?" She looks over to Ava for confirmation.

"Yes, your honor." Ava gives a nod before smiling over at me.

"Well, I'll be." Her smile grows a little larger and she does one single nod of her head. "You know, I've done many things in my life. Never did I imagine I'd add matchmaker to the resume." A smile takes over my face and laughter echoes throughout the room.

"Thank you, your honor. I'm not sure we would be where we are today if you wouldn't have made us stick it out," Ava says.

"Something tells me you two would have found each other again, one way or another. But I'll take the credit. Well, I guess that makes me pretty useless in this case. I wish you both many years of happiness."

"Thank you, your honor," Ava and I say in unison.

"You're dismissed. Have a good day," she says.

And a good day it is. I get to keep my girl until forever ends.

Today marks the start of forever with Ava.

We head out of the courtroom, and I have one burning image in my mind. Ava dressed in white. We missed that step, and it's eating at me. Not knowing what she would look like as my bride.

We get back in the truck, and my brain keeps turning, making me more quiet than usual.

"You okay?" She looks over at me with a hint of worry on her face.

"Hell yeah, you're officially Ava Ryder. Today is the best day." I grab our linked fingers and kiss her knuckles. And I truly mean it. Today is the best day of my life. But I have to wonder what her dream day would have entailed. We skipped that whole part. But she doesn't seem sad or that she's missing out. She flashes me a smile when I use her soon-to-be-official last name.

"Ava Ryder does have a good ring to it, doesn't it?" She grins once more at me before looking out the window while gears turn in my head.

We get back home, and I make an excuse to help the boys out on the ranch, but really, I need an expert opinion.

Walking into the big house, the large windows allow light to spill into the living room. It's my favorite thing about this space, all the natural light. Looking over to the kitchen, I spy the two people I am looking for.

"Ladies. I require some advice and, potentially, your services." Mabel and Aspen both pop their heads up from whatever they are baking on the counter. "Well, you know Ava and I had court today."

Mabel's face falls, and she places a lightly floured hand over her chest which luckily is covered by an apron. "Oh, Mav, I'm sorry."

I hold up my hand, wanting to stop them before they start panicking. "We didn't get divorced."

Both Aspen and her mother drop their jaws. Sometimes, I forget that Aspen is the spitting image of her mother. While Mabel's hair is grey now, and her face has a few more creases in it now than it did when I was a riled-up teenager, their expressions are the exact same.

"So you're saying that you two stayed married." Aspen holds up a whisk and points it at me, taking a few extra seconds to wrap her head around it.

I hop up onto the barstool that sits next to the counter, sensing it's going to take them a minute or two to come to terms with this. Ava and I didn't tell a soul. I didn't tell the boys, and she didn't tell Erin, her other friends at home, or Aspen. We just decided for ourselves and then got on with it. "Yes, that is exactly what I am saying. She's officially Mrs. Ryder."

"Holy shitballs, Maverick," Aspen says. Her mom rolls her eyes at her language. But I've heard Mabel drop some gnarly F bombs in her day, so I know exactly where she got it from.

"Yeah, so back to why I'm here." I tap the marble counter a couple times to keep their attention.

"Oh yeah, sorry. Go on." Aspen ditches the whisk in the bowl and leans on the counter, one elbow propping her head up.

"I want to plan a surprise wedding. She would want it to be small and simple anyway. But she deserves her day. And I want her to have it."

"From Maverick the bull rider to Maverick the romantic. Are you sure she would be okay with not planning it?" Mabel questions.

"Honestly, yes. I've thought about it a lot. She's had to plan every detail of her life, so I'd like to do this for her. And it won't be extravagant, but I want it to be her perfect day, hence why I need you ladies." I gesture my hands out to the two of them.

"Well, obviously, you have a terrible sense of style. If I'm being honest, so does Ava. It's probably best if you leave this in my hands," Aspen retorts. Jesus. I'm already regretting this.

"You're kind of an asshole, Aspen. Anyone ever tell you that?" I cock my head, expecting Mabel to give me the same look she gave Aspen. Except she's nodding her head in agreement. The motion causes a little chuckle to rise out of me.

"Everyday. But you all love me anyway." And we do. She is the little sister I never had. This whole family is the family I never had.

"Okay, well, I need you to get a hold of Erin. I want all of Ava's friends to be here. And I think Erin would be the best place to find out what Ava's dream wedding would look like. Do you think you could do that for me?"

"Yes." She nods her head, wiping her hands on her apron before pulling out her phone and wildly typing.

"And Mabel. Can you make the food? I don't think there will be a lot of people. Twenty at the most, but likely more around fifteen?"

"Of course, anything for you, my boy." She reminds me every now and then how lucky I am to have her, not with words but with the ways she shows up for me. My mom may not have chosen to stay around, but Mabel decided to love me like I was her own and I think the fact that she chose that makes it even more special and real.

"Alright, well, I'm going to go tell the boys."

"Wait, you told us before them?" Aspen's eyes grow wide. "Wow, I've never felt more special in my entire life." She holds one hand to her chest while gripping her mom's upper arm. The smile on her face is downright glee-filled.

"We need to work on how low you're setting that bar." I hop off the stool. I pick up my hat off my head as a sound off and run to find my two dipshit best friends.

Walking around to the barn, I hear a commotion. And where there is commotion, there is Weston. And where there is Weston, there is Rhett cleaning up his mess.

I swing open the door and head over to where we store the hay.

"You guys in here?" I holler out.

"Yeah, in the back. Counting bales," Weston's voice yells out.

I come around the corner and stop in front of them, slipping my hands into my front pockets. "You need help?"

"No, if Rhett could keep track, we would be done by now." Weston puts his hands on his hips and cocks his head at Rhett.

"If you could fucking count, we'd be done." Rhett points back at him. While none of us are blood brothers, you'd never be able to tell by the way we all bicker.

"Well, sorry to interrupt, but I need to talk to you guys real quick."

They both stop what they are doing and look at me. "You good?" Weston asks.

"Yeah. I'm better than good. You're looking at a married man." I stand tall and proud because being Ava's husband is the best title I've ever had.

"Did the judge deny the divorce?" Rhett prods. A mixture of shock and confusion is on his face.

"Nope, Ava and I decided that we want to stay married. She makes me the happiest man alive and I've learned my lesson on taking that kind of shit for granted."

Rhett smiles and does something we've never done—pulls me in for a hug. He taps my back twice and holds onto my shoulders. "Glad to see you're finally using that head of yours." He smacks the side of it. "You'd be a moron to let that go."

"I know. Also, I am throwing her a surprise wedding. So, I'm going to need a best man and a groomsman." They both cross their arms as their expressions get serious. "There's no way I can pick between you two, so I am going to let you two figure that out."

They stare each other down like they are sworn enemies.

"How do you want to do this?" Rhett asks.

"Arm wrestle?"

"Bring it on, noodle arms." That might not have been Weston's best idea. Rhett is a beast of a man. While none of us are small at over six feet, but Rhett is like a fucking lumberjack.

We make our way to the side office and I take a seat at the head of the table. The boys position themselves on each side of the table.

"On the count of three," I tell them. "One... Two... Three!"

Both boys grunt as they put their weight behind them and lean in. Weston's eyebrows knit together, while Rhett looks a little too calm for this to be looking like a challenge.

Weston, being the little fucker that he is, kicks his leg under the table, making Rhett lose his composure and smacks his hand down.

"You cheating fuck, but if you want it that bad, you can have it. I'll still be glad to stand beside ya, man." Rhett slaps my shoulder and stands up. Something tells me he knows Weston would want it more, and he lets him have it.

"Alright, I'll let you both know what I need from you here in a bit."

Walking out of the barn, I feel like the luckiest man in the world. Now it's time to plan the wedding of my girl's dreams.

Chapter 40
Ava

When I wake up, Maverick is gone, which isn't out of the norm. The second that man was cleared to do light work, he was out of the house. Having been in his shoes, I get it. The only entertainment he's really had is hanging out with me and playing cards. I wouldn't be surprised if he lights the deck of cards I played with him on fire the minute he is fully cleared.

The knock that raps against our front door this early nearly startles me. Rolling over, I grab my phone off the charger and check the time—seven AM.

Who the hell is at my door at seven AM on my day off? Sliding into my slippers to keep my feet warm, I walk to the door and swing it open. And then pick my jaw up off the floor when I see who's at the door.

"Erin, what the hell are you doing here?" My eyes feel like they are bugging out of my head. Erin bounces on her toes, clearly excited to be here. Her chestnut hair is tied up into a bun. Glee fills her eyes, which makes me a little nervous. She's only this happy when she's meddling or doing something she shouldn't.

"Well, are you going to let me in? Aspen's on her way, too."

I step back from the door and let her in. Still trying to wrap my groggy brain around what is going on. "Okay, but why are you both here so early?" Not that I am not happy to see her, but this is really early for her. She's more of the 'rise when she decides she's good and ready' type.

"Well, I have something to tell you. And I hope I was right about it."

Oh lord. "Okay…"

"Do you remember when that girl in college got married and you said the whole wedding planning thing seemed like way too much work and you would prefer to elope one day?"

My hackles go up immediately. "Yes. Planning a wedding was never something that sounded like a good time. What does that have to do with you being here?"

"What if I told you that you have the best husband ever, and he recruited everyone who loves you to plan you a surprise wedding…and it's happening today?"

For the second time today, my jaw is on the floor. There is no way in hell that man planned a whole wedding by himself. "Am I being punked? Did Aspen put you up to this?" I did eat her yogurt at work last week so I can see her getting back at me with extreme measures.

"No punking happening here, friend. I promise," she says as she makes a cross her heart motion with her hand. "You mentioned to him that a wedding would be nice, but that you wouldn't want to plan it and he wanted you to have a special wedding."

Tears fill my eyes because I didn't think that he was really even listening to me when I was rambling on about that only a couple weeks ago.

"Please tell me those are happy tears and we didn't shit the bed?" She asks as she bites her teeth down in a bared smile with eyebrows high, trying to stay hopeful. And I'd like to get some words out to tell her that this is the sweetest thing anyone has ever done for me, but words aren't working because I think I'm in shock.

I've had to do everything in my adult life alone. There were no parents to help me through school, to help me buy a car, or pick out an apartment. I was in charge of planning every detail. At some point, that becomes exhausting, especially when things tend to go wrong time and time again. Somehow, I managed to find a man who wants to take that load off me. That little piece of me that is a terrified eighteen-year-old girl heals instantly. I'm not alone and will never have to do anything alone ever again.

Blinking slowly, I mutter, "You're not wrong. But how did you pick a dress?"

"Aspen drove down, and we went to a boutique. Between what we both know about you, we picked one we thought you would like. It's simple and lace. And obviously it will make your tits look amazing."

My head tilts back with laughter because of course that's what she is worried about.

"So this whole thing is really planned?" Disbelief fills my tone because this seems too good to be true. A lot of things about my life recently feel that way.

"Yes. Your bouquet is made of your favorite flowers. The boys are getting the logistical side of things ready. The only thing you have to do is sit here, and let me make you pretty...er. You're already pretty."

"I really don't have to do anything?" The concept of not being worried about something is incredibly foreign to me. A part of me feels a little bit stressed at the lack of control of the situation, but the larger part of me is relieved that I'll still get to have my day and not even lift a finger.

A few minutes later, Aspen comes barreling in like a tornado, not bothering to knock. Her long brown hair is a mess, but she comes in with a garment bag in hand and stands in front of me.

"You already give her the spiel?" she asks as she goes to hang the dress on the closet door. Leaning over, she puts a hand on her knee and catches her breath.

"Yes. She was suspicious the second she opened the door and I'm a bad secret keeper," she then looks to me, "I was supposed to wait to tell you with her, but in my defense she was running late."

"Aspen, the garment bag would've given it away anyway." I hitch a thumb to the white garment bag now hanging off the closet door.

Maybe putting these two in charge of me wasn't the best idea. But I'm going to roll with it. Something new that I am trying out.

"Alright, I am ready to be pampered," I say as I lean back into the futon.

"Okay, let me get my makeup and stuff from the car." Erin gives me a wild smile that leaves me a little scared, but I laugh anyway.

A couple hours and a few mimosas later, the cabin resembles a beauty salon. Josie and Cami show up and I feel like I haven't stopped laughing in hours. If you had told eighteen-year-old me that this is where life would lead me, I wouldn't have believed you. But it is my life. I have the best friends in the world, a new bonus family and the best husband in the world.

"Alright, there," Aspen says, as she swipes the makeup brush across my cheek one last time. "You're done. Let's get you in the dress and then you can see yourself."

It's an-all-hands-on-deck situation trying to get the dress on. They make me keep my eyes closed the entire time, which makes it even harder, but eventually, they get me dressed and in front of the full-body mirror that Aspen brought over.

"Okay, on the count of three, open your eyes. One.. Two...Three.."
I open my eyes and gasp.

I'm shocked as I look at myself in the mirror. My blue eyes look piercing with the light pinks and brown shadowed across my lids. My eyelashes have never looked as full as they do today. My blonde hair cascades down my back in perfectly styled curls. And my God. This dress. My hands run down the soft lace. I couldn't have picked anything better for myself if I tried. It sits perfectly on my body. The sweetheart neckline swoops to show off my chest. And the bodice hugs me tightly until just past the hips and then flare out. The waist cinches me in. I almost don't recognize myself. Eyes bright and heart full.

"You look beautiful. Now let's get you to the field! It's time."

Maverick truly outdid himself. Our closest friends sit on hay bales covered by blankets. The aisle is lined with small metal tins filled with wildflowers from the meadow. And at the end of the aisle is an arch, draped with sage green and white linen. The empty spots are packed with bright wildflowers.

Maverick has his head turned, talking to Jack. Who I am guessing will be officiating the wedding. The girls have kept me hidden so he can't see me. They built privacy blocks out of wood pallets standing six feet tall. I take one last peek and then pop my head back.

Weston and Rhett stand at Maverick's side. Dressed in blue jeans, a button-up shirt, and a suit jacket. How he managed to pull all of this together last second is completely mind-blowing.

Aspen steps out from behind the pallet wall and makes herself seen. She looks to her dad and gives him a nod, letting him know we're ready.

I always thought that at this moment, I'd feel nervous. Wondering if I was doing the right thing. Be flooded with second thoughts, because overthinking and overanalyzing is pretty much a character trait for me, but none of that is happening. As I watch my closest friends walk down the aisle, all I feel is peace.

When my turn finally comes, I stand at the end of the aisle, my eyes immediately meeting Mav's. His strong jaw is clean-shaven, and the bright white smile? The one that's only for me? It beams at me the second I catch his eye. He's cleaned up so well, always in blue jeans, but his buttoned-up shirt is covered with a sports coat and of course, topped with a perfect cowboy hat. The walk down this aisle is the last time I will ever have to walk alone because now I'll always have him by my side. As I get closer, I see the tears that have gathered in his eyes, threatening to spill over. The toughest, strongest man in the world, and the sight of me is what brings him to tears. Never did I think being loved by someone would make me feel powerful and cherished, but that is how I feel here, standing with him at the altar.

Stepping up to the altar, Maverick meets me at the last line of seats. He encircles my hands with his and brings them to his lips for a quick peck before dropping one and walking to the altar. Rejoining both hands, we turn to Jack.

He smiles broadly at us and then at the attendees. "We are gathered here today to celebrate two things, the addition of Ava into our family, and the moment that Maverick pulled his head out of his ass and found someone to love him. Truly, a miracle." The few people we have gathered with us break into laughter, the loudest coming from Rhett and Weston. "Let us be reminded that there is no greater thing than to be loved through our failures, wins and all of life's tribulations."

Mav's turn to recite his vows comes and I feel butterflies erupt in my stomach. "Ava, for a long time, I thought bull riding would be the only thing to define me. And while I'm grateful for that, because without the sport and my passion for it, we wouldn't be here today. Today starts a whole new list of dreams for me and I'm looking right at the most important one. You and the life we set out to create together is my new dream. Whatever your hopes and wishes are, are mine. And I vow to pursue them with all that I have. There's nothing in this world I'm more thankful for than you. You breathed life into me at a time when I needed it the most. I promise to love and protect you with all I am until I leave this earth. You are my heart. I love you."

His words ricochet through my head all the way down to my heart. It feels too full, like it's bursting at the seams, and the only way to make more room is to let these tears of happiness fall.

Jack looks at me, his grin wide under his thick, grey mustache. I realize I'm completely unprepared. But telling the world how much I love Maverick isn't a hard thing to do.

"Maverick, you came into my life and turned every single thing upside down. But that led to things falling perfectly into place. Before you, I was used to doing things by myself. Carrying the weight of the world. Thanks to you, life no longer feels heavy. You've healed pieces of me that I didn't even know were broken. Sewing them back up and imprinting yourself so deeply into me that I can't even take a breath without feeling you deep in my heart. Loving you will be the greatest thing I have ever done. Wherever life leads me, I know it will be okay as long as I have you. I love you until forever ends, Maverick. Always."

When the part for rings comes up, I realize I don't have one for him. "Mav, I don't have one for you." My eyes are wide with a little bit of panic.

Maverick shakes his head, hands still in mine. "You didn't need one."

"What do you mean?" Of course he needs a ring.

"You see that guy over there?" He drops my hands and points to a man in the back row.

"Yes?" I question.

"When the ceremony is over, he's tattooing my ring on. You'll forever be inked into my skin like you are in my heart."

My eyes grow wide, and I almost can't believe that. The only marks on his body are scars, and now there will be his signal to the world that he's mine. That tattoo is about to become the most attractive thing about him in my eyes.

The ceremony ends with Maverick dipping me into a picture-perfect kiss. The crowd hoots and hollers.

"Get a room, you two!" Weston yells. Maverick puts me back into a standing position and kisses me one more time. My cheeks start to burn from smiling so much.

Maverick turns us, holding our hands up, showing us off to the crowd like I'm the grand prize. All the heartache I've lived through was worth it for this moment.

Since we get to skip the whole signing the marriage license thing, Maverick darts straight for the table set up in the back. I go to follow him, but he stops me. "Go enjoy our guests and your friends. I'll find you as soon as we're done." He leans in and kisses me while he squeezes my hand.

Erin and Aspen stand at the dessert table, and I hear them quietly arguing over it. "No, the white cupcakes should be up front, and the chocolate ones in the back. It's a wedding, it's supposed to be all decked out in bridal white."

The laugh under my breath isn't as quiet as I hoped, and both of them whip around to look at me. Both squealing when they realize it's me.

"Hi, babe! So, was it the wedding you always dreamed of?" Erin asks, taking my hand.

"It was more, so much more. And I had zero stress over the whole thing. Minus the one-second panic attack I had over vows and rings." Today was a dream. But it really isn't about the day, it's about the man I get to spend my life with. Today could have been an absolute disaster and I still would have been counting myself lucky.

"Well, you made for a very beautiful bride, and I'm glad you invited the rest of us this time," Aspen pokes fun at me, and I roll my eyes. But getting to share this day with them made it feel so much more real and special. I finally have a family of my own, and that's something I wasn't sure I'd ever have again.

Walking around, a few others stop me and congratulate me, and I make one or two stops by the dessert table, if not for desserts, then for some more time with Aspen, Erin, Josie, and Cam. It's so good having them all here.

I stand back from the crowd for a while and sip champagne. Basking in the moment. My eyes close and I think I finally feel what it is to be at peace. My mind is quiet and my heart is happy.

"Hey there, wife," Maverick greets as he walks over. His long-sleeve shirt is rolled up on his forearms and he's ditched his jacket. The late summer air is a little warm and I'm glad because all those years of holding on to a bull for dear life has left his arms corded with muscles and veins. It might be his sexiest trait.

"Well, let me see it," I say, setting my glass down on a side table.

He lifts up his finger and I grab his hand to inspect it. It's covered in a small Tegaderm film. The thick, inked dark band encircles his finger all the way up until it hits the front. The line goes all the way around, but he tattooed my initial on it. "Do you like it?"

I look up to him, tears brimming on my lower lash line. "I love it." He pulls his hand away and lays it above my beating chest.

The implication isn't missed. Because he's tattooed on my heart, too. Forever a little piece of him is ingrained in me. "I love you, cowboy." I drop his hand and put my mine around his neck. Sinking into the calm I feel whenever he's near.

He gives me one of those smiles that makes my heart skip a beat. "I love you most, Grandma."

Before I can give him a retort, he captures my lips, and it hits me that I will get to do this for the rest of my life. What a life that will be.

Epilogue

My truck comes to a halt at the end of the dirt road. Jack told me to meet him here and what he says goes, so I didn't ask any questions. The area is mostly abandoned; it has an old fence around it and a utility shed.

He stands, hip propped against the fence, arms crossed and back to me. Walking through the tall wild grass, I take the short walk and stand next to him.

"You know my family has owned this land for as long back as you can track. We've each raised our own families and passed it down, generation to generation." I study the look on his face; the setting sun reflects off the wrinkles that have gotten deeper with each year that has passed. He used to have strong, dark eyebrows, and the more time passes, the more they fade to gray. I sometimes forget how quickly life goes. It feels like it was only yesterday, I was ten years old, following him around in boots that were too big and trying to learn how to be a tough cowboy like him.

"One of the many things that makes this place so special." He looks over to me, studying my response, and a ghost of a smile turns his lips up.

"I've decided it's time for me to take a step back and let you boys take over. I've worked every minute of my last sixty years, and I think it's time for me and the Mrs. to slow down a little."

Shock fills me, I swore that he would be busting his ass on this ranch until the day he died. "Well, if anyone deserves it, it's you."

He nods his head. "Thanks, son. Well, I brought you out here today to talk about a few things. First, I'm handing over ownership of the land and the ranch. Weston will get thirty percent, Aspen thirty percent, and you and Rhett will split the remaining amount."

I try to find words because as much as I love this land, I never thought any of it would ever belong to me. I was happy just to earn my keep to get to stay here. "I. I. I—" shaking my head, I try to form a sentence, "I don't know what to say. I love this land and you guys. That is incredibly generous." Jack puts his hand on my shoulder and gives it a squeeze.

"You'll always be a part of this family. Your last name might not match, but your heart does, and at the end of the day, that's what makes a family." He gives me one more squeeze before dropping his arm. "Anyway, the land we're standing on right now is officially yours. It's got incredible views of the mountainside and would be a hell of a spot to raise a family if you want it."

My eyes roam over the chunk of land. The green grass and wildflowers will still be in bloom a little longer. Fall will be rolling around any day now, bringing in the falling leaves and a whole other scenery. All of it as pretty as the season before it. "This is too much." I shake my head. But as my eyes scan, I can see it. The life Ava and I can build. The babies that could run around the front yard. The laughter. A home. I can create the family I never had.

"I think it's just enough. I miss your old man more than words can ever say, but it has been an honor to watch you grow up and get to have a hand in raising you into the man that you are today." He purses his lips and gives a nod, swallowing back emotion. I've never seen this man cry, and I don't think today will start that. He's as tough as they come, mind, body, and soul. "Well, I am going to head back to the house. The wife is waiting for me." He pats my back a couple times, and I turn my head and watch him go. Turning my head back, I can't help but smile. This is the dream. Not winning buckles but having people around you who make you feel glad to be alive.

Reaching into my coat pocket, I pull out my phone and send a text to Ava, dropping my location and telling her to meet me at the spot.

Twenty minutes later her car comes up the road, which reminds me, she will need an upgrade if I don't want to pull her out of snow drifts all winter. She's officially a country girl, and we need to get her some 4x4 action.

Her car door closes behind me, and I turn my head and smile at her. Hopping up on the fence is a brave move, considering this thing is probably older than the pyramids. But it holds my weight.

"Whatcha doing out here?" She comes and stands beside me, resting her arms against the top of the fence.

"Oh, just planning the rest of our life." Actually, I think I've been doing that since the moment I met her. But even more so now.

"Wow, busy afternoon. Tell me, Ryder, what does the rest of our life look like?"

"It looks like a house right there," I point to a spot in the grass I'd want to clear out and put our house on, "and grass all around it so our babies can run. Maybe a dog or two?" I turn to look down at her and admire the way the light makes the faint freckles on her nose stand out. "I think we should make the kitchen face this way. That way our living room can be this view. I point forward, to where the mountains fall to a valley in the distance, and the sun shines through the peaks.

"I feel like I am missing something." Her eyebrows scrunch up, trying to put together what I'm saying. Probably not wanting to get her hopes up because this land is perfect for our forever.

"Jack is gifting us this land and making me twenty percent owner of the ranch and land. This is now ours, baby."

"Oh my God! That's amazing." She jumps into my arms, and her sweet scent wraps around me, making this ground feel even more like home. We've had a lot of talks lately about what was next for me now that bull riding is done, and I guess now I have my answer. All that worrying was for nothing.

"That it is. Looks like we'll have a busy winter. I want to break ground the second the ground melts."

She smiles up at me. "I love you, Mav."

Leaning over, I gently lift her chin and look her in the eyes. "Always?"

"Always." My lips meet hers and I can feel how good the rest of our lives will be. As long as I have her and this Wyoming air, I'll have all I'll ever need.

Acknowledgements

If you picked up this book, thank you! Every time you read an indie author's book, we get our wings.

This is my favorite thing that I have ever written and I am so glad that I got to share it with you.

There are quite a few people who this book wouldn't have been possible without. First off, my bestie Caitlin who convinced me it was the right decision to abandon a quarter done manuscript and start from scratch two months before my scheduled editing slot. It was one of the best decisions I have ever made, and I wouldn't have done it without the extra push. And if that wasn't enough, she was also my very first alpha reader!

My author wife, Mindi, who listened to me plot out this book over voice message a million and four times. Thank you for always being there to bounce ideas off of, and have menty b's with. I love you, grandma.

My beta readers, Amber my bull riding expert and Jenna my hype girl, thank you so much for taking the time out of your busy lives to help make this baby shine. I appreciate you all so much. Bryanna, a special thanks to you for all the extra work you did for me, I am so happy I had you in my corner. Hiring you was probably the BEST choice I made for this book.

My coworkers, Jess, Renee and Cory. Jess and Renee have to listen to me in detail explain things a million and seven times, and they are just as excited on time one million and seven as they are the first time. They are two of the most supportive friends I have ever had and I am forever grateful for them. And Cory, for being voluntold to proofread every single book I write before I publish because she is the most detail oriented person you will ever meet, it might be her personality, or it might be the seven cups of coffee she drinks a day, who knows.

Finally, thank you to my readers, with each book I've gained new readers, and new friends. If you didn't know, I love to yap, and I love that I've found new yapping friends just from putting some words on a page. I am forever grateful for you for being apart of making my dreams come true.

Also by

Check out my Love Island Duology on amazon or at my website
https://www.ellejordan.com/

To stay up to date on new book news, head over to my website and
subscribe to my newsletter!

Stay tuned, Weston's story is up next and it looks like his old flame is
coming back to town.
Find me on social media!
TikTok: ellejordanbooks
Instagram: KindleKween_